**DO NOT REMOVE
CARDS FROM POCKET**

ALLEN COUNTY PUBLIC LIBRARY

FORT WAYNE, INDIANA 46802

You may return this book to any agency, branch,
or bookmobile of the Allen County Public Library.

The Widow of Oz

Also by Kathryn Lasky Knight

ATLANTIC CIRCLE *(nonfiction)*

TRACE ELEMENTS *(fiction)*

The
Widow of Oz

Kathryn Lasky Knight

W · W · Norton & Company

New York · London

Published simultaneously in Canada by Penguin Books Canada Ltd,
2801 John Street, Markham, Ontario L3R 1B4
Printed in the United States of America.

The text of this book is composed in Goudy Old Style,
with display type set in Goudy Handtooled.
Composition and manufacturing by
The Maple-Vail Book Manufacturing Group.
Book design by Jacques Chazaud.

First Edition

Library of Congress Cataloging-in-Publication Data

Knight, Kathryn Lasky.
    The widow of Oz / by Kathryn Lasky Knight.—1st ed.
      p. cm.
    I. Title.
    PS3561.N485W53 1989
    813'.54—dc19   88–28330

ISBN 0-393-02669-8

W. W. Norton & Company, Inc.
500 Fifth Avenue, New York, N. Y. 10110
W. W. Norton & Company Ltd.
37 Great Russell Street, London WC1B 3NU

1 2 3 4 5 6 7 8 9 0

I am indebted to the following people for their distinguished work in the fields of primatology and paleoanthropology: Irven Devore, Alison Jolly, Sarah Blaffer Hrdy, Barbara Smuts, Jane Goodall, Adrienne Zihlman, and the late Dian Fossey.

It should be noted that the character of Ella Voight is a unique and wholly original creation and bears no resemblance to any actual person.

I would also like to thank David Pilbeam for guiding me in my research. It was in David's class at Harvard that I first encountered primate studies. His insights must inspire anyone who tries to grasp the nature of our primate ancestors.

July 5, 1988
Deer Isle, Maine

The Widow of Oz

1

Every time Dorothy Silver returned to her living room after going to the bathroom or her bedroom, she expected to find no one there. But always there were the little clumps of people. Not that she minded. Good heavens! What would she do when they all did leave and she was left alone in this half-furnished, half-finished condominium? It did seem almost exactly half done: the painters had painted the "dining alcove"—a term Dorothy loathed—white, whereas she had asked for a rich, bean-soup red. It constituted only one-third of the floor space in the living area, but drop cloths and a ladder with a can of latex paint on its platform were still in place.

When Dorothy's son, Peter, suggested that they remove the drop cloths and ladder because of the heavy traffic of the condolence callers, Dorothy resisted. It was the only flash of bitterness she had shown since Ira had died.

"You realize of course that all the floors in this five-hundred-thousand-dollar condominium are pure concrete. There isn't even any plywood! Therefore, eighty percent of the floor space has to have wall-to-wall carpeting. It's actually written in the condo bylaws. Can you imagine! Wall-to-wall carpeting mandated for the major living areas. It's supposed to be the same as I picked for the living room. But there's been a delay. I just hope it's the same dye lot." She paused in the middle of this diatribe and sighed ruefully. "So much for the Heriz we had back in Lincoln." The Lincoln house was not many miles away but it was a world apart from this Boston condo.

So drop cloths and the ladder with the paint can were to be left to discourage the callers from delivering their condolences on the bare, sound-transmitting floors. It would be unseemly to give verbal solace on top of concrete. It would not be solace. It would be vibrations without origin. She had, of course, never planned this occasion. However, if one could plan ahead, as Dorothy now thought, wouldn't it have been much more comfortable to receive condolences in the north end of the Lincoln living room with those marvelous cherry floors, covered with the eight-by-ten Seljuk rug? So comfortable, so absorbent. Everything seemed to reverberate here.

If Ira had died four weeks earlier . . . Good God! What was she doing? What in heaven's name was wrong with her?—wishing Ira four weeks less of life, a life already cut short at fifty-four, just so she could receive . . . She did not finish the thought. She clenched her hankie and stared at her knuckles. It is true though, she thought, that four weeks ago she would have been in the lovely old rambling house and not here in Church Tower condominiums where dining rooms were reduced to alcoves and closet doors were hollow-core. What really was the matter with her? Why couldn't she stop thinking about the goddamn condo, and grieve—she inhaled sharply—how? Properly, grieve properly as should a widow who had loved her husband. That sounded so stupid. But she was stupid. Every time she started thinking about Ira, life without him, she ended up thinking about the damn condo. What in the world would she do here without him? The move, after all, had been his idea. She clenched her hands harder and tried to will widow-ish thoughts upon herself before walking into the living room to greet new callers. It seemed unusually quiet as she walked down the short corridor from the bedroom.

There were not little clumps of people but one large knot, hushed, the people's heads bent as if examining something. How odd, she was thinking, and just at that moment she caught a glimpse of her mother's deeply tanned face, the pouched pale eyes filled with a kind of childish terror, her nut-brown hand like a tiny claw half covering her mouth.

"Who would ever?" It was her son, Peter, speaking. Dorothy felt her chest constrict with fear. "What now?" She forced out the words. And then they all turned toward her and looked up, their faces clutched with guilt like children caught in a naughty act. But there was something slightly absurd about the scene that dissolved Dorothy's initial terror and suggested that something mildly ludicrous might be in the offing.

The people, of course, were not her children except for two—Peter and Sophie, who were in their late twenties. There was Peter's girlfriend, Ella, a robust young woman whom Dorothy had only just met and who seemed to reside quietly, watchfully, behind masses of crinkled red hair that foamed around her face despite gargantuan barrettes intended to sub-due it. There were two of Ira's colleagues from the Mass General Hospital and their wives, and Ira's receptionist and nurse. And then there were Dorothy's parents, Beebie and Gordon—short, squat, wrinkled and ridiculously tanned from a long winter in Juno Beach, Florida.

"Talk to your mother," her father said, urging his grandson forward with his hand.

"Talk to her?" Beebie Lipman muttered rhetorically. "What is there to talk about? This sicko!"

Sicko? Had Dorothy heard her mother correctly? Her mother had never, as far as Dorothy knew or could even imagine, used that word.

"What is going on here?" Dorothy's voice rose.

"Mom, I'm sure it's some sort of mistake. Weird coincidence, that's all." Sophie strode briskly toward her mother. She looked so pretty, Dorothy thought, when she dressed this way—loose, open collars, not those severe androgynous, dress-for-success tailored suits. At least she didn't wear ties or ascots. For the life of her, Dorothy couldn't figure out why there was all this neck gear among young businesswomen. Sophie said only middle management types succumbed to these masculine sartorial flourishes. It seemed, Dorothy mused, such an oddly restrictive and uncomfortable form for penis envy to take. Sophie, of course, could wear pink ruffles and still come out on top in a negotiation. But what in the world was going on here in this room right now?

"What are you talking about?" Dorothy was utterly perplexed. "What's a mistake? What's a weird coincidence?"

Sophie had taken her hand and was guiding her toward the dining room table, which of course was now the dining alcove table. It was not in the alcove at all now but in the bay window overlooking the Charles River. The knot of people separated to make a passageway for her. It all seemed slightly ridiculous. Wasn't this precisely the way crowds parted for royalty? Everybody was expectant and terribly somber. It was almost as if they were holding their breath in one collective lung. But for the first time in days Dorothy felt a trace of mirth. She felt lurking within her the antic shadows of all sorts of untoward responses that were contrary to the lungs full of breath and tautness of mood that flanked her every step.

"There," Sophie said.

"Oh," Dorothy said slowly. The word hung in the air, round and calm. On the table before her lay a red T-shirt. Scrawled across the chest in white script were the words *Surrender Dor-*

othy. The tail of the *y* swooped back and upward forming a broom with the figure of a witch riding across the red sky.

Dorothy felt a small bubble deep inside her, and then like a silvery stream the laughter came and she was seized with a fit of giggles. She clutched her arms and bent forward slightly. She was vaguely aware of a hand on her back.

"What's she doing? . . . Laughing or crying? . . . Well, I never!"

She could not stop laughing to explain. But she could never really explain anyway. Lucky she didn't have to pee. She would have wet her pants right there on the wall-to-wall. Run for the drop cloth! This made her laugh even harder. She had to sit down or she would fall. No chair, of course! So she collapsed right there onto the floor in a kneeling position. There was a collective gasp.

"Don't worry! Don't worry!" She raised her hand and waved it jauntily to signal that she was fine.

"Dorothy!"

She opened her eyes and through her tears saw the violently painted toenails. Her mother's feet were the color of Moroccan leather except where the straps of her beach sandals had left little white crucifixes that showed now in her open-toed pumps.

"Dorothy!" Beebie's voice was sharp. "What is the meaning of this?"

Of what? Of her laughter or the T-shirt or both? Dorothy knew perfectly well what her mother was asking for. But now for the first time ever that Dorothy could remember, she felt intimations of a mirthful defiance. In fact she was, although she could never admit it, laughing at them. So she looked up at the little nut-brown figure of a woman. "Meaning of what, Mother?"

For a moment Beebie seemed taken aback. "Of your laughter." She paused and swallowed. "Of this T-shirt."

Dorothy moved onto all fours now as she attempted to quell

her giggles and get up. She felt a hand underneath her arm. It was Peter's. She took a last look at the toes before rising. Did she imagine it or were these toes growing slightly impatient? Thickly horned and painted bright as geraniums, did they suppress a little tattoo that they longed to tap as they awaited an answer from this suddenly obdurate and newly unfathomable daughter?

"Mother," Dorothy said getting to her feet at last. "You remember from the book when Dorothy first sets out after meeting the wizard, or is it before when she's still on the yellow brick road and the witch skywrites with the broom?"

"I know the story perfectly well, Dorothy." Beebie refrained from adding that it was before meeting the wizard that the witch had inscribed the sky with the warning and the demand for the ruby-red slippers. "You need not repeat it."

"Well, I just thought . . ." Dorothy made a nervous little fluttering gesture with her long fingers and swept back one of her gray curls. There was a slight stammer in her voice and still the undercurrent of laughter. "I thought, Mother, for the benefit of those not familiar with the story . . ." She was sure that Ella would not be familiar with such stories. When would she have had time for fantasies and fairy tales? Hadn't she decided to be—what did they call it—yes, a primatologist, that was it. Hadn't she decided that in kindergarten? Ella appeared absolutely impassive behind a hank of red hair that had escaped from the barrette and tumbled like a cataract, obscuring half her face.

"Who's not familiar with *The Wizard of Oz?*" Beebie's pouched eyes blinked incredulously.

"Well, at least our . . ." Dorothy hesitated. "Our family's . . . uh . . . interest in it."

"Dorothy is named for the Dorothy in the book." Gordon Lipman nodded matter of factly to Jack Cohen, Ira's associate at the Mass General, and his wife, Lita.

"So, Dorothy, darling," Beebie's face creased in perplexity, "who could have done this to you? It's sick. Just when Ira dies to receive this."

It was slightly unbelievable to Dorothy that the power of the stupid story could make inroads into this situation, that there could be this commingling of childhood fantasy with adult tragedy. That they could all be so upset. But she knew how they were. She knew. She always had known.

"Mother, I'm sure it's some sort of silly coincidence. You know, of course," Dorothy said turning to Al Fischer, "that Margaret Hamilton, the actress who played the witch in the movie of *The Wizard of Oz*"—Good Lord, she thought. It was as if people had to have an exegesis to follow this nonsense. "Well," Dorothy continued. "She died a few days before Ira did."

"A very odd coincidence!" Beebie added. The pale tobacco eyes narrowed.

"Mother!" Dorothy wheeled around. "It is not an odd coincidence. Numerous people died the same week that Ira did. Now is there any card with this shirt?"

"No," said Beebie with more than a hint of triumph in her voice.

How could this squat little lady who played eighteen holes of golf a day and mah-jongg five times a week, who cooked four briskets a month and wore Bermuda shorts—how could she have succumbed to such a degree in her imaginative life to this fantasy?

"I'm sure there is a card," Dorothy said. "You just haven't looked. Where's the package or box that it came in?"

"There," said Peter. "It was partly torn open. That's why we opened it the rest of the way."

Dorothy held out the package and squinted for lack of her reading glasses. "Well, of course!" She sighed contentedly. "See the postmark? It's from England. It must be Monica."

"Why Monica?" Beebie asked.

"She happens to be the only person I know in England.

There's probably a card in here somewhere." Dorothy shook the box and reached in. "Ah! I feel something." She pulled out a card and held it aloft. "Look! Monica, of course." She waved the iridescent notecard in the air. "It's one of her darling little light cards," Dorothy said, briefly studying a picture that looked like a photograph of an oil slick. "Oh, Ella!" she said, turning toward the young woman. "You would really get on with Monica." In truth, Dorothy was not sure they would get on at all but somehow she had felt a need to break the present mood and Ella, still impassive, nearly unreadable, seemed comfortably neutral. "Her field, of course, is entirely different from yours. She ponders stuff about light and matter. What's it called again, Peter?"

"Quantum electrodynamics."

"Yes . . . yes, that's it. A far cry from your primate behavior studies, Ella. But I know you'd get on."

Ella seemed not especially animated by this prospect and peered at Dorothy through the stream of red hair that fell down her face. Dorothy continued less energetically. "See this card? It probably has something to do with photons or electrons. Let's see, what does Monica have to say?" She flipped the card over and began to read.

" 'Darling, heard on the BBC about Margaret Hamilton's demise. Florinda had just found this shirt in Falmouth on her holidays' "—Dorothy broke away from the note at this point. "Monica has four beautiful daughters—all with names like English floral scents or sachets." She continued reading. " 'She thought of you. Now that the Wicked Witch is dead I guess there's no one to surrender to. So fly high. Hope to make it over this year. Love M.' "

There was a shocked silence.

No one to surrender to. The words gave Dorothy a slight jolt.

"She didn't know about Ira?" Ella asked.

"No. No . . . ," Dorothy said.

"We tried to call," Sophie explained, "but the housekeeper said they were all gone for several days."

"I'm glad you found the card, but I still think it is very odd. Very weird," Beebie said. "I would be very upset if I were you."

She would be very upset if she were me. How profoundly odd, her mother's saying this, and yet how entirely familiar it was. Hadn't her mother always assumed this interchangeability between them? Now something seemed to coalesce, to harden slightly within Dorothy. She took a deep breath and reached out and patted Beebie's arm, but she looked at no one in particular. "You would not be upset if you were me because it's your story and not mine."

Beebie appeared absolutely stunned.

2

❧

Back in the thirties when Dorothy was born there had been a brief vogue for naming baby girls after popular literary and cinematic heroines and personalities. There were Scarletts, Vivians and Ramonas, among others. Beebie had chosen to name Dorothy after Dorothy Gale of *The Wizard of Oz*. Ever since, her family and friends had bestowed all sorts of Ozian mementoes and memorabilia on her, including, when she was five, a wire-haired terrier already named Toto.

She never changed its name but kept a secret name for the dog, Ruff, which she used when they played alone. She felt the name fit what a terrier was, with its stiff, coarse swirls of salt-and-pepper fur and low, gravelly bark. She felt that this was the proper way to go about naming a living thing—with an ear attuned to some inherent quality, something genuine and immutable about the creature. So, although she later realized the name was not "distinctive," it was original because it matched the dog's being, its essence.

The callers had all left. It was almost eleven o'clock in the evening. Dorothy lay in the double bed and thought about the afternoon scene. She had pretended so well until this afternoon. As a child she had worn the sky blue gingham dresses with the deep white collars, outgrowing one after another from toddlerhood to junior high as her mother replaced them in her closet. When the movie of *The Wizard of Oz* came out in 1939 and Dorothy was seven, Beebie braided her hair just like Judy Garland's.

The Dorothy Gale look had lessened somewhat as Dorothy Lipman grew older. By the time she was fourteen her mother agreed that French braids were not the hairstyle with which to enter high school. But there were always those occasions that would warrant a reminder or reference to the story. After she and Ira had moved into the condo, a plant arrived from Beebie and Gordon with the note, "Gee, Toto, I guess we're not in Lincoln anymore." She wondered if they remembered that they had sent the same message twenty-five years before, when they moved into the Lincoln house after Ira had finished his residency in New York: "Gee, Toto, I guess we're not in the Bronx anymore."

It was not that Dorothy Silver disliked the story of the Wizard of Oz. It was just that she had never been entirely comfortable with the way things happened to Dorothy Gale. Tornadoes tore her house up from the prairie, plunking her down amid Munchkins, killing a witch in the process of landing; flying monkeys abducted her; fields of poppies drugged her. It was all so random. Dorothy Gale seemed like a piece of flotsam, a dry leaf blown about by a maverick wind or rogue prairie currents. If one had to be passive, wasn't it better to be like Emma Bovary and couch oneself in elaborate ennui? She worked the scalloped edge of the bedsheet between her fingers, bunching the monogram together. And yet it could not be denied, even if she did not feel inside the story, that now things had certainly happened to Dorothy Silver in a seemingly random way. Had she not been torn up from Lincoln and put down here in this strange land? Not amid Munchkins in Oz but Yuppies in the Back Bay. This was Ira's idea of freedom: no lawn, no house maintenance, kids grown up. "We're too old to be Yuppies, Ira," she had said.

"What do you mean, 'too old'? You're never too old. Besides, who said anything about Yuppies—not to mention, Dorothy, that you were the very first Yuppie ever. Who had a cappuccino machine in 1959 other than Italian restaurants?"

So the house had landed in the form of a condominium and with a cruel twist—oh, she should not go on like this. Instead of a wicked witch's feet sticking out from under, it had been Ira's. He was wearing his nylon shorts and bright blue running shoes when he collapsed not five blocks away in the public gardens, the very same gardens she had brought the children to from Lincoln to ride the swan boats and retrace the path of the ducks in the book *Make Way for Ducklings*. But now there would be no retracing, Dorothy thought bitterly. Fifty-four years old! A distinguished cardiac surgeon. Why couldn't he have listened to the signals of his own heart? Of her heart!

She heard a soft knock at the door. A tremor of shame ran through her. She was not shocked but slightly sickened by her own bitterness. She tried to compose her face.

"Yes?"

"It's me—Ella."

"Come in, dear." Oh, Dorothy thought, she was a wicked witch under all these "dears" and scalloped linens.

Ella loomed like a violent sunset in the door frame. Good Lord, she'd never seen her with her hair completely down! There were masses of it. How did she and Peter ever sleep in the same bed, as they apparently had been doing for the past four months? It would be like having a third person. A ménage à trois.

She had only met Ella for the first time five days ago. When the news came through about his father, Peter had flown back from Kenya with her. They had been planning to come within a week anyway. She had known about Ella for several months. Peter, always a diligent correspondent, had written about re-meeting an old school friend. She had been slightly ahead of Peter at Berkeley and had already established some reputation for her work done on Barbary macaques and pygmy chimpan-zees. Peter kept referring Dorothy and Ira to articles written by Ella in various scientific journals. Dorothy, always assidu-ous in trying to keep up with her children's interests, had duti-fully plowed through articles in *Scientific American, Natural History, Smithsonian* and *Discover* which bore titles like "Infan-ticide in Nonhuman Primates" or "Dominance and Sexual Hierarchy in Pygmy Chimpanzees" or one that Peter told her was supposed to be very witty yet terribly on target entitled "Keep Your Pants On, Desmond Morris: The Myth of the Male Orgasm as an Evolutionary Strategy."

In Dorothy's mind, Ella, with her obsession about sex and death, was a humorless version of Woody Allen. One evening as she and Ira were reading in bed and Dorothy had been working her way through yet another article of Ella's, she turned to Ira. "Why couldn't this Ella be teaching monkeys sign lan-guage? Or there was that cute picture on the cover of *National Geographic* of that chimpanzee or gorilla—I get them mixed up—taking a picture. They were teaching it art or something. Why couldn't she do that?"

"You better get it straight which one's a chimp and which one's a gorilla." Ira had laughed. "Forget about the orgasms in the Rhesus monkeys."

"Rhesus macaques it was, dear."

"What's a macaque?" Ira had asked.

"Well, it's not a chimp or a gorilla."

"Is that the one you read me about the clutch reflex at the time of ejaculation?"

At that point they had both started laughing. Ira had clutched her and that was the last time they had made love in the Lincoln house before moving to the condo.

She supposed she had Ella to thank in part for being the catalyst for that. Now Ella stood before her in the doorway. What in the world could Dorothy have to say to someone whose head spun with tales of monkey infanticide and images of primate orgasms?

"I forgot to tell you, Dorothy," Ella said, walking a few steps into the room, "that your stockbroker called earlier. I took the message. He said did you want to put a stop loss order on Regency Electronics at six and that he would buy some more Deluxe Check if it got down to forty-six." Ella held a small scrap of paper in her hand which she glanced at as she delivered the message.

"Stop loss order?" Dorothy said vaguely.

"Yes." Ella looked at her searchingly.

She expects me, Dorothy thought, to know what all this is about. She who writes about chimpanzees' social hierarchies by the light of a hissing kerosene lamp in African jungles, not only does she know all that but she knows what a stop loss order is. Dorothy wondered why she felt so defensive. Poor girl, walks right into the middle of this family tragedy. Has to meet us all at the same time. She shouldn't blame Ella for being smart.

"You know what he means?" Ella asked softly as someone might ask a child whether she understood a word or a simple math concept. The taste of panic welled in the back of Dorothy's throat. She had been caught! Caught by this wary and too gentle teacher.

"Uh . . . No . . . Well, yes, yes . . . I think so." She paused, inhaled sharply. "Of course I want to stop my losses." Dorothy felt her mouth curl into an ugly little line. Would Ella miss the bitter little joke?

"Maybe you should talk to Sophie," Ella advised.

"Yes, of course." She began fingering the sheet again. "Here!" Dorothy said, suddenly reaching for a box on her bedside table.

"Try one of these. They're awfully good. Someone brought them."

"What are they?" Ella asked, walking across the room. Dorothy felt it was like a bonfire moving toward her.

"Very good candy—chocolates with a praline center. Better than Godiva—more expensive, too. Here, sit down." She patted a place on the bed beside her. What had come over her? Why was she sharing chocolates, inviting this intimacy with this young woman whom she hardly knew and seriously doubted she could ever like even though her son seemed to be in love with her?

Ella bit into a candy, worked it silently in her mouth and rolled her eyes in approval. Well, at least she could appreciate good chocolate.

"How do you stay so skinny, Dorothy?"

"Well, I don't make a habit of eating chocolates in bed." Now hadn't Emma Bovary done something like that? Dorothy thought.

"But you're some kind of food expert, aren't you?"

"Hardly. I write occasional articles on food and cooking. Sometimes gardening." She might as well include all her subject areas.

"How do you stay so thin, though? You're like a rail. You must like to eat?"

"Some."

"Some what?" Ella asked, perplexed.

"I mean," Dorothy laughed, "I'm not a big eater."

"I am," Ella said.

"I would imagine you'd burn it off tromping about chasing those troops of, uh . . . animals."

"Not that much. These are great." She rolled her tongue about in her mouth, roving for remnants.

"Have another one."

"Are you sure?"

"Of course."

Ella reached for one and tucked a large freckled leg under her bottom as she sat on the bed. The thick curtain of hair swung forward, obscuring her face entirely. It was like having a slightly animated stuffed animal perched on the bed.

Dorothy suddenly felt completely comfortable. "You know something, Ella?"

"What's that?"

The head turned but the face was still barely visible. "Well, this is something I overheard Al Fischer saying that I wasn't meant to hear but I heard it anyway. Don't say anything to Peter or Sophie."

"Yes?"

"Well, you know they did an autopsy on Ira and of course it was myocardial infarction."

"Peter and Sophie know that."

"Yes, but I overheard Al saying to Jack Hirsh that . . ." Dorothy paused. "I don't know why I'm telling you this." Ella was silent and absolutely still. "Al said that Ira's arteries looked like cottage cheese."

Ella turned her head slowly and ran a hand through her hair, tucking it behind one ear. Her eyes, a rich golden brown, opened wide. "How could he be in that bad shape and not know it or feel it—him a cardiac surgeon?"

"I know," Dorothy said. "But I guess it happens all the time. We just expect more from doctors—at least that they'd be more medically attuned to themselves."

Ella sat impassively. The hair she had tucked away had come loose. The crinkled curtain was drawn closed once more, but Dorothy could feel herself being watched through the hair. Was this how Ella studied her nonhuman primates, stalked her macaques and pygmy chimpanzees through the dense rain forest growth, parting branches, disentangling vines to observe them with her sly amber eyes? Dorothy was suddenly very irritated with herself. Why had she told Ella the thing about the cottage cheese? She would undoubtedly enter it into her "field notes" on Dorothy.

May 18, 10:45 P.M.

Made contact with the mother. For several seconds after the mother was informed of call from brokerage house, she stared vacantly into space. Subsequently mother offered chocolates, patted nest, signaling observer to sit. Seemed exceptionally disturbed by informal autopsy report comparing the lining of the deceased mate's arteries to cottage cheese.

And what had been that afternoon's entry?

Mother exchanged hoot series with alpha female. Mother subsequently assumed the conventional posture of submission, but then rose to chestbeat and exchange further hoots. Made gruntlike sounds about the Wizard of Oz.

Oh, *why* had she mentioned the cottage cheese? And what did this girl know about Oz? Even if it were not Dorothy's story, Ella would not know why it was or wasn't. The child had no capacity for metaphor. How could she? For God's sake, this girl had actually analyzed the dung of monkeys. There was a footnote in one of her articles referring to it. And she had measured clutch reflexes and uterine contractions during orgasms of Rhesus monkeys. Now why in God's name had Dorothy ever offered chocolates, and told her about the cottage cheese?

3

❧

"The Ashes Issue"—in all fairness to Beebie, there had been a preposition inserted that tempered it slightly by breaking the alliterative susurration. So it became The Issue of Ashes. Still Dorothy had jerked when she heard her mother say it. She caught Sophie shooting Beebie a sharp, dark look, a look that only Sophie could deliver and which she used sparingly with a dead-eye accuracy. It said, "Get your golf cleats out of here."

Beebie and Gordon stuck around for another day or so. Dorothy had been purposely evasive about The Ashes Issue, as she now thought of it. Nobody had spoken to her directly about the disposal of the ashes. She was not supposed to have heard them talking, but Beebie had a gravelly voice that simply never got into the register of a whisper even with the mushy sibilance of words like *ashes* and *issues*. There was a lot, Dorothy realized now, that she was not supposed to hear but sometimes overheard. It concerned all the vital things directly connected with herself and her life as a widow. But she was not supposed to hear about it—at least not directly.

Just as in French there was a special tense, the historic present, reserved for use only in literary expression, so Dorothy surmised that for new widows, fresh ones, there was reserved a special indirect form of address. The purpose of this form was quite the opposite of the historic tense. Instead of creating a sense of immediacy, of flow between past and present, the aim of this tense was to amputate the past and to form a new linkage between the present and the future. One, of course, was not supposed to hear about the future on the spot, directly, but to become a guileless eavesdropper on one's own future.

There had been no violation when Dorothy heard Beebie's hoarse voice. That conformed to the new grammar of fresh widowhood. No, the violation in this case was one of language itself, word choice. Fresh widows were not supposed to jerk in horror over vocabulary. One, after all, could not simultaneously jerk in horror and eavesdrop in innocence. The Ashes Issue was a phrase designed to fracture the shell-thin facade of guilelessness. Her children, her parents, and occasionally Ella were often talking in hushed voices, or just out of earshot, about her life—the condo, the painters, the insurance, "nice weekends" in New York to visit Sophie, a trip to Florida next winter—who knows, maybe even Africa?—and there was the boat, what should be done with the boat? Would Peter and Sophie use the boat enough to justify keeping it? Well, certainly not Peter. His field season in Kenya was not compatible with the sailing season on Martha's Vineyard. Sophie couldn't see having time, not with the four-part utility bond issue package she was helping to choreograph—her biggest deal yet, 400 million dollars. "Four hundred million, phew!" Ella gasped. The conversation quickly turned not to Dorothy's present and future at all, but to the children's—Sophie's, Peter's and Ella's—which seemed right, appropriate.

But now Dorothy was ready for some direct address.

"The issue of the ashes," she said quietly the morning after

Beebie and Gordon had left. Peter, Ella and Sophie were standing around in bathrobes on the drop cloth in the dining alcove drinking cappuccino. "Do you want me to get more of a head on that for you, Ella? Peter didn't do a very good job steaming it." Ella gave her an odd look. What could be the meaning of that? Dorothy wondered. Here her possible mother-in-law-to-be was trying to be as nice a hostess as possible under rather trying circumstances. The girl was totally charmless. Dorothy was just trying to enhance her morning coffee. Ella loved cappuccino. She had somehow never tasted it until coming to Dorothy's. Dorothy was stumped as to how this could have been accomplished unless the poor girl had spent her entire life in the bush, which she had not—although there was something rather feral about Ella. Well, she would persevere.

"You know, the steam spigot on the machine is all gummed up. It's a little hard to work. So I'd be happy to go in and perk yours up a bit." Ella declined. Dorothy had been about to say how Ira never wiped it down when he fixed himself the occasional evening cappuccino with whiskey and that was why the spigot was all gummed up. She caught herself just in time, just before she jerked again, and this time there was no one to blame except herself. *Ashes*, not *steam*, she reminded herself, was the subject at hand.

"I've given some thought to this matter—the ashes." Even with Beebie and Gordon gone, this was going to be slightly more difficult than she had imagined. At that moment the telephone rang.

"I'll get it!" Ella said quickly and ran toward the kitchen.

Dorothy could hear Ella answer the phone. "Yes, yes, I'll see if she can talk."

What does she mean, she'll see if I can talk, Dorothy thought. "It's for you, Dorothy. It's Monica in London."

"Monica! In London! How can you ask if I can talk? Of course I can!" Dorothy was more than irritated with Ella. She'll see if she can talk. You bet she can talk. She was not one of her little field primates, dearie! "Dearie"—there, she had thought it, the witchiest word in her arsenal of terms of nonendearment for her dreary little might-be daughter-in-law. But one could hardly be dreary, she supposed, with all that red hair. The silent mutterings swirled through her head as she walked quickly to the phone. She slopped a bit of cappuccino on her robe.

"Monica! . . . No . . . No . . . So good to hear from you. No, of course you couldn't have known. . . . Well, mother did at first say whoever sent it was a 'sicko.' " Dorothy giggled. "That was before we found your card."

Dorothy heard herself answering the questions about Ira's death, providing the details in brief, truncated phrases—"in the public gardens . . . no, no . . . yes, they tried to revive him . . ."

Monica apologized and continued to make gentle conversation but Dorothy was not really listening. Instead the scene a few days before of the entire family standing around her dumbfounded by her convulsions of laughter replayed with delightful vividness in her memory. Now, how could she explain that to Monica? The sheer delight of it. Poor Monica had probably been flagellating herself hourly since realizing what she had done. It was not that she wanted to tell Monica that she needn't feel bad. What Dorothy really wanted to explain was just how good she had felt at the time. She wanted to share it, to tell her about that sudden euphoria that had washed over her like summer rain, that feeling of release from pretending anymore about the silly story.

Odd she had not thought about the T-shirt and the entire scene that much since then. Something had stopped her. The memory of euphoria had vanished, simply melted away. She had felt good, really good. At the time she knew she had. But now she had to tell herself so. Convince herself. She knew she was right, too, about the story and being "outside" of it.

Just now Monica was rattling on about "condo life." How did Dorothy like it? She would never have imagined her in a condo, giving up the garden and all. "How did it happen, Dorothy?" What? Dorothy was slightly lost in the conversation. She had better attend more closely. This call was costing Monica buckets. How did what happen? Dorothy had already briefly explained about Ira and the running in the public gardens, the coronary. "The condo, sweetie! How did you wind up there?"

Dorothy paused. She felt all her sinuses clench as if trying to dam up a hole in the dike. For the first time she felt she might actually cry. But she did not. "Well, Monica," she sighed, "I don't know. It just happened." And she thought of that dry leaf blown about by maverick prairie winds. The very condition she hated most about Dorothy Gale had indeed been her condition.

"Things have just been happening to me lately." She felt her voice crack. She felt Ella stealing glances at her over the deflated head of steamed milk. Peter and Sophie were plopped on the drop cloth absorbed in the *Boston Globe* and the *New York Times*. But Ella was the ever diligent observer of primate life. Damn her! Had there ever been anybody as invasive? If she would just get a haircut there would at least be less of her. Dorothy turned her back on the dining alcove and faced the blank kitchen wall. "Things are just happening to me—so . . . so sort of randomly." She spoke very low.

"What? Monica! Now what do you mean, I'm talking like a physicist—quantum mechanics? For heaven's sakes . . . I have to *start* thinking like one, you say?" Her voice grew stronger. Monica really could cheer one up. "Well, my dear, that might be a bit difficult. We've already blown the graduate school budget. Besides, I am not so endowed—either with boobs or brains." She would have liked to steal a glance at the old primella-tologist on that one. Yes! The old lady can talk quite casually about boobs, not that she has much to talk about . . . oh, forget it, she thought. . . . "What's that, Monica? I couldn't quite hear . . . 'an unruly swarm of random events'?

Yes, I would say that is a very apt description of my recent life. And there's nothing morally wrong with it. How can there be? It's no one's fault."

That's the problem! She almost said it out loud. She hadn't planned the move and Ira hadn't planned to die. So why was she so mad? Monica was now saying something to the effect that she had not been talking about "wrong" in the moral sense and had continued with something about particle bombardment as a metaphor. . . . "Yes. Well, I am feeling rather bombarded, but your analogies are getting a bit abstract for me. Remember, I'm your basic 'domestic engineer,' as all those desperate homemakers used to call themselves. . . . No. Just a memorial service. I was just about to discuss with the children what to do with Ira's ashes." It sounded strange but right to Dorothy. "Yes." She swung around and faced the three young people in the alcove. "I think we'll take his ashes down to Martha's Vineyard. The boat is already in the water and the weather is supposed to be beautiful for the next few days. Peter can sail us out into Vineyard Sound and we'll scatter them there . . . Yes . . . Yes . . . Okay. Thanks for calling, dear. Love to Rupert and that bunch of beautiful girls of yours."

"Mom, you never liked the Vineyard that much or sailing, for that matter," Sophie said.

"Well, it's not my ashes. They're Ira's and he loved the Vineyard. So that makes sense." What did not make sense was that he was dead and got to be where he wanted to be and she was alive and was stuck in a place she loathed. That made no sense at all. But she wouldn't say anything. Nor would she tell them that there was a time when she did like, no loved, sailing. But that was a long time ago, and she tucked it away like a cheating mate would tuck away a delicious infidelity. There was a part of her that did not want her children to know just how larky and antic she could be or had once been. To be savored, some pleasures needed to be sequestered.

4

᠙᠑

Dorothy had been on a few boats in her life, but certainly never in this situation—sitting in the cockpit with an L.L. Bean canvas bag containing a jar with her husband's ashes. It was in fact the first time she had ever boarded *Ventricle* without having absolutely stuffed this canvas bag with fresh baguettes, bottles of wine, cheeses, pâtés wrapped in plastic, boxes of homemade chocolate truffles and bottles of sun-dried tomatoes.

It suddenly struck Dorothy that if in a single word she had had to describe the difference between sailing with Ira and sailing with Monica as she had nearly forty years before, it would be "bags." It was not Ira's fault at all. It was her fault, really. Again it was just one of those things that had happened. She could picture the pier before they left on one of their weekend cruises, with its mustering of canvas bags, insulated carryalls, hampers, coolers and duffels.

With Monica in the days of the *Dory Dear* on Lake Michigan, there had been one brown paper bag with two tuna fish sandwiches and one bottle of soda pop. They limited themselves to one bottle because if they both drank a whole one they always had to pee. There was no head on the boat so the only choice was peeing down the daggerboard slot. They had done this occasionally until the bright summer day when LaPolk ("Polkie") Fitzgerald, a sophomore at Yale and as far as they could ascertain the only Yalie on Lake Michigan, sailed round the point on the blind channel where they had anchored for lunch. There was Monica mid-pee, astraddle the center board, haunches pointing toward Sault Saint Marie. It was the most mortifying experience two fifteen-year-old girls could have. There was only one possible runner-up in what they called the terminal embarrassment sweepstakes: a bride farting at her own wedding, loudly.

Every summer from the time Dorothy was thirteen until she went away to college, she would visit Monica and her family at their Harbor Springs summer cottage. They would sail endless days on the *Dory Dear*. Everybody else sailed fast, sharkish little boats like Lightnings and scows, but Monica's family, slightly eccentric and with a keen sense of aesthetics, had always taken to the more seakindly shapes of salt water boats. Thus for the nearly fifty years they had been summering in Michigan, they had imported a series of dories—all bearing alliterative names. There had been *Darling Dory*, the *Dory Dear*, *Dory D. Vine* (that one had been built on Martha's Vineyard), *Dory Delight*, *Dory Devil* and the first one for which they had bought cushions had been christened *Dory Deluxe*.

So when Ira had first proposed that they buy a sailboat some twenty years before, it was the little pine *Dory Dear* with its gentle hull, curves sweeping fore and aft into elegant peaks that Dorothy had first imagined. How silly, she realized. Of course they would have needed something bigger with two kids and their own friends and their children's friends. She had just never imagined a plastic boat. But that was exactly what Ira had bought—a Morgan 35, which to Dorothy looked just like a Clorox bottle.

It was all a far cry from those larky sails on Lake Michigan, taking turns being skipper, eating tuna sandwiches, peeing in the daggerboard, ranking embarrassing moments on scales of 1 to 10, talking sex, Yalies and wedding gowns. It shocked Dorothy to realize now as she sat in the cockpit that she could not remember one actual or specific conversation she had had on the *Ventricle* with guests, people who were their closest friends. She could recall categories or probable conversations: food, medicine (Harvard Medical School, the MGH), prep schools, of course, when Sophie and Peter were of that age, college admissions, when they were at that age. But the words, the facial expressions, the laughter did not come back. It was as if the affective content of the experience was mired in the details of the task of a weekend cruise. On the bare bones of the *Dory Dear*, all of the human detail stood out in bold relief against the calm tableau of wind, sky, lake, pine spars, canvas and rope. Now there were heads to be unclogged, a butane stove to be cautious about, bright spinnakers to be lofted with style and precision, elaborate menus to be designed.

Dorothy did extraordinary things on boats. She made soufflés that rose like bronze cumulus clouds in gimballed ovens that swung through alarming angles of sea travel. On rough anchorages she injected freshly made crème pâtisserie into puff pastry shells she had made and transported from Lincoln. It seemed extraordinary to her now, after thinking so much about Monica and the days of sailing the *Dory Dear*, that below in the galley there was actually a pastry tube along with a box labeled "Cajun Survival Kit" containing exotic blends of spices more fit for the bayou than the Atlantic.

Peter now stood at the helm looking as if he were hoping for a bit more wind to speed things up. But the slow pace under the impeccably blue skies was fine as far as Dorothy was concerned. She sat in the cockpit on the lee side, the jar of ashes in the canvas bag tucked between her legs and the seat. Sophie sat across from her. She too scanned the water for a darker ruffling that might indicate more wind. Ella seemed not to care about the wind in particular but instead appeared to be alert to a whole concatenation of things. She had walked to the bow and, straddling the forward stay, hung her bare feet over and let what little wind there was play through her hair which streamed back toward the starboard quarter of the boat. Her nose was freckling up already, giving her a burnished look to match her hair. Indeed she looked to Dorothy like a plump, freckled figurehead suitable for a nineteenth-century square rigger. For such a full face, however, she had no trace of a double chin. The chin was delicate and slightly squared. The face, despite its general chubbiness, was made to cut through gales. Dorothy could just imagine the straight little nose and angled jaw plowing through a surging China Sea, foam flying off the freckled cheeks, hair streaming straight behind like licks of fire, the fearless chin cocked for Java.

"Wind's about gone, Mom," Peter said as the sails began to luff.

"Oh dear, I hate to have to use the engine. It's so lovely and calm."

"Why do we have to use the engine?" Ella asked, walking back from the bow. "We don't really have to get anyplace."

Peter and Sophie looked at Ella oddly as if trying to decipher what she meant exactly. But of course! Dorothy suddenly realized that Ella was perfectly right. One patch of pretty water on the sound was as good as the next for this. Ella plopped down next to Peter. Her pants' legs were still rolled up. She raised her bare leg and crossed it squarely over her other knee. Peter rested his hand lightly on her calf. The other part, the better part of Ella's invasiveness, Dorothy realized, was a kind of soothing inertia, a capacity to wallow in the "thereness" of a situation, to suspend herself from all other constraints that had to do with time and compulsions.

Dorothy looked at Peter and Sophie, still scanning the water for a hint of wind like nervous mustangs in a box canyon. She loved them dearly, her own high-strung thoroughbreds, her driven, overachieving baby boomers, but here was Ella making an art form out of complacency. Something within her cried "no fair." She admired it and wanted to steal it for her own babies but she did not want the rest that came with it—the invasiveness, the natural superiority. She did not imagine that. She knew it was there. Ella from the plains, Ella from Hays Springs, Nebraska, Ella who had never gone to prep school but who indeed had to "prep" at the state agricultural school before winning a scholarship to Berkeley. Ella had in fact achieved distinction equal to, if not beyond, that of her own high-powered children. She was not jealous of the achievements per se. She was envious of the simplicity with which it had all been done—the lack of folderol. She coveted it in precisely the same way she coveted those old days on the *Dory Dear* when sailing had been a simple lark with a nice breeze, a bag lunch and a shared bottle of soda pop. How had life become so complicated?

Ella was right, though. They were not going anywhere in particular.

"We'll scatter the ashes right here," Dorothy said briskly.

"Okay," Peter said, and began letting out on the mainsail and luffing up into the vanishing wind.

"How do we do this?" Sophie asked. Her voice was tight.

"Well," Dorothy said. "I think if we move toward the stern, that's where there's the most room for us all to stand. I haven't prepared anything to say." She supposed she should have brought a poem, or a prayer book. But then it would have been just like the pier with the mustering of canvas bags before the weekend cruises. Instead of Brie and wine and French bread she could imagine carryalls full of poems and sonnets and scriptural verses about death and the everlasting. And then,

of course, the voices of one's own family sounded so odd recit-
ing such things that they would have had to bring along a
rabbi—or perhaps an out-of-work actor—and before you knew
it there would be a tape deck and a cantor, and it would be
an elaborate burial at sea and they would have to have lunch
and wine and—oh God, this was how life became so damned
complicated!

They began moving toward the stern, Dorothy clutching
the container of ashes. Peter held her firmly under one elbow
and Sophie stood beside her with her arm around Dorothy's
waist. Ella stood next to Sophie. The sail slapped indolently
with the rocking of the boat and the last whiffle of wind. She
felt Sophie and Peter tense beside her as the seconds passed
and yawned into a minute or more. They wanted words, she
felt, but she could not give them. She heard Sophie begin to
hum a jagged little melody in the back of her throat. She felt
Peter's hand tighten on her elbow. She began to take the lid
off the container. She slipped the top into the pocket of her
windbreaker.

"Do you want to take some, Peter?" He looked straight down
into the jar. His tangled dark bangs cast an antic shadow across
his eyes. He reached in and took a small handful. He did not
really look at what he held, nor did Dorothy. The boat rose
up on a swell and Peter dropped the handful over. Dorothy
next offered the jar to Sophie, who in one smooth motion
thrust in her fist then leaned out and released her ashes, her
hand poised like an asymmetrical star over the water. Dorothy
was last. She poured the remainder into her hand then stepped
forward and leaned out over the rudder. There was absolutely
no wind now. The ashes did not even swirl or fly up. There
was no unruly swarm of random particles. They drifted with
lazy inevitability on the black surface of the calm waters and
lay there in a kind of wordless everlasting good-bye.

Dorothy stared down at the fine white dust and then at her
wedding band and the diamond engagement ring. The rings

would outlast them both. What had once slipped her ring onto her finger was now ashes drifting calmly on a black sea toward Cuttyhunk. What if one little ash had on its course through the air between jar and sea been blown upon her ring? Oh dear, was she succumbing to pathetic fallacy or what here? She could remember her old English professor at Smith quoting Ruskin on Kingsley's "Alton Locke" concerning the horrific line about the "cruel crawling foam." " 'The foam,' " the old professor read from Ruskin, " 'is not cruel, neither does it crawl. The state of mind which attributes these characters of a living creature is one in which reason is unhinged by grief.' " And this produced the falseness of effect known as pathetic fallacy. A fine kind of widow she was, trafficking in such things. But there was not wind enough for randomness to conjure up a pathetic fallacy today even if she were slightly unhinged.

"Mother, I think we should start the engine."

"Yes," Sophie said quickly.

"Why?" Dorothy asked.

"Well, I just think . . . uh . . . you know . . . it's time," Peter said.

Did he mean time to say good-bye? She did not think so. Just time to leave this place where a father's ashes clung to the water's surface.

The values of matter had changed. They, the living, were still ruled by the laws of gravity, but Ira was ashes and had passed through to the realm ruled no longer by dimensions of volume and gravity, but by area and surface tension. On this windless day his ashes refused to scatter, to be borne aloft and vanish.

"Just another minute." She leaned over the rail to watch the white and gray dust. She could feel Sophie and Peter growing restless. "Okay," she finally said. "Start the engine. We'll go."

There was a cough and a sputter of the diesel, then an unpleasant grinding of the gears.

"Oh shit!" Peter muttered. "Didn't Danz fix this gearshift?"

"Give it a touch of reverse. That's what Dad always did."

Suddenly they were speeding backward. Dorothy lurched against the rail.

"That's more than a touch, Peter!" Ella cried, grabbing Dorothy's arm to steady her.

"I can't get the goddamn thing out of reverse!"

"Oh no, Peter!" Dorothy exclaimed.

"Do something, Peter!" Sophie squealed.

"You all right, Dorothy?" Ella asked.

"I'm fine. I do think we are catching up with the ashes, however."

Ella opened her eyes in shock. It was the first time Dorothy had really caught Ella off guard. There was such innocence, though, in her shocked appearance that Dorothy felt somehow drawn to her.

"Dorothy, you are something else!" Ella whispered conspiratorially.

She wanted to say yes, but she just winked at Ella instead. She really must be coming unhinged but this was not pathetic fallacy—even if they were motoring in reverse onto Ira's ashes.

The boat was actually going backward in circles now quite fast. They had caught up with the ashes. They were now providing, by virtue of their wake, a set of nonrandom pressure waves that were stirring the ashes into little frenzies on the surface. Sophie was screaming at Peter to do something for God sakes.

"Why don't we just sit down here, Ella. I'm no help at all in a situation like this."

So they both sat on the stern and watched the swirl of water and ashes. Dorothy wondered if they could create enough agitation for the ashes to break from the water's surface and fly.

The boat did not want to get out of reverse.

"Why do we keep going in circles?" Sophie yelled.

"Where do you want to reverse to? Spain?" Peter muttered

as he wrestled with the recalcitrant gear lever.

Dorothy's mouth turned down as she tried to control an ominous gurgling of chuckles that welled up within her. She kept her eyes locked on the spot where the ashes still floated in an effort to concentrate. The ashes were starting to disappear. To where she did not know. They just seemed to vanish in a traceless manner, not into the air as she now realized she had hoped they would. Dorothy did not believe in an afterlife any more than she believed in Oz. But she knew she was a creature of metaphor, and loved the notion of spirits, like escaped kites, swept up in windy ascents of freedom without peril.

There was a grinding noise. The boat suddenly slowed its backward circular course then plowed straight forward. This was good-bye then, she thought, and from somewhere deep within her memory a voice crept back over the decades. " 'Now you are a scholar, Trotwood,' said Mr. Dick . . ." From out of a *Dory Dear* summer spent reading Dickens, she let the voice wash over her. " 'You are a fine scholar. You know what a learned man, what a great man the Doctor is. You know what honor he has always done me. Not proud in his wisdom. Humble, humble—condescending even to poor Dick, who is simple and knows nothing. I have sent his name up, on a scrap of paper, to the kite, along the string, where it has been in the sky among the larks. The kite has been glad to receive it, Sir, and the sky has been brighter with it.' " The voice stopped. Yes, Dorothy thought, it would have been nice if these last bits and flakes had swirled aloft among the larks.

5

"Oh, I think she'll love it!"

"It's going to look great. Here, Ella, can you put those daffodils in something?"

"I think if we can get some of her old familiar things in place it will really help."

"I wish we could get her to hang up some of these pictures. That's one thing that you cannot do alone."

"She says she has to think about where they should go."

"I wish she'd start thinking."

Dorothy could hear the children talking back and forth. She was at the front door with a Mrs. Emory who lived down one floor and was inviting her to a little cocktail party next week to meet some of the neighbors. The children on the way back from the Vineyard had decided to get the place really "fixed up." It was more their need than hers. She seemed to sense that before they left her to pursue their own lives doing wondrous things that would make impacts on the world, they had to make sure their mother's niche was in order. So she could . . . what? Go to cocktail parties with people she had never met before?

What exactly did they expect her to do here? She really wished the kids would get out so she wouldn't have to pretend she was going to do something, so she would not have to make nesting noises. She was finished playing house and she did not know how to play widow or new neighbor, and she hated having to try to sound alert and knowledgeable in front of the kids when the lawyers and stockbrokers and insurance people called. She wanted to be able to act dumb, sound dumb and be bitchy. And most of all she did not want to have to keep talking about Ira with them.

"Well, I'll try and make it." She smiled thinly at the Emory woman whom she could see was trying to peer over her shoulder into the rest of the condo to see how it looked. Dorothy said good-bye and turned to see what nesting intrigue Sophie, Peter and Ella had been up to. The three were standing expectantly in the not-quite-furnished living room. "Well, how do you like it?" asked Sophie brightly.

So this was one of the old familiar things to be put in place that was supposed to ease the transition from Lincoln to Boston, from wife to widow. The lovely Bokhara rug, the color of old rubies and deep within its ruby spectrum a lambent pulse like the ancient flicker of distant stars. But here against the oatmeal-colored wall-to-wall it sat dull and lusterless—diminished, relegated like an old vicomtesse at a village church social without even a rumor of past fire. It was most definitely out of place. But she would not let on. She smiled and murmured approval. She would take it up tomorrow, immediately after the kids left. They were all taking the nine o'clock shuttle to New York—Sophie to Wall Street and her four-hundred-million-dollar utility package deal, Peter and Ella on to Nairobi via London to begin once more piecing together the oldest families' first histories. And Dorothy would roll up one family's history into a tight, ruby-red sausage.

Later that evening when Dorothy was in the kitchen Ella came in. She was wearing a thin nylon robe with not much on underneath it. Her large, pendulous breasts hung under the robe like shimmering aqua melons. Her hair with no clips raged like a brushfire under the harsh overhead light. It was as if the Venus of Wilendorf had come to life in Dorothy's kitchen. Ella reached for an apple from a basket of fruit.

"So you're not wild about the rug?"

Dorothy wheeled around. "I never said anything."

"Well, I could sort of tell," Ella said, hoisting herself onto a bar stool.

"Oh you could, could you?" She really did not feel like being a diplomat anymore.

"Yeah, frankly, Dorothy, you seemed uh . . . kind of generally pissed."

"P— . . ." She started to make the sound but couldn't.

Dorothy was profoundly shocked. This was way out of bounds! She inhaled sharply. "Young lady . . ." Good Lord, did she sound like a relic or what? But she would continue. "I do not know precisely what the rules of the road are in your profession, but I am going to tell you right now that if you are going to insist on doing your primate observation routine on me, this primate is going to speak when spoken to. First of all, although I cannot stop you from observing, I can request that you reserve your judgments and opinions and keep them to yourself. If I'm p-p-pissed, as you say, it's my piss." Dorothy's hand fluttered. "I didn't mean it quite that way. It's my anger and it is not up for analysis. Do you understand?"

"Yeah. Except for just one thing."

"What's that?"

Ella looked directly at her. "I think it's good to be angry."

Dorothy rolled her eyes. God spare her. How banal! Couldn't Peter have found someone else? Anyone else? Her children were more original than this. They deserved better. Now she was really angry. "I know, that's quite the style these days.

Isn't it? Therapeutic anger. Good to let it all hang out. Well, guess what, dearie? I come from a long and venerable tradition, a bygone era where people carried dance cards, diagrammed sentences, declined Latin nouns and in terms of emotion, well, prevarication and repression were the name of the game. So if I am angry I shall do my best to hide it from my children, and if it is 'good,' as you say, to be angry, you and they will be the last to know if I am."

Dorothy turned and swept past Ella. When she reached her bedroom she realized with a shock how wonderful she felt. She would never give Ella the satisfaction of knowing this, of course, but the sensation must have been akin to the aerobic high in jogging that runners were always carrying on about. Maybe Ira had had one just before he died. She had consoled herself before with the notion that when Ira had dropped dead there had been very little pain. Jack Cohen had tried to reassure her of this. "Maybe a little nausea . . . a kind of vague crushing sensation in the chest at worst. I mean, Dorothy, he literally dropped while running according to the young man who was jogging just behind him . . . no pulse, nothing." She had pondered what a "vague crushing sensation" would feel like, but now she found herself hoping that just maybe he went out in a blitz of euphoria. She supposed not, though, for it was all related to oxygen, and the point of massive coronaries is that they are anaerobic, not aerobic—thus the nausea and the vague crushing sensation. Well, it was a nice thought. A very nice thought for an angry lady.

6

The following night Dorothy sat barefoot on the painter's ladder in the dining alcove. Her mouth pursed, she glared at the text of *David Copperfield.* " 'And his beautiful wife is a star,' said Mr. Dick. 'A shining star. I have seen her shine, Sir. But . . . ' " Why was she doing this? She should shut the book right now, but she read on. " 'Clouds, Sir, clouds.' "

"Oh, by all means, let's read about the clouds!" Dorothy muttered. She continued reading. " 'There is some unfortunate division between them. Some unhappy cause of separation. . . .' " Dorothy scanned the passage quickly. " 'It may have grown up out of almost nothing.' " She slammed the book shut, angry with herself. She had just gotten out of one story, by God if she were going to get trapped in another. The memory of the Dickens passage had gnawed at Dorothy since the day on the boat. But she had waited until the kids had left to look it up. It had meant going down to the storage room in the basement and bringing up several boxes of books and unpacking them until she found the dog-eared copy of *David*

Copperfield. It was not the same copy from the summers in Michigan, but an old one of Peter's from his undergraduate years at Harvard. It was now eleven o'clock at night. It had taken her an entire evening to lug the boxes, unpack them, find the book and then the passage. The upshot was that she had been made miserable by reading about wives like "shining stars." What did Dickens know about women anyhow? He was a monster who had used, abused and finally rejected his own wife, leaving her fat, ugly, depressed and with ten children.

She was no shining star but she was no Catherine Hogarth Dickens either! How had that happened to poor Mrs. Dickens? She supposed it was easy back then—a product of Victorian marriage, the suffering female demanding attention until she finally turns into a whining, silly old slob.

She looked about her. Now that she had actually unpacked three boxes of books, she supposed she should shelve them in the recessed bookcases in the living room. She did need her books around. She realized that she had missed them more than the furniture. She got them shelved quickly and stood back. She could see both the living room and the dining alcove from where she stood. The Oriental rug that she had rolled up that morning rested against a wall. She had also removed a few other, smaller pieces of furniture, "old familiar things," a footstool with a needlepoint inset, a small cherry parson's table. It did not really look bad now. There was nothing left to mock a previous life. It didn't look like home exactly. Not at all really. There were books on the shelves flanking the picture window which framed the Charles River. There was a ladder on the paint-splattered drop cloth, still with the bucket of latex paint. The place was more like a stage set, and she did not dislike the effect at all. It seemed impermanent and ready for action, which seemed rather paradoxical to Dorothy. She would call the painters tomorrow and tell them to hold off. She would tell them she wanted to consider yet another color.

So now the kids were gone, the rug rolled up, the main character in place. But the main character was not behaving right. She was not crying and the condo, although empty, was filled not with the reverberations of the loneliness of a new widow but with anger. And when the anger ebbed there were always the swirling eddies of guilt. She had to tread carefully so as not to be caught in the undertow. Young people like Ella didn't know about guilt. Their anger came clean. It was a have-your-cake-and-eat-it-too situation with them. And that was enviable. What, after all, was the use of being angry if one had to feel guilty? Anger was not like illicit sex. It was not enhanced by feelings of guilt. Such an expert she was becoming! A guilt maven.

Dorothy had tried to make amends for her outburst to Ella before they had all left. But it was an awkward attempt made even more so by Ella's warm smile and readiness for complete understanding, again suggestive of Ella's belief that all of these feelings were somehow therapeutic. But beyond the nods and the smile were the dispassionate eyes of the field observer. She could imagine the entry . . .

At 1900 hours there was an outburst. Although the old female had lost some of her former position during the bereavement and the dominance hierarchy had been disturbed with subadult male and females directing nesting matters, she was biding her time until subadults left to assert her preferences. Alone the old female was approached by the newcomer subadult who exhibited aggressive behavior. The old female gave cough-threats, a soft bark-like grunt uttered through partially opened mouth directed down the hierarchy by higher-ranked to lower-ranked individuals, indicating slight annoyance. It was to function as a mild warning. The newcomer ignored the warning and pressed on until the old high-ranking female was forced to give wraaa-barks typical of those in a clearly agnostic context. By the next day, however, the old female made the soft woo woo's of attrition and initiated some grooming behavior.

Dorothy would stop thinking about Ella. This was a simply ridiculous indulgence. The girl was not that bad, and she certainly did not deserve that much thought.

The next morning Dorothy had just taken her coffee into the living room when the telephone rang. It seemed as if the ringing sound was in a stereo that was slightly out of register. There was the regular ring from the kitchen and then a sharp echo. Of course! The new cordless phone that Ira had brought home the day before he died. Peter had just hooked it up the morning they left. Dorothy realized that it had either not been working or she had not received any phone calls in twenty-four hours. But it was definitely working now and she did not know where the damn thing was, although she could hear it screeching. She looked about. The sound was coming from the dining alcove. How could such a noise, such a thing, get lost in a place without furniture?

She moved toward the ladder. It seemed to be coming from that region. She stepped on something. It squawked. "For goodness sakes!" she muttered, and reached down. The phone was in a deep fold of the drop cloth, ringing madly. "Shut up! Shut up! Now how do I work this thing?" It bore no resemblance to a phone, with its confusing array of command buttons and antennae. There were simply too many things to push: a privacy button, a redial button, a hang-up button. The phone kept blasting away. "Goddamn, how do I say hello?" Dorothy shouted out. She was madly pushing buttons. "Would you shut up!"

"Dorothy!" a small gravelly voice piped through the square patch of tiny holes in what Dorothy assumed to be the receiver.

"Mother! Whoops! I have you upside down." How one would ever know which end was the ear end and which was the mouth was beyond comprehension. "Mother . . . Mother . . . you sound so . . ." She hesitated. "Miniature." Indeed it was as if there were a tiny little Beebie incarcerated within the receiver.

"Put up the antenna, Dorothy!" Her father sounded little, too—Munchkins!

"This thing has an antenna?" Dorothy asked of no one in particular and held the receiver several inches away, trying to examine it. "Oh, so it does." She quickly extended the antenna. "There we go."

"Now we can hear you," Beebie said, swelling to normal size in Dorothy's ear. "So how's our baby?"

"Goo."

"What? I'm having trouble hearing you again." Beebie was shouting.

"Good," Dorothy said. "It's just that I've never used this cordless phone before. Ira bought it and Peter set it up for me. It seems rather complicated. I don't know why anybody would need one."

"Well, if you have a garden and are outside," Gordon said. "But you don't have a garden now so . . ."

"Gordon, what do you mean she doesn't have a garden? The condo has that lovely little courtyard garden. She can go down there anytime."

"Well, I mean she doesn't have a garden like she used to."

This was a typical long-distance call between Dorothy and her parents: Beebie and Gordon wound up talking to each other.

"As a matter of fact . . . Dorothy, are you still there??"

"Yes, Mother, I'm still here."

"Well," continued Beebie, "I went down there the morning we left and there was a fellow turning over the beds. I bet they have them planted by now. Anyhow we're glad to see you're taking initiative."

"What initiative?" Dorothy asked.

"The phone. You're using it—a newfangled device. Ira would be proud of you."

A newfangled device for a newfangled widow, Dorothy thought.

"Hey, Beebie, tell your daughter what you did yesterday."

"Oh, Gord!"

"What, Mother?"

"I had a very nice golf game."

"Don't be so modest, Beebie," Gordon urged.

"Okay, okay. I broke ninety."

"Mother! That's great! You're seventy-five years old and you broke ninety. Seventy-five-year-olds don't do that!"

"First of all, darling, I am not seventy-five. I'm seventy-four and a half. And secondly, yes they do—Rose Farber did it two years ago."

"Is that the lady with the wire-brush hair and false eye-lashes?" Dorothy asked.

"Yes, Rose. She's in my mah-jongg group too."

"She should have a chromosome test—her score might not count. No, Mother, this is great!"

"Well, thank you very much. Listen, Dolly, I'm sending you some of those good bagels from Toojays. We went there last night."

"Did they have the brisket?"

"No, just on Tuesdays and Thursdays."

"What'd you have?"

"I had the blintzes. What did you have, Gordie?"

"I forget."

"How can you forget? You said it kept repeating on you all night."

"Oh, the corned beef. It's the way they cut it."

"Dad, it can't be the way they cut it that gives you indiges-tion."

"No," said Beebie. "It's not the way they cut it, Gordie. It's the way you chew it. You don't chew your food and you know I was just reading in the *Miami Herald* that the average size piece of meat that people choke to death on is the size of a package of cigarettes."

"I chew my meat better than that, Beebie."

"Listen, enough about us already," Beebie said. Shoot! Dorothy thought. She had really been enjoying the conversation. "How's by you? How's it going?"

By "it" Dorothy assumed her mother meant widowhood. "Fine. Fine."

"As well as can be expected," Gordon offered.

"Right." Her dear father—always with *les mots justes,* shoring up the emotional dikes, providing easy ramps of transition out of sticky verbal situations. None of this let's-let-it-all-hangout stuff. Ella seemed as silly and as abstract as a cartoon figure now.

"Are you getting the condo work under way again? When are the painters coming?" Beebie asked.

"Tomorrow," Dorothy lied.

"And I understand the Bokhara rug looks gorgeous in the living room."

"Yes," Dorothy replied, staring at the blank wall-to-wall carpeting. "How did you hear that?"

"Peter called from the airport before he and that girl flew off to Africa."

"Mother, it's not 'that girl.' "

"Ella—forgive me. But honestly, Dorothy, your father and I feel that she's a little . . . a little . . ."

"Weird," Gordon said.

Dorothy never thought she would be in the position of defending Ella. "Well, she and Peter apparently share a lot."

"How can they? She's so . . ."

"Weird." Gordon finished the sentence.

"Well, Peter's a little weird," Dorothy replied.

"He is not," Beebie said fiercely. "He's a perfectly normal, brilliant boy."

"He likes living out in the bush and digging up dead people's bones. Some might think that's weird."

"Well, it's not. Besides, it's fossils and he's a brilliant paleontologist."

"Well, Ella's a primatologist," Dorothy persisted.

"That's monkeys and it's weird."

"Oh, Mother!"

"Listen, enough of them. What are you going to do today?"

"Uh . . . I don't know. Unpack some books."

"Be careful. Don't stoop over. Bend from the knees," Beebie cautioned.

"All right. I'll do that."

"But you really need some fresh air. Listen! I have a wonderful idea."

"What's that?" Dorothy asked. She was looking out the picture window which was being bisected by a rower's shell slicing down the Charles.

"You need to get outside and get some fresh air."

"I'm watching an MIT or Harvard student right now through my window. It's lovely."

"No," Beebie said. "You need to be out there. Here's my idea. Take the cordless phone and go all the way down to that darling courtyard and see if we can still talk."

"Mother?"

"Do it."

"Oh, my God."

"It'll be good for you."

She was sick of doing things that people thought would be good for her, but then again arguing about it wouldn't do her any good either. "Okay," she said, heading for the front hall. This was ridiculous. She would simply not do it. She would lie. Suddenly it seemed that a charming adventure was at hand. "Okay . . . I'm heading down the hall to the front door." She slammed the coat closet door and turned on her heels and walked to the kitchen. "Okay. I'm waiting for the elevator." The broom closet had a louvered door on a track. "Here it comes!" She slid the louvered door open and then shut.

"That's very clear," Beebie said. "I can hear the elevator door."

Dorothy smiled. This was great fun. Maybe she should go into sound effects. She grabbed a whisk broom and brushed over the receiver.

"A little staticky . . . ," Gordon was saying.

Dorothy lowered her voice and continued to brush the receiver. "Well, we're going down now."

"We can still hear you!" Beebie's voice exploded like pellets through the whisk broom.

"Okay! We're here," Dorothy said. She slid open the louvered door, but remained in the broom closet. She looked about for her next prop. From the dust-cloth bag she grabbed a terry rag and put it over the receiver. "Okay. I'm walking toward the lobby."

"We can still hear you. You sound farther away but the static is gone."

She grabbed another rag. "How do I sound now?"

"Dimmer."

"I'm approaching the garden," Dorothy said. She took down the entire rag bag and thrust in the receiver, then yelled into the bag, "CAN YOU HEAR ME NOW?"

"Barely," came the voice like fine-grained sandpaper.

"WHAT?"

"Barely."

"LET ME MOVE CLOSER TO THE COURTYARD ENTRANCE . . . Is that better?" She took the receiver out of the rag bag.

"A little . . . yes . . . yes. . . . Now how's the garden?" Just at that moment the doorbell rang.

"Just a minute, it's my . . ." She caught herself just in time. "Listen," Dorothy said through four dust cloths. "I better be going now."

"Just tell me one thing. Did they do the azaleas?"

"Yes . . . Yes, they did them. Better go."

"Call us from your garden again. We love you and remember . . ." Dorothy thrust her hand with the receiver into the rag bag and clicked a button.

7

They had certainly "done" the azaleas. Little crescent-shaped beds had been carved out at precise intervals along the courtyard walls and in each a bright coral-pink azalea squatted. Like little ballerinas in tutus, they deep-pliéd into the mulched crescents. A rigid strip of impatiens flanked a north-facing wall. The condominium building had actually been erected as a superstructure on top of the shell of an old church. It was five stories high and enclosed the garden space on three sides. In the middle of the grass plot was a mound of silver artemisia belted by petunias. The attempted design was that of a cloistered garden. But it had backfired somehow and the resulting effect was that of being in the bottom of a landscaped well over which a small square of sky had been permitted to hover.

Dorothy had stood in many an ardent new gardener's first "real" garden. She was accustomed to garish splashes of color and the relentless symmetry of excessively formal designs, but this was different. There was something quite bizarre and inappropriate about this garden. On one hand it seemed a cross between a putting green and a cloister. Yet it was hard to imagine either a golfer or a monk feeling particularly at ease here. There were two little stone benches against far walls, but no paths leading to them. The immaculate square of grass with the artemisia preening in the middle suggested acts of trespassing. A cloistered garden would invite one to walk at a measured pace in attitudes of reflection and contemplation. Here one walked to escape and longed to climb out of the hole. The garden was showy but hardly cherished. There was something profoundly forlorn about it. This was not the gaily patterned garden in which circles and squares of plantings bloomed like the decorative geometry of a Persian rug. Instead it was more like a child wearing makeup—glazed and confused, cut off from its nature.

Dorothy imagined that this was how child prostitutes must appear in exotic brothels patronized by sick old men. There was something truly perverted about the garden, literally turned the wrong way, inside out. It seemed to die under a spell of garish colors and disastrous symmetry. On top of the west wall, part of the original building which rose only twenty or so feet, was a statue of a winged angel. She was turned partly away from the garden. Her hands seemed tense and her wings too small. Dorothy turned abruptly, vowing never to set foot in the garden again.

She had planned to take a stroll down Commonwealth Avenue. There were many grand old buildings, once private homes, that had now been purchased by nonprofit organizations. The first she came to was the archdiocese of Boston's Division of Education. She found the snarl of roses behind its unkempt hedge a relief from the mulched crescents of azaleas. Next came the Scientology Center. There was a pathetic little array of marigolds, a very poor advertisement for such energetic proselytizers. One was constantly encountering their minions in the neighborhood.

Then there was the New England School of Optometry. Its
yard was a raggedy little postage-stamp affair with too many
different things plopped in it. Whatever happened, Dorothy
wondered, to the notion of a square of pea gravel with a few
stone urns of spring flowers and cascading ivy? Unless a building hosted one of the magnificent Commonwealth magnolias,
the gardens looked terrible and were totally unimaginative.

Dorothy did not know where she was walking. She could
not really imagine having errands in this neighborhood. If one
were of a religious bent, yes, there was much to do. The only
"practical" store was the most ludicrous grocery she had ever
encountered. It catered exclusively to the Yuppie population.
One could buy raw shish kebab sticks in marinades to take
home and cook. They sold these with small packages of mes-
quite charcoal, "suitable for the hibachi." For eight dollars
there was a minuscule portion of pesto sauce in a darling container. There was Sacher torte by the slice, an array of sauces
with raspberry vinegars and pink peppercorns. One could place
an order now for fresh brioche for "that Sunday brunch."
Croissants were apparently out of vogue.

Dorothy needed a new pair of nylons and it pained her to
realize that the nearest place she could purchase them was
Saks Fifth Avenue, two blocks away. Buying stockings at Saks
seemed ridiculous. When she had lived in Lincoln she had
loved making trips to Saks. But they were for special pur-
chases—a spring suit, a gown to wear to a hospital fund raiser.
It was an event to come to Saks, go shopping and then lunch
at the Ritz.

What happened, Dorothy wondered, when "events" became
part of the flow of everyday life? Did life become trivialized
then? Could there still be ritual? Before they had moved to
Boston, there had been this ebb and flow between errands and
trips, between schedule and ritual, between what was com-
monplace and what was an event. In Lincoln one drove to get
stockings and one walked in gardens and rarely on streets.

Now everything was different. And here Dorothy had just walked the entire length of Commonwealth Avenue and found herself at the Ritz Carleton where once she had lunched on delicate shrimp salads with women friends.

Across from the Ritz were the public gardens where her husband, against all actuarial charts and self-knowledge, had dropped dead. The gardens years ago had played gracious host to the ritual of retracing the ducklings' path with her children, in springtime. Now they had become the scene of a tragic event, the result of which must be coped with, dealt with, accepted and mainstreamed into her life until the actual event lost its sharp edges and became smooth with time, part of a continuum of this thing called life.

How had she happened to get here? Here, to the bottom of Commonwealth? She could barely remember the walk. She looked across and saw mothers and children walking through the winding paths toward the duck pond, flanked by flotillas of spring blossoms. She crossed the street to see the people more closely—mothers, children, babysitters, men and women on their lunch breaks. She walked through an entry gate and down a paved path for several yards. The pond showed through clouds of dogwood and flowering crab. Along the paths were rectangular beds loaded with catface pansies. Then came the rectangles solid with tulips. Now this is how a garden should be, thought Dorothy. This was the urban translation of what the great English designer Russell Page meant when he wrote about the formally patterned garden in its juxtaposition to an incalculable and wild world. A patterned garden was to be reassuring, a reaffirmation of people's authority which was extended toward the edge of the wilderness whether it was a forest or the Kansas prairie of Dorothy Gale.

In this case the wilderness was the city. But the public gardens were not rigidly patterned or overwhelmingly symmetrical as was the one in Church Tower. There was a problem, after all, with too much symmetry. The perfect balance, Dorothy thought, suggests a paranoia, an obsessive fear of chaos. The loosely patterned garden never fears frenzy but in its gentle order provides the possibility for chance, for a kind of randomness that might offer surprises but no tornadoes.

Dorothy had just passed a fifty-foot bed in colors that undulated from creamy pinks to deep reds when suddenly the color ended, and instead of a rectangle full of tulips there was a forest of blossomless stems. She remembered now reading in the paper how vandals had come through and decapitated the bed of flame-tipped orange and red tulips. Ira had even mentioned noticing the bed on his runs through the gardens.

Dorothy stood and stared. She pinched her mouth together. Was she actually going to cry? She, the fresh widow who had not yet really wept for her husband, in a matter of seconds felt her face slick with tears for four hundred goddamn tulips. And the more she thought about it the more she cried because she knew that the tears were not for Ira but for herself. She was terribly ashamed because the long and the short of it was she could not cry the first-class tears of real grief but instead these chintzy little tulip tears of anger. It was the difference between one-hundred-dollar-an-ounce perfume and dimestore cologne. One scent lingered. The other grew stale. With real tears she imagined feelings of relief and ennobling calm. These tears merely begot tension and more anger.

She looked up through the scrim of her tears. The garden and its life had turned wavy. She saw trees and children and more flowers but they all seemed to be losing their identity in some fundamental way. It was as if reality were breaking up before her. Shapes and forms were becoming atomized. A light of cognition seemed to dim within Dorothy's brain. The children's heads intermingled with the tulips and other blossoms. They hovered in the air like disembodied splotches of color. The mothers became formless darker blobs. It was as if she were losing her bearings and becoming a dazed wanderer in a world of lifeless abstractions.

Dorothy felt panic well up within her. She had to get out of this place, this garden. But she could not go back to the other place with its garden, the little child whore looked over by the angel with the midget wings. If she could only go back to Lincoln—not forever, just for a little bit, to get her bearings. She had once been a wife, a loving wife, a mother with children, real children—funny, dear little things with moods and sassiness and love and wit who had grown into smart, dear big people who knew more about everything than she did. But she was still their mother. Yes, she must, if only for a few hours, get back to Lincoln.

She rushed to Church Tower and went immediately to the garage for the car. Within twenty minutes of leaving the public gardens she was driving west on Storrow Drive. She stole glances toward the river on her right. Light dashed against the water at harsh angles and golden slivers sliced down the river as crews practiced. White triangles bobbed in the glittering river light as fleets of sailing dinghies crisscrossed the Charles. On the banks college students sunbathed and played Frisbee and, thankfully, it seemed to Dorothy as if the visual world were beginning to reassemble itself. The domed cupolas of Lowell and Leverett houses rose across the river.

Dorothy swung into the right lane to cross the Larz Anderson Bridge. This was an unnecessary wiggle in her route. It would have been more direct for her to cross the river farther up, but she longed to drive under the arc of sycamores on a particular stretch of Memorial Drive. She needed to drive through that arcade of dappled light. She would not, after all, dash madly back to Lincoln, but proceed at a measured pace with some ceremony. For Lincoln was now the event and needed the attending ritual.

Memorial Drive flowed into Mount Auburn and Fresh Pond Parkway. Dorothy followed the parkway another mile and a half to the traffic circle which shooed her onto Route 2. This was the same route that Ira had driven for twenty-six years, twice a day, in his quest to mend the chambers of the heart, to darn the valves and to patch arteries. He was a seamstress of the heart with his small, slender fingers. He could sew anything. When moths ate a hole in his favorite herringbone jacket and Dorothy took it to the tailor who had supposedly performed his invisible weaving magic, Ira had roared. "He calls this invisible? The guy must be blind!"

That evening Ira brought home his heart tools and, with the matching thread that Dorothy had found, set to work. Within an hour the hole had been transformed, rejoined with the rest of the body of the fabric. Dorothy got out a magnifying glass. There was no trace of where the hole had been. The pattern ran flawlessly, slanting at just the perfect angle and then reversing direction in the new row.

Route 2 made a hard left turn to the south and west. In a minute there would be a sign for the Lincoln turn but she decided to come in the longer, more circuitous route through Concord Center. Another ritual, she supposed. But it had been to Concord Center that she had driven for her stockings, her dry cleaning, her marketing, her errands in the old station wagon.

They sold the station wagon the day after they had moved to Church Tower. They did not need two cars anymore since Ira could walk to work and it was ridiculous to have a station wagon in the city. Dorothy knew that this all made perfectly good sense. So if they could collapse what had amply housed twenty-six years of conspicuous consumption into a two-bedroom condominium, they could certainly be comfortable in the small, upholstered confines of a BMW. What was there to haul around now? There were no kids or car pools, and with no garden there were no more fifty-pound bags of peat and lime and mulch. So what did they need all that space on wheels for?

She was now coming into the center. She had just passed the Brigham's Ice Cream parlour when she noticed the new brick facade on the storefront next to it. Miss Hewitt's was certainly still there, wasn't it? Dorothy pulled over. There was a parking space right in front. She could see there was still a café curtain drawn across the bottom half of the window. She walked toward it and, coming right up to the glass, she peered in. Ah yes! A feeling of relief swept over Dorothy. There was a row of little girls in pale pink leotards and tights inscribing *ronds de jambe* on the floor with their pointed toes. They were so small, tiny little waistless things, with pooched-out tummies. This had to be the pre-ballet class for four-year-olds, Dorothy thought. And there was Miss Hewitt, her white hair twisted back, her body still elegant, a birch among saplings. "We shall now walk like queens into the studio," Miss Hewitt would announce and thus a class would begin. Six or ten or a dozen little girls, their hair pulled back in elastics, their faces alert, their tiny bodies pink and keen, would spread their arms and follow Miss Hewitt into the mirrored room.

Miss Hewitt could summon children as no parent or teacher ever could or would. She summoned them to grace and intimations of elegance. They became primas to themselves without ever knowing the word. Just as Dorothy never thought of Ira as a surgeon but instead as a seamstress with nimble, beautiful fingers, so she thought of Miss Hewitt not as a ballet teacher but as a cultivator of the most sensitive and illusive of human instincts. Miss Hewitt was "the still unravished bride of quietness" from the Grecian urn who stirred within those little pink bodies notions of truth and beauty.

They were running now diagonally across the studio floor, trying their *jetés*. They appeared as pink smears against the mirrors and sunlight. Miss Hewitt was standing and observing. With her tall dance master's baton in hand she tapped out the rhythm. She put the baton aside and ran into the gap. She sailed across the space in one leap—a silver swan splashed with sunlight. The little girls followed, leaping a bit higher. Dorothy turned away. She did not want to be seen. She suddenly felt very old and very stiff, with no stirrings of truth or beauty.

It was late afternoon by the time she drove up to their old house. She would go up and ring the bell. Joan Murray, the new owner, was a lovely, sweet young woman. Dorothy would explain that she happened to be in the neighborhood and thought she'd stop in to say "hi" and could she perhaps sit in the garden a moment? She rang the bell and waited a minute. No one seemed to be coming. She rang again and waited. Then she walked around to the back. The Murrays' two cars were in the garage. Of course, she remembered now. Joan Murray had a sister in California who was getting married. The whole family was going. Well, now she didn't have to make any excuses about sitting in the garden.

She followed the walk which was actually a brick path fringed on both sides with hosta and ferns and lilies of the valley. The thyme that Dorothy had planted between the bricks was just coming up. The path flowed into an elliptical brick terrace presided over by a golden rain tree in its center with wild ginger growing under it. Spring bulbs crowded up along the edges of the terrace. It looked just the same. Joan Murray had kept it exactly as Dorothy had planted it. Even the furniture and the stone tubs were still in the same positions, brimming with ivy, and the small pots of miniature white cyclamen were set amidst the ivy.

To the right of the terrace was the small vegetable garden with the cages already on the tomato plants and a few ruffled leaves of lettuce just up. Dorothy's eyes swept the lawn. Good Lord! Joan Murray finally had the nerve to do what Dorothy never did: take down the grape arbor.

It had always disturbed Dorothy that she could tolerate so easily the extraordinary banality of a grape arbor. But tolerate it she had for some unfathomable reason. She would have never imagined that tidy little Joan Murray, "prepped out" as Sophie had put it, in her Talbot wardrobe, would beat her to the punch and tear down the grape arbor.

The arbor had separated the sun and the moon gardens. Dorothy began walking toward the far end of the yard where the arbor had once been. She did expect changes in the moon garden. When the Murrays had come to look at the house originally, she had sensed that Joan had felt the moon garden a bit weird with its white moonflowers, many of which were night bloomers. Ira had not helped with his anecdotal material. "Yep!" he had said, "we sometimes call Dorothy the Spider Woman. You know that movie? Naw, you kids are too young. It was a favorite of mine as a kid. Sherlock Holmes battles the Spider Woman, the little old lady who grew night-blooming plants in her London basement. That's our Dorothy!" It had fallen flat, as family jokes and stories often do outside the boundaries of bloodlines.

The prize of Dorothy's night bloomers was her own son, Peter. When as a child on summer nights, unable to sleep or awakened by a nightmare, he would run into her and Ira's bedroom wanting to get into bed with them, Dorothy would take him by the hand and lead him downstairs, out the back porch to the terrace, past the rain tree. Barefoot they would run across the lawn to the moon garden where they would sit on the little bench side by side and breathe in the fragrance of the night-blooming jasmine. They would become used to the night and Dorothy would tell Peter about the people who loved the stars so much they could not fear the night.

Once she had lost a baby in the moon garden. Between Peter and Sophie she had become pregnant. She had spotted throughout the first two months and one very hot August night, feeling crampy and unable to sleep, she had walked out to the garden to sit. Ira had come home very late from an emergency and he came to sit with her on the bench. When she got up there was a big red stain on her nightgown. The baby had bled away in the moon garden. Poor Ira! The dear seamstress was so shocked and disoriented. There was simply no way he could stitch up the baby within her womb again.

Peter had grown to love the moon garden. About the time he was nine or ten years old he had made a series of small signs. Using silver luminescent paint, he had inscribed quotations that had to do with moonlight as well as werewolves. He called them nightlights. There were words from favorite horror movies and from old nighttime children's stories. She had been proud of Peter's love and care of the garden, for it truly represented a triumph over all the dark little goblins that had invaded and haunted his nights as a youngster. She wondered if the signs were still up. She had always removed them for the winter. But she had put them out early this year, a few weeks before the Murrays moved in. She approached the moon garden cautiously. She knew that Joan Murray must have changed it. Yes. There was a ring of pink impatiens. In another month it would thicken up and creep through the alabaster flowers, the pink stealing away small pieces of moonlight.

There was only one sign left, the one under the forsythia. *And still within the summer's night / A something so transporting bright / I clap my hands to see.* That one had been Dorothy's choice from Emily Dickinson. "Hmmp!" Dorothy grunted. There would be a little less hand clapping once those pinks took over.

All of the other small signs had been taken down. The spot under the wolfsbane was empty. Once there had been a sign with a quote from an old horror movie made back in the forties. *Even a man who is pure at heart / And says his prayers by night / Can become a wolf when the wolfsbane blooms / And the autumn moon is bright.* Some of the words were creepy. Some were lovely like the *Goodnight Moon* verse from the old children's book. How had that verse gone? Dorothy wondered. How could she forget that lovely book? Hadn't she read it every night to one or both children for years?

Ira was never home from the hospital in time to put the children to bed. She had always done it. The hard part of the job was rounding the kids up, the it's-time-to-go-to-bed and the attendant whining and procrastinations, the raucous baths and the bathroom left a sodden mess. The good part was tucking clean little children into beds, reading the bedtime story, turning off the "big light" and turning on the "little light," the wet hullabaloo of minutes before dissolved. A quiet enveloped the upstairs and with it came the gentle ritual. First, Peter checked under his bed for monsters. He then placed his monster bat beside his bed along with a can of hairspray—for not only would the hairspray sting but it would make the monster's eyes stick shut so it couldn't chase Peter.

Sophie, a strangely fearless child, would rearrange her stuffed animals. She had endless configurations for them. Sometimes they sat at tiny tea tables. Sometimes they manned battle stations or guarded the dollhouse or elaborate block castles that Sophie had built.

"Ready?" Dorothy would call. "Ready!" two little voices would answer. First she would go to Sophie's room and read *Goodnight Moon* and then she would go to Peter and read it again. She had discovered the book when Peter was two. He did not even begin to tire of it until he was five or six. And now she could barely remember it. She had read it almost nightly during all those years. Perhaps the sign with the verse from the book was still in the garden shed. Could she get in there? She suddenly remembered that there was an extra key wedged behind a shingle. She had never used it. It might still be there.

It was. She felt like a thief as she put the key in the shed door. What if the Murrays suddenly appeared? How would she explain it—"The Return of the Spider Lady"? She opened the door. The dank, chilly air rushed at her. "Oh, dear!" Dorothy whispered as she saw an entire wall still stacked with stuff that was supposed to have been hauled away. The shed had become a bit of a dumping ground during the packing-up process, and Mr. Emerson had been paid to come and take away this final load. He had apparently not done so. The Murrays should not have to contend with this, the debris of a previous family's life. There were old bike tires, the mildewed, ripped canvas from an old trampoline, a cracked aquarium. She poked around a bit searching for the signs which seemed to be nowhere in sight. She lifted a piece of plywood from a stack under the potting table. A centipede scurried out from under it and into a crack in the concrete floor.

The crack! Dorothy nearly gasped out loud. How could she have forgotten that day? She had been starting seedlings in trays. Sophie, who was three at the time, had sat beside her on a stool helping when suddenly she had fallen off and smashed her chin on the concrete floor. There had been blood all over the place. Luckily it had been a weekend and Ira was home to stitch her up.

Afterward, with Sophie still whimpering, Ira brought her back into the shed. "Sophie!" he said. "You're not nearly as bad off as that floor. Look!" he said pointing to the crack. "Did you do that when you fell?" Sophie giggled. "I did that!" She pointed gleefully at the crack. Then Peter had come in. "What happened to all the blood?" he asked. And before Dorothy could say she had cleaned it up, Sophie giggled raucously. "The crack drank it." Poor Peter had nightmares about vampire cracks and did not come near the shed for weeks. Dorothy crouched down now and ran her finger along the crack. Had it all really ever happened? Had she had this life so filled with blood and giggles and growing things?

She looked up. There was a stack of collapsed packing boxes against one wall. Sticking out from behind the stack was a familiar shape. What was it? Something from one of the kids' rooms. She pulled the stack of cartons away from the wall. Out tumbled the old Mickey Mouse lamp. She unscrewed the body from its base. No bulb. She was curious to see whether it would still work, so she unscrewed the bulb from the light over the work table, put it in, then plugged the cord into an outlet and pushed the switch. A dim light showed through the accretions of dust. Indeed it was as if the light had traveled from a distant time, a distant star. She remembered how in the moon garden she had spoken to Peter of such things as they watched the stars' reflections in the small sunken pool. She would tell the strange story of how light traveled so fast but came from a star so distant that the light they saw in an evening could have left its star on its journey to the garden before there were even humans on Earth. The moon garden had become a cozy place to talk about the vastness of space, the immensity of time and the fears of a little boy.

Dorothy licked her finger and rubbed the dirt off Mickey's face. He beamed more brightly. She unplugged the lamp and coiled up the cord. She would take the Mickey lamp back with her to Boston.

It was almost dark now. She would go back to the moon garden, and ignoring the pink impatiens, she would sit on the bench of the Spider Woman for a while and wait for the night and the moon. She sat quietly, the Mickey lamp on her lap, and watched the burning shades of the sun garden, the cutting garden directly opposite with its poker-hot reds and garish pinks and yellows, grow pale in the fading light. The first stars appeared and a three-quarter moon began its climb. The night-blooming lilies had already opened and moths addicted to the sweet fragrance were paying their dark visits. Water lilies and star reflections floated on the calm dark sea of the sunken pool. The moonlight now came splashing down to join the stars and the water flowers. Dorothy watched. The garden began to glow—the blossoms of the white forsythia hanging like suspended snowflakes, the spikes of columbine and vesper and Siberian iris, the yucca filamentosa with its ever silent white bells. She sat there all night, her sweater wrapped tightly around her.

Finally the moon stole away to another night in another place. The dawn broke cool and gray. She turned east to face the old rose crescent with its fragrant antique varieties of musk and damask and cinnamon and China. A tincture of pink spread through the gray until the sky for one brief instant appeared to Dorothy like the shell of a transparent egg, and the sun spilled over the edge. The moonflowers had long ago closed and Dorothy got up stiffly and walked toward the crescent of roses. There was a haughty little apricot-colored tea rose that dared her to pick it. Dorothy looked down at it. She had planted the bush twenty-six springs ago when she had been pregnant with Sophie. "And what am I to do with you?" she thought. "Pick you? Take you with me?" And when it faded was she to put it between the pages of a heavy book until the rose became squashed and ugly, the color of tobacco? And in this shabby immortality it would try to lay claim as a fragile memory of a fragile past. There was something rancid about it all. The hideous tenacity of all those flattened corsages pressed between books' pages. The mockery they made of the past. She grew flowers. She banished goblins. And she helped scared children not to fear the night. But she did not press flowers between the pages of fat novels. It only made stains on the story. Dorothy turned and walked out of the garden.

8

For months after Ira's death Dorothy's mailbox at Church Tower would be stuffed with the most impersonal communications about the most personal aspects of an individual's life. There was a constant stream of stuff from their lawyer and insurance people, but it did not take Dorothy long to realize that she was on the widow's mailing list. She was receiving communications from quarters that knew far less about her life than the lawyers or the insurance folk, but they did not hesitate to get into the act. Almost daily there were pamphlets for cruises catering exclusively to widows and financial planning classes for estate management. After she had returned from Lincoln she sat on her ladder with the morning's mail and found herself reading an unbelievable letter on very sedate stationery about "that problem you can never feel comfortable discussing with your lawyer, your children and probably not even your doctor—**sex for widows over fifty.**" From this point on there was a promiscuous use of boldfaced type.

"We know," the letter went on, "that it's hard to get out

and meet new people after all these years with your loved one. And just because your loved one is gone does not mean that your **natural urges have gone too.** Sexual activity in widowhood is not only **natural** but **healthy.** In studies conducted with over 1,000 widows and widowers . . ." Dorothy skipped down past the statistics that related sexual activity to declines in everything from osteoporosis to constipation, to the next bit of boldface words—**an appropriate partner.** "We know," the letter continued, "that it's difficult getting out to meet new people after all these years. Now with the advent of AIDS, the sexual revolution is over. If initiating conversation with new people is hard, just imagine how hard it is asking if they have had a recent **blood test.**" Dorothy read on. "In lieu of a live partner in which conversation is difficult and safe sex cannot be guaranteed, we offer to send you at an extremely low price a device in a **plain package** with **no markings whatsoever** as to the contents . . . all parts guaranteed . . . runs on D-cell rechargeable batteries."

Dorothy was stunned beyond words. She did not know whether to laugh or cry. She tried to imagine herself dead and Ira left alive with all his natural urges in boldface. She certainly would not want him to get AIDS, but then again she hated to think of herself replaced by D-cell rechargeable batteries in some inflatable vagina. She did hope that if it had been Ira, he would not have fallen into bed with a nurse. If the banality of a grape arbor bothered her, the idea of Ira and a nurse was absolutely intolerable. If he had to fulfill urges it should be with someone sexually stupendous, but not too young. Joan Collins perhaps. As for herself, Dorothy simply could not imagine or put a face on a would-be partner other than to know that this device was not it. She tossed the letter into the wastebasket along with one on a Caribbean cruise. There was another envelope in an unfamiliar handwriting. She opened it up and out tumbled a twenty-dollar bill. She glanced to the bottom of the note. It was signed Ella.

Dear Dorothy,

I'm afraid I have left a couple of things behind that I am really going to need in Africa. First, and most important, are some notes in a folder for an article I was working on. The folder is in the bottom drawer of the bureau in the room Peter and I were in. The mail is so unreliable between Boston and Nairobi. Could you Xerox the notes and keep a copy just in case, as a backup? Also another article that I was doing for Primatology Journal *was supposed to be sent to me in galley proofs in care of you at your place. Could you also forward that when it comes?*

Many thanks for welcoming me at such a difficult time. I am sorry that I was never able to meet Ira. And I also apologize if I overstepped the boundaries when I guessed that you did not particularly like the rug. In an odd way it reminded me of something in our house once that was all wrong and totally out of place. Peter and I will have two weeks in Nairobi before we head for different directions in Kenya. But we will be rendezvousing every few weeks. Again many thanks.

Yours,
Ella

Dorothy reread the note. The thin paper trembled in her hands. For some unfathomable reason this felt like the first genuine communication she had received since Ira's death and it felt good. In its curious way it had more resonance than any of the carefully worded sympathy notes she had received from their old friends, or Ira's colleagues and patients. She wondered what the something was that someone had once put in Ella's home. She knew so little about Ella really. She had remembered when she had asked Ella where she came from, her answer seemed so peculiar. "Are you from Omaha?" Dorothy had asked. It was about the only city in Nebraska she had ever heard of. "No," Ella had said. "Hay Springs, Sheridan County. It's near the Niobrara River."

It was as if she came from some raw uncharted land, so vast and empty, so bereft of traditional reference points, that only large chunks served as indicators. Thus one spoke in terms of counties and river boundaries. Dorothy imagined scenes from Willa Cather—sensitive, tender people leading complicated interior lives against harsh landscapes. She pictured farms where steaming pans of milk were brought straight from barns on winter mornings into a kitchen with a woodburning stove. She imagined front rooms, a parlor with a piano gleaming like a tantalizing monument to a world that would in some ways always seem unattainable and impenetrable. She pictured a little Ella in a sunbonnet, a few red curls escaping, her chubby fingers pounding out *Au clair de la lune*. And there would be a frail, beautiful mother dressed in faded calico rocking in a chair with her gossamer dreams of culture and art and cities. Dorothy tried to imagine what the something could have been that was "totally out of place." She could not imagine. A Picasso? A Chippendale secretary?

She read the note one more time, then went into the guest bedroom. In the bottom drawer was the folder. There was a stick-on label with a title in Ella's handwriting. *Sisterhood: Beyond Alloparenting in Primates*. Dorothy opened the folder. There were several different-colored index cards. The pink cards were titled *Aunting Behavior*. Dorothy flipped through them. They contained notes about aunting behavior in Rhesus monkeys, Barbary macaques, orangs, Capucin monkeys, yellow baboons. The blue cards dealt with *phenotypic matching* and had the subtitle *sister recognition patterns*. The yellow cards had the heading *reciprocal altruism* and the white cards contained all the information that one ever dreamed of wanting to know about homosexual behavior in both nonprimate and primate species, particularly as witnessed by Ella among female pygmy chimpanzees. A myriad of subtopics included such items as *mutual masturbation as outlets for tension;* one had the hyphenated initials G-G. Dorothy pondered these letters for several seconds wondering what their meaning was. Good girls? Gorilla groups? Beneath the initials were three phrases: *homosexuality an evolutionary strategy? Stopgap measure? Stopgaps as evolution.*

She then turned the card over and after reading a fairly elaborate description of pygmy chimpanzees spreading their labia and cozying up to one another, realized that the initials G-G stood for genital-to-genital contact. There was one other card entitled *Slam-bam-thank-you-ma'am—orangutan rape.* The most interesting note of all, though, was not on a card but scribbled on the inside of the folder: "To see evolution in action we should look for failure—the drought year, the marginal habitat, the relict population whose range is dwindling to zero, and to watch and see who dies. Some points on the graphs do not show species' adaptations but ill-adapted populations making the best of where history has stranded them on the margin of their niche."

This quote was attributed to a certain Alison Jolly. She carefully copied the quote onto a card of her own and taped it to her vanity mirror. There was a kind of sweet irony in thinking of her half-million-dollar condo as being on the margin of a niche, and of herself as a member of some relict population, ill adapted, making the best of where history or Ira had stranded her. She became so fascinated with the concept that she eventually ordered Ms. Jolly's text. Although much of it was very boring for the uninitiated, or at least for those primates who were not primatologists, Dorothy found Jolly's broad interpretations and conjectures about evolution intriguing and quite readable. One had to look hard for them, though, buried as they were between graphs and tables in chapters with off-putting headings like "Interspecific Relations."

One of the most eloquent renderings of these notions was found in the chapter titled "Is Food Limiting? The Howler Controversy." From these passages came the quote Ella had written down. The howlers were howler monkeys in Guatemala. The ostensible point of the passage was to illustrate a little academic battle concerning short-term versus long-term sampling studies of something called "optimal foraging behavior." What interested Dorothy was not the academic teapot tempests, but Ms. Jolly's more general insights. What, for example, did the author mean by "history"? First she had used the word *nature* and then, later on in the paragraph, *history:* "making the best of where history has stranded them." Even more perplexing for Dorothy were the author's allusions to randomness and chance which she guessed were a part of history.

A few weeks later Dorothy received a warm and heartfelt acknowledgment from Ella. The notecards, in spite of the shaky postal routes between Boston and Nairobi, had arrived safely. The mission had been completed and there was no reason to have expected more written communication to occur between them, but Dorothy was still curious about Jolly's use of the words *history* and *nature.* There was, she thought, history and there was natural history. History, it seemed to Dorothy, was a kind of sweeping narrative. It was played out by figures against fabulous backdrops and tapestries of violence and grandeur. Natural history was a small-scale affair that led to contemplations about the wonderful and mysterious world of, say, the beetle or the inchworm or whatever. History was not ordinary life. History was extraordinary life. She was so occupied with these questions of history and nature and marginal niches that she decided to write to Ella about them. She sat down in the slants of gold light that streamed through her window to ask about history, both natural and unnatural, and chance and random change.

Dear Ella,
(She paused. She really did not know how to begin such a letter. Did one come right out with the questions? There seemed to be no transitional material. She who had spent a lifetime reading novels, gardening books and cookbooks suddenly found herself in the midst of a textbook entitled

THE WIDOW OF OZ / 75

The Evolution of Primate Behavior. There was no prece-
dent and there were no transitions. So she continued.)

*I'm glad that you received the notes in good order. I
have a confession to make. I read them all. I became fascinated by a quote on the inside of the folder you had scribbled and attributed to Alison Jolly. I subsequently
purchased Jolly's book, most of which I found beyond me
and consequently less than scintillating from the "lay primate" point of view.*

*But in chapter 5, the one on ranging, I found Dr. Jolly's
remarks on evolution in action quite intriguing. What
intrigues me the most is her use of the word* history. *She
says, or rather writes, that* "to see evolution in action, we
should look for failure—the drought year, the marginal
habitat, the relict population whose range is dwindling to
zero, and watch and see who dies. Some points on the
graphs do not show species' adaptations but ill-adapted
populations making the best of where history has stranded
them on the margin of their niche." *I have never thought
of history in quite this way. I just don't quite catch the
meaning of the word in Jolly's context. Then again when
she speaks of behavior as "neutral" and random changes in
behavior it gets rather murky for me. Is she still talking*
history *here?*

Basically my questions are these:

*1) What's the difference between history and natural
history—aside from the fact that one happens to people
and the other to plants and animals?*

*2) What do primatologists and biologists mean when
they talk of chance? (I know what my friend Monica the
physicist means. It all has to do with haphazard movement
of subatomic particles. But is it that chancy all the way up
from the atom to the howler monkey?)*

                                           Best,
                                           Dorothy

Two weeks later Dorothy received a postcard.

> *Dear D——*
>
> *Will write more later, but here's the quick answer to your questions. 1) None. There's no real difference between history and natural history. Remember history begins when things screw up, i.e., wars, plagues, volcanoes, tidal waves, etc. The figures just differ—kings, queens, as opposed to dinosaurs, lemurs. 2) Yes. Life's a crapshoot.*
>
> > *yrs.*
> > *Ella*

9

Dorothy had succeeded in delaying the painters for almost five months. They had not seemed particularly upset that she had been so indecisive about the color in the dining alcove, wavering, as she told them, between bean-soup red and the linen white they had mistakenly used on the one wall. They had after all been flat out over the summer months with more work than they could handle, and because of the particularly dry summer they were loath to spend clear, sunny days on interior jobs when they could be painting acres of exterior stuff.

The truth, however, was that Dorothy did not give a hoot about the color of the dining alcove walls. That was purely a secondary issue. But she had in fact become quite attached to the ladder, the paint-speckled drop cloth and the work plank on sawhorses. At sunset she would often sit on the fourth step of the ladder using as her cocktail table the foldout support for the paint bucket. She would sip her Scotch and soda while watching the river. The plank on the sawhorses, which was where the buffet should have been, made a very nice desk. She would usually have her breakfast there.

She had taken to buying huge bouquets of cheap flowers, the kind they sold in supermarkets rather than the fancy flower shops on Newbury Street. It was quite amazing to her how any colors in the flowers interplayed quite dramatically with the splatters on the drop cloth, ladder and plank. She had bought an entire bucket of those cheap dyed carnations. The colors of the flowers erupted into a candied lapidary splendor when placed on the drop cloth.

It was ten o'clock on a Wednesday morning and George from the reception desk downstairs had just hung up, saying that Bill Conover, the painting contractor, was there and wanted to come up and see her. Dorothy knew the moment was at hand. She had rehearsed a little speech. Bill Conover was sweet, and she knew for a fact that he was continually harassed by demanding and petulant clients. He had even said that he was eternally grateful to her for not being in a rush. But now he obviously had the time and for efficiency's sake wanted to finish up the job. She walked to open the front door as the bell rang.

"Well, Mrs. Silver . . ." His gangly frame filled the doorway. "How are we doing? And by the way, here is your mail," he said, handing a stack of letters and magazines to Dorothy. There was a letter from Ella on top.

"Oh, thanks, and I'm doing just fine, Mr. Conover."

"And have we come to a decision about the color in the dining alcove?"

"Well," Dorothy inhaled deeply and sighed.

'It's not that bad, is it?" he said good-naturedly.

"No! No!" Dorothy laughed. "Come on in. I'll explain it." She knew that he must really think her weird. The alcove was either going to be red or white. What could there be to explain? "Would you like a cup of coffee?"

"Sure. Why not?"

Dorothy poured him a cup and then led him into the alcove. The space was slashed with light. A prism that Sophie had sent flung spots of slowly twirling colors that floated across the concrete floors.

"Flowers look nice," Mr. Conover said.

Bless him! Dorothy thought. He was making the job easier.

"I'm glad you noticed, Mr. Conover, because they have something to do with what I've decided to do here. Now this may sound weird." She paused. Bill Conover's face appeared as placid as a sea on a windless summer day. Dorothy chided herself. She knew that nothing sounded weird to a contractor. They were seasoned explorers in the wilderness of families' secrets, obsessions and dreams. Every psychoanalyst should be made to sign on with a contractor for a year's internship. Bill Conover set down his coffee mug on the ladder and slapped his hands together loudly. "Okay! Try me."

"Well," Dorothy said, looking about the room and smiling. "Basically I like the room the way it is."

"You mean you like it white."

"No, not exactly. I like it with this one white wall on the river side and the others the way they are."

"Bare." It was a statement, not a question. Mr. Conover did not even indulge in lifting an eyebrow, which would have in the contractor's repertoire of facial expressions constituted an aerobic exercise.

"Right-o." Dorothy was truly enjoying this conversation. "Of course I will pay you for the work you've already done up to now."

"You already have."

"Well, for the bedroom, kitchen and living room but not for this wall, Mr. Conover."

"The wall is on me, Mrs. Silver."

"Oh no, Mr. Conover." Dorothy shook her head. "There's primer and there's one coat already and you might not want the wall to be on you when you hear the second part of my proposal."

"I'm not an Indian giver, ma'am. It's yours, prime coat and all."

"Well, I wanted to ask you if I could purchase . . ." Dorothy breathed in deeply and squeezed her eyes shut, then launched into her list, "the ladder, this drop cloth, plus the other one that you left, the plank and the supporting sawhorses."

When she opened her eyes Bill Conover's face was as tranquil as if she had just recited a grocery list.

"It's yours. House gift."

Dorothy's face broke into a smile. "Oh no, Mr. Conover."

He had ambled over to the unpainted wall by the makeshift desk. He leaned forward and took out his reading glasses and put them on. "What's this—phone directory?"

"Yes, my children's numbers and a few others. It's easy to have them right in front of me there."

"Good idea. Do you have any grandchildren?"

"No, not yet."

"Well, when you do you can have a wall just for them to draw on."

"What a charming idea. But Mr. Conover, I really don't want you to give me all the drop cloths and ladder and sawhorses. Please let me pay you something for them."

He looked about at the flowers, the drop cloth, the twirling prism. "Naw, I like this idea of yours." A colored bubble of light slid across his face. "Jelly beans," he said. "The whole place looks like jelly beans."

When Mr. Conover had left, Dorothy settled down with a second cup of coffee at her desk to read Ella's letter.

Dear Dorothy,

I got the galleys. Thanks loads. Things are gradually sorting themselves out here. This is, of course, the hardest time. I call it the time of double habitation. The new crew of graduate students has to be habituated to life in the field and the baboons have to be habituated to us. We are working with the same Troop #8 that I observed last year. It has shrunk a bit. There were 60 baboons eighteen months ago. Now the troop is down to 55. Four of the males are confirmed emigrants to troops 9 and 6. One elderly female we suspect has died, as well as an ailing adolescent. Two infants are gone, possibly picked off by lions or perhaps victims of infanticide. There are two other young males that we think have probably emigrated. Tally that up and it adds up to ten missing. The deficit has been partly made up for by five births since I was gone. There are three "black" infants and two browns. They are called black because when baboons are born they have a very dark velvety coat. At around seven months it is replaced by a brownish pelage.

One of the black infants, Willy, was a bit of a surprise. Willy's mother, Ginger, had only begun to have menstrual cycles when I first came out here two and a half years ago—it's actually called estrous cycles with baboons and if you are a baboon you don't have a "period." You are said to be cycling. Usually baboons will have their first estrous cycles somewhere between four and six years old. They do not conceive until one to two years after that. Ginger seems to have broken the mold. When I was here ten months ago she was just getting ready to have her first cycle. Now she has a black infant, the one we named Willy.

There is a male who was Ginger's mother's consort, that means sexual partner. We never had much occasion to observe him. He seems now to be hanging around with

Ginger and taking a real interest in her infant. Although
it was confirmed to me by Barb Feldman who observed
here last winter that Fred was not Ginger's consort. (His
name had been Fritz but when he teamed up with Ginger
we thought, gee whiz, can't let that one go by.) So it is
not out of paternity he is taking this interest. It does seem
lucky for Ginger, however, for as a mother she is a bit
awkward and she is not particularly high-ranking. Nor was
Ginger's mother, Dot, for that matter, but Dot did have a
knack for having relationships with high-ranking females,
mostly through baby-sitting and aunting behavior.

Willy is adorable. Last night I spent the night hidden in
a clump of fever trees near the sleeping cliffs that the
troop often uses. Fred was reclining following an afternoon
of voracious foraging. Ginger was grooming his paunch,
separating the hairs, picking out the grit. He was totally
relaxed when up comes Willy who literally somersaulted
across Fred's belly. Fred extends his index finger and pokes
gently at Willy who then comes back and begins bouncing
on Fred's stomach. Ginger tries to push Willy off. But
Willy keeps coming back for more, intent on playing. Fred
is more than tolerant and keeps touching and stroking
Willy as if to reassure him that it is okay and occasionally
he reaches up and touches Ginger as if to reassure her that
Willy's rambunctiousness is just part of being a kid. This is
why it's good to have Fred about. Ginger, so recently a kid
herself and now thrust into motherhood, seems somewhat
at a loss. She loves grooming Fred and being with the
adults. She's gotten in with some of her mother's high-
ranking cronies when Dot will let her, but at times she
does seem rather confused about Willy.

Did Peter write you about the skull they found over at
Olduvai? Very exciting.

Best,
Ella

10

Sophie had planned Dorothy's New York visit with her usual meticulous care. There were theater tickets and tickets to a big show at the Met. Sophie's secretary had made dinner reservations at Café des Artistes for the first night, a very good Italian restaurant on the second night and the third night it would be a late after-theater supper at the Four Seasons. Sophie knew that her mother eschewed anything too trendy or that was too self-consciously nouvelle cuisine.

"Art as art. Food as food," Dorothy said as she took a bite of the smoked salmon. "They do a nice job here." She had not cooked elaborately or eaten out anyplace special since Ira had died. And although the salmon was really stupendous she could not say she had missed it all that much. There was some little part of her that cringed when she thought of all those dinner parties she had once given. There was something so overwrought about them—fresh raspberries in February flown in from Peru to a fruitier in Cambridge, ridiculously thin asparagus, oysters grilled on rock salt and flamed with sake.

It suddenly struck Dorothy that there was nothing "over-wrought" about her life these days. Cheap flowers in buckets, thick chops broiled nicely, accompanied often by a frozen vegetable and an inexpensive wine. The waiter had removed the salmon plate and was now bringing her scallops of veal loin in a Madeira sauce with braised radicchio on the side and wild rice. It was the best meal she had had in months by all conventional measures, but she knew that in a matter of days she would forget it. She would not call her food pals Ginny and Barbara and Eloise in Lincoln and report, as she had in the past about various gastronomic adventures. That simply was not how she lived now. This exquisitely rendered meal would sink into oblivion while one of her most memorable ones would be a dinner she had had almost six weeks before when the corn was at its peak and she had driven out to a farm stand in Belmont where one picked one's own. Dorothy had picked six ears of corn, driven directly back to Church Tower, steamed them immediately and uncorked a bottle of very cheap Spanish champagne that the local wine shop proprietor had recommended. That was a memorable meal. She had sat on the floor in the living room using the coffee table for the huge platter of corn. She had taken her last glass of champagne sitting on the ladder looking out at the river which was scalded orange by the setting sun.

"Mother," Sophie said looking down at her plate. "I'm worried about you and that condo."

"Well, it's a little too late for that!" Dorothy replied tartly.

"No, I don't mean it that way really. I'm worried that you don't do anything with it."

"What do you mean by 'do'?"

"Well, Mother, you haven't fixed it up at all. Whenever I ask if you've hung up any pictures or brought any furniture up from the storage room like the buffet you say 'no.' For God's sake, you haven't even finished painting the dining room yet."

"Alcove—they call it an alcove."

"Alcove schmalcove. It's like you're camped out in the god-damn place." Sophie looked directly into her mother's eyes. "That's it, isn't it? You are thinking of this as just temporary."

"Not at all," Dorothy replied. But Sophie was lost in her own train of thought. That fabulous mind that could put together bond issue deals, arbitrage its way through millions, was now going into an overdrive perhaps reserved for the clos-ing steps in the financing of a quarter-of-a-billion-dollar deal. Sophie was listening but she had her own agenda.

"You're thinking about moving, aren't you, Mom? Or, oh God . . . you're scared of dying."

"We're all scared of dying."

"But, Mom, you're scared because of Daddy and you're thinking it's going to happen to you and that's why you're not fixing the place up and . . ."

Dorothy leaned over and in a very soft voice whispered, "Hush. I am not scared of dying anytime in the near future. I am fifty-two years old and I am not thinking of that dumb condo as a way station to heaven or a campground out in front of the pearly gates."

"Well, then, how come you're so disdainful of it?" Sophie was in a confrontational mode. One of the dear things about Sophie, Dorothy had always felt, was her ability to slide so fluidly between confrontation and consultation. The transi-tion was nearly seamless and certainly served her quite well in her business of negotiating at Lowmann and Gold. It was not number crunching, as Sophie had once said. "That's for the underlings. It's people crunching—knowing when to be com-bative and when to be cooperative."

"Well, if I am disdainful it is because it is dumb. Five hundred thousand dollars for flimsy window frames, a hollow-core door on the bathroom, those concrete floors." Sophie was rolling her eyes.

"Mom, you and those concrete, sound-transmitting floors. It's like a dirge with you."

"Yes, I suppose so," Dorothy conceded. The waiter had just come and handed them dessert menus. "Shouldn't we concentrate on dessert now—ooh, beach plum sorbet."

"No. I want to concentrate on you and this condo business."

Good Lord. She had forgotten how tenacious Sophie could be.

"Now look, Mom," Sophie's voice grew warm in a blend of good humor, confidence and cajolery. No wonder, thought Dorothy, they let this child loose with millions of dollars. "Don't you think these defects, the concrete floors, etc., would become somewhat less noticeable if you would furnish the place? You would be able to stop with the dirge already."

"No, darling." Dorothy shut the menu. "I did, by the way, replace the hollow-core door on the john."

"Well, good for you. So why not bring up the buffet and paint the alcove?"

"Don't you see that the more I try to make this condo look like home the dumber it becomes?"

"What?" Sophie was utterly perplexed.

How come it had been so easy with Mr. Conover? And here was Sophie with her zillion-dollar brain looking for all the world like some not-very-bright kid stumped by a simple math problem.

"Look, dear. I don't want you to worry. I am not camped out there waiting to die. As a matter of fact I've just joined a health club."

"You have?"

"Yes. And it's filled with bright young things like yourself with fabulous minds and fantastic bodies. The steam room is amazing. All these beautiful young bodies talking deals—networking, as they say. That pretty lawyer that Peter knew at Harvard . . ."

"Lacey Concannon?"

"That's the one. She belongs. She was just made a partner in Hale and Doerr."

"So you've joined and you 'network' in the steam room. What does this have to do with the condo and the furnishings?"

"I was just trying to point out that I am not dying. I am alive and well in my flexi-stretch class, which is a sort of low-key aerobics. I'm living a little differently, that's all."

"How do you mean?"

"Less complicated. I don't need or want all that furniture from Lincoln. That's why I sent some to you."

"Well, it is the you-can't-take-it-with-you syndrome."

"You said it. I didn't." Dorothy was irritated now and Sophie knew it.

"Don't get pissed. . . . But, Mom, what do you sit on in that place? There's only one couch."

"A ladder."

"A ladder?"

"Yes, and I'm keeping two drop cloths for the concrete, sound-transmitting floors."

"You're what?"

"Mr. Conover calls it the jelly bean look."

Sophie gave her the most incredulous stare. Dorothy felt that this must be precisely the way all relatives stared down their next of kin just prior to deciding to have them lobotomized.

"Who is Mr. Conover and what exactly is the jelly bean look?"

"It's apparently better than what they had installed upstairs."

"Is this Conover guy a decorator and what did he install upstairs?"

"Smoked mirrors. And no, he is not a decorator. He's a contractor, painting mostly. I think I saw the man of the smoked mirrors in the elevator the other day. A real double-knit sort.

Don't tell me!" Dorothy raised her hand in a defensive gesture. "I know. I'm a snob."

Sophie laughed. "Maybe he'll invite you to an orgy."

"Well, I wouldn't traffic with a double knit."

"Oh, no!" Sophie tried to mask her surprise that her mother would even make a rebuttal, let alone a humorous one, in this area. Sophie thought of sex as a discrete area, a block of activity that never overlapped with work, just like the athletic activities she enjoyed. When there was time she made a point of going skiing and she skied very fast and very hard. She had sex the same way, in allotted time blocks, space made available by her schedule and the appropriate man. Her real recreation was her work. She enjoyed the business entertaining that went with it, the clothes and most of all the deals. It all formed a kind structure for profit.

"I don't think Dad really imagined a double-knit guy with smoked mirrors when we bought there." Dorothy sighed.

"So what's with the jelly bean look and this arbiter of taste—Conover?"

Dorothy explained briefly over dessert.

"Mom." Sophie shook her head in disbelief. "You now have one wall painted, one that you scribble phone numbers and reminders on, the floor covered with drop cloths and a ladder is your favorite piece of furniture. Some people would say that you're getting a bit eccentric, to put it mildly."

"Well, aren't you glad that I delayed it until you were past adolescence? Remember Jane Rosborough in her skating skirts and good fairy outfits? An anathema to her own children. Those poor kids of hers living in a state of perpetual mortification."

Every dinner during Dorothy's three-day visit had its agenda or topic which Sophie skillfully introduced. At Café des Artistes it was the condo and its furnishings. At Sal Anthony's it was money—Dorothy's portfolio and her desire to donate the royalties from Ira's text on cardiac surgery to the Children's Hospital; Sophie's advice to hang on to the Schlumberger a bit longer. And over each meal, usually during dessert, Dorothy revealed some small bit of information that caused Sophie to raise an eyebrow as she began to perceive glimmerings of a new tack on life by her mother. At Sal Anthony's it was the *Wall Street Journal.*

"You're reading the *Wall Street Journal* now?"

"Yes. My subscription to *Gourmet* ran out. After twenty-five years I decided not to renew. It got boring. Joseph Wechsberg is dead. M.F.K. Fischer hardly ever writes for it anymore."

"So you replaced it with the *Wall Street Journal?*"

At the Four Seasons they had been discussing Ella and Peter's relationship. Just after the waiter had set down the dessert Sophie leaned over her profiterole. "Mom, you're kidding? You and Ella have been corresponding? Whatever about? I thought you could barely tolerate her."

"Well, she's more tolerable in letters."

"What in heaven's name do you write about in letters? Peter?"

"No!"

"Well, what?"

"Primatology."

There was the incredulous stare again.

"Monkey fucking?"

Dorothy squeezed her eyes shut quickly in a prim little gesture she had honed over the years that was designed to show contempt for obscenity and foul language. She had once washed Peter's mouth out with soap when he had come home, a swaggering nine-year-old, his mouth full of newly acquired foulness. He had on this occasion tried to impress the cleaning lady by referring to something being as much fun as a "fuck in a rolling doughnut." But Dorothy had hated the punishment as much as he did and had actually squeezed shut her eyes as she held him in a headlock and scoured out his mouth with a bar of Ivory. Peter, his eyes opened wide with horror, for it was the most violent thing she had ever done, had a close-up view of his mother's clenched face. Sophie, standing off to the side, had a fairly good view too. Their mother's face squeezed shut in the grip of this outrage must have become etched like some optical tattoo on their brains. It was indeed a kind of extreme form of retinal fatigue where the image of the clenched face had persisted even though the original stimulus, the bar of soap, was no longer needed by any of those involved. Dorothy simply made that face and everybody tasted Ivory and talking dirty stopped.

"It's not just monkeys', or in this case baboons', sex lives. It's much more."

"I know. I know," Sophie said. "But, Mom, she does have a gift for scintillating titles."

"Yes. I agree. I had to forward her galleys for an article that came to my place. They were supposed to come in May when she was there. Guess what the title was?"

"I can't."

" 'The Pleistocene Prostitution Hypothesis.' "

"No!"

"Yes. It's a wonderful article attacking some expert's theory about the origins of monogamous behavior and human evolution. You know, the males bring home the bacon, the females tend the kids. This all leads to monogamy. He gets steady sex and paternal certainty. She gets provisioned."

The corners of Sophie's mouth were curling into scrolls of disgust. Her nostrils flared. "It's such a goddamn narrow view of the true dimensions of being profit-oriented."

Dorothy gazed with near rapture at her daughter. Sophie was so sharp, so tough. Dorothy knew that not many found Sophie lovable. But she did. It was not simply militant feminism with Sophie. She was beyond that. She was too clever and original. It wasn't only a sense of justice or righteousness. It was really that even from her profit-oriented stance Sophie appreciated as much as anybody the rich variety of life. She was in her own peculiar way the least narrow, most unprejudiced person Dorothy knew. She was driven. She did have her life organized into rigid areas. But the driving force, the fuel that fed the fire, was a gut belief in all the deals that could be made by all the players.

Dorothy spent her last afternoon in New York, before taking the shuttle back to Boston, in the Frick Museum. She had first come there as a college student, down from Northampton, to do a paper for her art history course. Her favorite painting back then had been a small Boucher which was a charming portrait of his childlike wife on a chaise longue. Dorothy had in those days prided herself in not getting caught up in the obvious favorites—Ingres's *Man in a Red Hat* or the eternally popular *Polish Rider* by Rembrandt which was now under a cloud of doubt as a possible forgery. The issue of its possibly being a fake had just been raised a year before and Dorothy had felt a slight flush of vindication reading about it in the *Times,* even though it had been over thirty years since she had consciously or subconsciously decided to eschew the easy favorites. The day the article had appeared in the *Times* their old friend Halsey Winthrop had come up from New Haven where he was a professor of English at Yale.

"I never had cottoned to that Rembrandt," Dorothy had said that evening over dinner.

"Your unerring sense of style." Halsey had commended her.

Dorothy had enjoyed the compliment. Most of their friends were medical people. Halsey was one of the few from Ira's college days whose life was dedicated to literature and the liberal arts. He taught courses with titles like "The Literary Mind of the Middle Ages." He could discuss troubadours and trout fishing in nearly one breath. He usually came to Boston to buy maritime art and Oriental rugs. His home was filled with both— John Marins, Fitzhugh Lanes, Bokhara rugs and rare editions.

Ira and she had adored his visits. The friendship had gone

back to when both Ira and he had first entered Yale as fresh-
men. At that time Ira was one of the few Jews at Yale and had
felt, as he once told Dorothy, that he was probably the first
Jewish person Halsey had ever met. Halsey was drawn to things
a bit offbeat. He was a collector of sorts and it was for this
reason Ira had believed the friendship first started.

For whatever reasons the relationship had begun, it flour-
ished into a genuine friendship over the year and, if anything,
it was Dorothy and Ira who had come to think of Halsey as
something rare and different among their friends. He was their
own private Renaissance man, a cross between someone out
of an L.L. Bean catalogue and Lorenzo di Medici. He came
complete with great art, slightly shabby clothes, wacky old
aunts and well-selected passions such as trout fishing, canoe-
ing and Sherlock Holmes. There was an occasional gorgeous
girlfriend, but these never amounted to much in terms of a
relationship. He was a man whose primary relationships would
always be very hearty, robust friendships with people like Ira
and Dorothy, or certain favorite students or special aunts and
uncles. He was a man who enjoyed writing scholarly articles
about romantic love as portrayed in medieval literature as
opposed to actually pursuing it in life.

Now Dorothy was in the Boucher room of the Frick Museum.
She had just dashed by the dubious Rembrandt and was standing in front of the small portrait she had always thought so
charming. It now seemed fluffy, banal and totally insipid. How
could she have ever been drawn to it? Looking at it now had
given her much the same feeling she had had once when she
had looked at an old high school prom picture of herself. She
had been overdressed in some fussy confection of tulle and
organdy with too much makeup and underneath it all she had
appeared terribly bland. It was not that the Boucher portrait
was bad; it was just that she could not understand how it had
ever touched her. And yet as she had whisked by the once-
reputed Rembrandt, *The Polish Rider*, something had caught

her eye. Had it been the movement of the horse in stride, or was it some nuance of the alertness in the rider's eyes? How could she have caught such shades walking by so quickly? She headed back toward the Rembrandt.

It was all that and more. It was the movement and the keenness in the young rider's eye, and the precariousness of his journey against the bleak landscape. And to think it was probably all a fake, and she knew as she stood there that she liked this fake better than she had ever liked Boucher's ditsy wife. For thirty years had it been possible that she as the viewer had been the fake? Had posed, had fabricated a taste, a false love for the small portrait, a true, verified Boucher, for all the wrong reasons, those perhaps of false pride that had to do with being cultivated and tamely iconoclastic? Dorothy had wondered why she had endured the banality of the grape arbor so long, and now she wondered why she had succumbed to the Boucher. Well, she thought, Halsey might be disappointed.

11

The night she returned from New York she dreamed not of Boucher's distracted, shuttle-brained wife but of Ira. It was the first time she had dreamed of him since he had died. It was a summer evening. They were having a cookout with some of their oldest friends, people like the Levines and the Nobles who had long since moved away. They were still living in Lincoln, but the children were grown and Ira had returned. Everybody in the dream knew he had died but now he was back. No one was supposed to say anything about Ira's return. As she passed a tray of rumakis Dorothy managed to tell each guest not to comment on it. It was somewhat like a warning a hostess might give to her guests about the presence of an alcoholic fresh from drying out: Don't mention anything about his condition; just give him ginger ale.

The most bizarre part of the dream was that no one at the party seemed to find the situation the least bit extraordinary, except for Dorothy who with an increasing sense of panic, paced about the brick terrace sneaking glances at Ira through the yellow veil of the golden rain tree. She would try desperately not to look, but every once in a while Ira would catch her eye and wave jauntily at her. She could feel the panic rising within her like a bubble until at last she screamed through the strands of tiny yellow blossoms, "You're dead!" And Ira's face simply crumpled like a disappointed child's.

She had awakened trembling, with a terrible pit of fear in her stomach. She tried to calm herself down. Of course, she had told herself, it was a very strange dream, but she suspected that it was not an unusual dream for people who have lost a spouse. Probably a normal phenomenon in a stage of grief. Still, no matter how typical this dream might be she found it unnerving, not because of the obvious impossibility of someone returning from the unreturnable. No, there was another reason, far more disturbing, one she could not quite grasp. It was like one of those uncatchable images that lures, tantalizes and then escapes just as one is on the brink of apprehending it. Ira himself had been such an image since his death. Dorothy had not been able to really picture Ira. His image and even his voice would slip away. Now the dream had brought back his physical presence with startling clarity but the sense of profound disorder, of frightening disturbance, had a reason beyond that of a dead man's return.

All day long she would think about the dream, or the illusive reason it had disturbed her so much. And every time she would get even close to the faintest glimmer of insight, it was as if all the systems would close down and her mind would jump to something else. Often it would jump to the Boucher painting of the ditsy wife. She began to think of the painting as a test pattern, the kind that appears on television sets before networks resume broadcasting for the day.

She had analyzed the dream from every angle and now even her analysis had begun to fall into a predictable pattern. She knew what was weird—Ira coming back. There is, after all, no going back for the dead or even for some of the living. The business of a widow is to move forward, to go on. Did she perhaps feel a little guilty for screaming at Ira in her dream that he was dead? No, someone had to say it. She was the wife, the hostess. The kids weren't going to say it. Okay, so maybe she had felt a little guilty but the image of that crumpled face had started to fade almost immediately. However, this sense of disorder was not caused by feelings of guilt. Guilt was too easy. Guilt was as banal as grape arbors. There was something beyond guilt, she told herself, and then the image, the Boucher test pattern, would pop on the screen and everything would shut down. A little later she would begin again. The dream occupied her thoughts for a full week. She had no trouble sleeping at night. She never dreamed it again. Her nights were strangely dreamless, like dark blanks between the days. But each morning when she woke up she had this pit of fear in her stomach which she knew was the residue of the dream, a sort of high-tide mark of where the dream had reached before it had ebbed away into her blank nights.

Still she could not figure out the reason for the fear, only that it was linked to a frightening disorder, a kind of chaos that seemed to be at the invisible heart of the dream. The fear dissipated almost as soon as she got up and started moving, but despite the fact that its hold on her was weakening she still wanted to know what its source was. For a week she told herself that it was not guilt. The patent disorder, the reversibility of the finality of death, although weird, was not the cause of her apprehension. To a certain extent she prided herself on her ability not to mingle fantasy and reality, dreams and actuality, as she felt her mother had in her fundamentalist reading of *The Wizard of Oz*.

She had hoped, when her preoccupation with the dream did not subside, that she would finally become bored with it, or with analyzing it. But this did not seem to be the case. As she was walking down Commonwealth Avenue one bright morning in late October, her mind was again seized by a vague, upsetting sense of the anxiety with which she had wakened that morning. It had never revisited her during the day, never in her "upright" waking hours. The fear had come in the previous days only during that penumbral part of the morning, in that half light of first waking between the shadow of the night and the brightening rim of a new day.

Now in the new morning as she walked briskly down Commonwealth to her health club for her ten o'clock flexercise class, she knew she should not be feeling this anxiety. It should be far off. By this time of the morning she was usually into an objective analysis of the dream, not experiencing these feelings of undiagnosed fear. She quickened her pace and began her usual pattern of analysis. Within half a block she realized that it was not working at all. She was not even making it to the usual point before the test pattern appeared. She decided to change tactics. Suppose she did follow that facile track of guilt and suppose she said yes, it was a damned weird dream. It might have been only a dream but still the dead just don't come back. And how come this was the first time she had even been able to visualize Ira—in a dream and not of her own free will? And how come she could still not really visualize him?

As she walked through the entrance to her club she was still haranguing herself. She picked up a locker key from the attendant. So busy had she been with her internal dialogue that she had neglected to request her favorite locker. She sat down on the bench and began undressing. It didn't take her long. She always wore her exercise clothes under her regular clothes and brought along fresh underwear to wear home. She wore a black leotard with the "Surrender Dorothy" T-shirt Monica had sent her, bright red tights and matching red Reeboks. She had felt obligated to wear them since she had bought the stock—her first independent market acquisition since Ira's death.

She thought she looked rather devilish in this black and red

combination. She went to the mirror and pulled her gray curls
back in two bunches, fixing them with elastics. If she had
been as completely outfitted as her fellow classmates, she would
have been wearing a matching headband. But, as she told
Sophie, she felt it was a little *de trop* for someone her age. The
leotard, the T-shirt, the bright red tights and the gray pigtails
were enough already. She resumed her analysis along the guilt
track. All right, so she had been angry about the condo. Who
wouldn't have been but . . . She was getting stuck again. She
walked into the gym. Oh dear, she thought, the instructor was
Tom which meant heavy metal music that sounded like elec-
tronic volcanoes from groups with names like Twisted Sister
and Quiet Riot. She preferred the light, frothy show tunes
that Betty, the other instructor, played.

"Okay, ladies! Let's hang it up!"

There was a wail, and an explosion fulminated from the
speakers. The women went to the high bars which were about
six-and-a-half-feet high. This was the first exercise. Nine women
grabbed the high bars with both hands and let their bodies
drip "like molasses." This was not easy given the thumping,
frenetic tempo of the instruments. "Like MO-lasses, ladies.
Let it all HANG OUT. Strrrretch and go for it!"

The first time she had done this, Dorothy could only stand
it for five seconds. Now she could hang for forty-five seconds.
The count was now twelve. So I feel guilty, she thought, as
she approached the twenty-second mark, but guilt is not fear
and so I am angry. Ella would be so pleased . . . letting my
anger hang out—literally. But you can't be angry and scared
simultaneously. She pictured anger and fear diagrammatically,
as in one of the Venn diagrams from her college logic textbook. She could not visualize an overlap or a point of inter-
section between the two circles representing anger and fear.
The face, however, the vacant little nincompoop face of
Boucher's wife was beginning to creep into the periphery of
one of the circles. Scat! she hissed silently. She thought suddenly of her little dog Ruff, the one everyone else had called

Toto. Her mind lurched forward. Gee, Ruff, I guess we're not in Lincoln anymore. We're letting it all hang out in the Back Bay Health Club. Thirty-eight! Maybe she'd try for fifty-two today. Maybe she wouldn't.

She dangled on like a leaf turning in the wind. Her hands grew numb. Things had happened to her. She had been more inside that story than she had ever believed but now there was a twist in the story. Dorothy dropped off the bar at forty-eight. She dropped not from fatigue but shock. She had finally arrived at the crux of the dream, the very simple truth that was within the dream: Lincoln, the scene of the majority of their life, had become as gray as the Kansas prairie. The class had lined up now to begin the next exercise but the words of the book had begun to come back to Dorothy. They came to her in thin patches, like scraps of fog blown by wind. *Once the house had been painted . . . but the sun blistered the paint and the rain washed it away, and now the house was as dull and gray as everything else.* . . . The women had started to do waist bends. Dorothy still stood on the floor where she had dropped.

"You okay, Dorothy?" Tom asked.

"Uh . . . yes, of course. Just a little tired. I'll rest a second on the sidelines."

But she left the exercise room and went to sit on a bench in the locker room, which was empty. She stripped off all of her clothes and walked into the steam room that was filled with hissing white sound and swirling with vapor. She put her towel down and leaned back staring off into the thick warm fog. So this *Dorothy*, she thought, does not want to go home after all. For in the dream she realized that Lincoln had become as grim and bleak as the prairie, and she saw a grim bleak prairie wife just like Aunt Em, only it was herself. How could that be? That was her home. For her it had been that place of beauty and magical power. She had been so happy there. What was the meaning of this gaunt, colorless dream figure she recognized as herself?

Then as if through the scrims of a dream, only it was actually the steam, she saw another face. The silly little wife from the painting. She sat up straighter on the warm, wet bench. The dream was not real. The life was real! She was no longer frightened, just stunned. Stunned and sad. She felt as if she had lost an entire life, or what she had thought had been a life. And if this were so, she had lost it not through death but because it had never really existed. Her own life led simply, directly and singly over the last few months seemed suddenly more real than anything that had preceded it. Had that previous life been such a gossamer construction? She had tended her kids, her flowers, her husband. That had satisfied. She had never longed for more. That was enough. That is enough.

If she had looked back at this point and seen for herself the distinguished career of Monica, would it have seemed so much more substantial? She doubted it. But why then did life now, despite the tragedy of Ira's dying thirty years too soon and leaving her where she never wanted to be, seem not better but more real, more substantial? And she herself seemed more real, although in all honesty at this point she could barely see her own feet through the steam.

The walls of the room and even the door were obscured. She heard the door open, however, and saw an amorphous figure enter. A dark mass in the clouds of steam moved toward the tile benches.

"I don't want to sit on anybody," a voice said.

"I'm down here," Dorothy replied.

"Dorothy, is that you?"

"Yes. . . , is that Lacey?"

"Yep. Did you hang on to your Schlumberger?"

"I didn't, Lacey."

"You're kidding? I thought Sophie told you to."

"I know." How would she explain to Lacey that it had actually been a kind of perversity that made her sell it against Sophie's counsel. She didn't quite understand it herself but again it was a part of her that seemed new, although she was beginning to feel rather at home with it. "Well, you know I just, well, it's hard to explain, Lacey, but I just hated sitting around either watching for the bottom to drop out or for it to recover."

"I wish I had done that—not sat around."

"You're a busy lawyer, Lacey. You have a lot of things on your mind. I'm just a widow lady." Dorothy laughed. "And it gets boring sitting around watching your money."

"Oh go on, widow lady!" Lacey said. "Anyhow I'm taking a bath on this Schlumberger."

"Oh dear, I feel terrible. Sophie is usually so right on these things. I'll tell you what I'll do. I have a sort of tip that so far seems to be working out all right."

"What's that?"

"I took my Schlumberger profits and—"

"You had profits?"

"Darling, we bought the stuff when you were probably in kindergarten."

"Okay, so you took your profits and what did you buy?"

"Microtron—semiconductors. The company's into some new product development for DRAMS. You probably already know what they are but I didn't. It means dynamic-random-access-memory."

"How'd you get into that?"

"It's the same strategy I tried a month or so ago with a fiber optics thing. Not my strategy really. It's Sophie's. I figured if it worked there it might work here. Except there is one danger and even though it is temporarily alleviated it is still a risk."

"So what's the risk?"

"The Japanese. I guess they're always to be contended with in this sort of thing, but right now forecasters are anticipating a DRAM shortage since they think that the Japanese are going to be forced to reduce production."

"Why's that?"

"Some new guidelines put up by the Japanese Ministry of

Trade. They are actually anticipating that these guidelines will happen. I have no idea what the guidelines are or how they are supposed to affect all this. But they say that this along with the weak dollar is supposed to drive up exports as well as domestic sales. It's all rather mystifying to me but I'm still taking the warning seriously."

"How'd you find all this out?"

"That's odd. A magazine for the man who lives above me, a man I have never met and all I know about him is that he has wall-to-wall smoked mirrors—my contractor told me this—well, his magazine got in my box. It was a kind of trade journal for the semiconductor industry. So I read about this Microtron outfit and the Japanese thing in a kind of news briefs column in the magazine. I just thought, Why not try and apply Sophie's strategy here? I called my broker. He thought it sounded good and it's done very nicely over the last several days. But I must caution you. It really is just a quick, short-term thing. You want to get in and get out at just the right time. Mort, my broker, said that there will probably be a rise again in Japanese production of at least ten percent by the second quarter of next year. I mean, it's no sure thing that this improvement will continue."

"Dorothy, you surprise me. I'd take you for a straight blue-chip type."

"Well, I am, dear, I really am. But as I was saying before, money is really quite boring, especially just sitting and watching it. So you try to fiddle with it a little bit and you come up with these oddities and variations. Listen, dear, I had better get out of here before I become a wet noodle. How is your father, though?"

"He's going to go for the bypass. He wishes your husband could do it."

"Who's doing it?"

"Cortepeter."

"Oh, Steven Cortepeter. He's wonderful. He was a student of Ira's."

"Good. Oh, and the name of the company?"
"Microtron."
"Great. I'll call my broker."

When Dorothy emerged from the steam room she nearly laughed out loud at her reflection in the mirror. Her hair, still held in elastics on either side of her head, had frizzed into two silvery cumulus clouds. Her face, bright pink, peered out between them. Jesus Christ, she thought, she didn't look any more like Aunt Em than the man in the moon. The merry widow, or indeed the fresh widow. Now she knew that if she turned around, and she began to laugh to herself, there would be two bright pink spots the size of peonies blooming on her skinny old butt. Ira had never failed to comment on them. Indeed he preferred that she not get dressed immediately after a shower. There was something rather quaint about Ira's notion of what was sexy. But he had called the two rosy marks "erotic" rather than sexy. She did miss that. He was awfully clever about sex and all that. Now hadn't that been real? She asked herself as someone might ask a child one was trying to convince that all was not lost.

Dorothy combed out her hair, dressed and left the club. She was no longer frightened as she walked up Commonwealth Avenue. Her step was lighter but with every step her feet seemed to tap out a little rhythm on the pavement.

It—had—to—be—real—it—had—to—be—real to the tune of "It Had to be You." For Lord's sake, she thought, this was ridiculous. She had had two children. Was she going to have to look at her rear end every night after showering to convince herself that she had had a real husband and a real life in a real place? And if that were not real, what exactly was this now? How could she feel more familiar with who she was now than with the person she was before?

12

There was no pit of fear in her stomach when she woke up the next morning. But she did have two questions: Why had Dorothy Gale wanted to get home? That *was* the central theme of *The Wizard of Oz*. And why did Dorothy Silver *not* want to, especially since where she was now could hardly be considered a land of great beauty and magical power? The condo garden alone was the most hideous thing she had ever seen. Why then had Lincoln turned gray and grim in her dream? Had she been fooled all these years into thinking it was something that it was not?

As a matter of fact, Why had she thought, as she had yesterday, of Ira as being clever about sex? What indeed was her basis of comparison? Zero. He was the only man she had ever slept with. And to think how daring she had thought herself at the time because she had slept with him before they were married. Sophie had once asked her if she had, and she had answered truthfully. "That was kind of wild for the early fifties, Mom," Sophie had commented. Dorothy had cut off the conversation for she was never very comfortable discussing sex, especially her own sex life with her children. She had, of course, neglected to tell Sophie that they had slept together before they were married but after they were engaged. About one minute after. She cringed now to think about it. Ira had slipped the ring out of one pocket and in his other pocket was a condom. Was that what being clever about sex was?

No, she thought, being clever about sex was Rosalie Barrows's strategy for getting around the three-feet-on-the-floor rule that many Eastern women's colleges enforced or tried to enforce. The rule went roughly this way: when a woman entertained a man in her dormitory room, the door had to be open a specified amount and three out of four feet had to be on the floor. Rosalie got hold of a wooden leg which she became very adept at setting up in the most convincingly chaste positions.

The rationale for sexual abstinence in those days was something to the effect that fellows did not marry girls with whom they had slept. This was what a lot of mothers, especially Jewish or Midwestern mothers, told their daughters. Even back then Dorothy knew that it was probably not true, but she was such a tractable child that if she had really doubted, she would never have questioned her mother. She would have just played along, rather, as she had when everyone called her dog Toto and she had kept her own secret name for him. She quietly accepted things. She knew this about herself. She was an acceptor, rather than an asserter. It had presented few problems because things were generally comfortable for her. She was smart insofar as school things had always come easily. She was fairly pretty and there was really very little need to carry on about anything. She did not particularly like that quality in her mother that drove her constantly to assert herself about every issue, no matter how large or small.

Beebie seemed to need to do this for almost metabolic reasons. She had such an excess of physical energy that it provided another outlet for her, like golf did. She needed to exercise an opinion on everything. Asserting was just another activity for Beebie. She asserted herself to express her opinion and to make sure it was realized. Now Dorothy understood that the whole Oz thing in a sense was a tidy way of asserting for Beebie and was a perfect vehicle for her mother's personality. Through the fantasy she could camouflage the quirk nicely while making a game of furnishing a kind of childhood for Dorothy, including everything from naming her and the dog, to clothing her, to buying toys for her.

It wasn't just the fantasy that appealed to Beebie. It was also the convenience of it. Beebie had liked the notion of this "theme" for her daughter's childhood in the same way and for the same reasons that she did most of her cooking on one day every two weeks and froze the meals to carry them through for the next fourteen days. The fantasy, just like the precooked meals, provided a kind of prefab structure or format for daily living—especially for those who do not relish the nitty-gritty charms of the quotidian. In a sense life went on automatic. Therefore one could devote more time to the other, more amusing things it had to offer. It was convenient for a person like Beebie, for it gave her time to pursue her sports and her mah-jongg games. She had become an expert in cooking, wrapping and bagging entire meals. Gordon called her the deep-freeze specialist. Dorothy sometimes wondered if other people thought he was suggesting that she might be frigid.

This of course was back in the days when every other article in *Ladies' Home Journal* or the *Reader's Digest* was about frigid wives. Dorothy was certain that this was not the case with Beebie. She felt that her mother was probably a pretty hot number in bed if only because of her energy level and athletic prowess. But Beebie had probably enjoyed it too for she would sometimes caution Dorothy not to "do it" before getting married. She would roll her eyes merrily, smile slyly and exclaim, "Save it!" as if to say there is something there to relish and don't let guilt interfere. Of course, the converse was that if perchance you don't "save it," by all means let guilt spoil it for you.

Dorothy realized that for women of her own generation it wasn't at all the case of men not marrying a girl they had slept with, but the inverse—girls feeling they had to marry men they had "done it" with. Suppose she had not slept with Ira when she had become engaged—Would she have gone through with it and married him? It seemed so odd even to question it now.

Dorothy got up and went to the kitchen and made herself a cup of coffee. She brought the coffee out to the ladder in the dining alcove and sat down on the bottom rung to watch the river. She guessed that she would have married him. But she remembered that during the last semester of her senior year, when they had become engaged, she had lived in a desperate fear of something happening to Ira, that he might get killed driving from New Haven to Northampton. That she would become "widowed," as it were, before she had ever been married. And that although she would not have been in a state of disgrace, she was not yet exactly in a state of holy matrimony—and she was desperate to get there fast. She had never felt that way before she had slept with Ira.

Had marriage, then, become a kind of corollary to sleeping with Ira? She had always thought that she loved him, but where was the proof? It suddenly struck Dorothy that, if she remembered correctly from her high school geometry, corollaries did not need proofs. She went over to the sawhorse desk where she kept a dictionary alongside the telephone directory. She turned to the C's and quickly found the word. **Corollary** 1: a proposition that follows with little or no proof from one already proven 2: a deduction or inference 3: a natural consequence or effect, a result.

Dorothy's brow knitted. It seemed to get worse as she read on: [Middle English: *corolarie*, from Latin *corollarium*, money paid for a garland, gratuity, a corollary; from *corolla*, small garland, diminutive of corona, garland. Corona].

When, Dorothy wondered, looking at the first definition, had her love been already proven? And was it a natural consequence that from the engagement ring the condom followed? Dorothy laughed out loud. The echo rebounded sharply. "Well, my, my, my," said Dorothy to herself. She slammed the dictionary shut.

The telephone rang.

"Ginny! You're back! When did you get back?"

It was Dorothy's old friend Ginny Harrison from Lincoln, back from a summer on Martha's Vineyard. "Why are you back so early? You never get back before the end of October."

"Dorothy! How could you forget?"

"Forget what?"

"Henke!"

"Henke! Oh, good God! I completely forgot. When does he get here?"

"Tomorrow."

"Oh, yikes! I guess I can do it."

"Well, if you want we can certainly change it to my place."

"No, no," Dorothy said. Hesitantly, she cast an eye around the condo wondering just how she would explain the state of deshabille of her "home."

As if on cue, Ginny then asked, "How does your place look? It better be sensational. Remember that's why you never came down to the Vineyard." There was a pause which Dorothy did not rush in to fill. "Yes?"

"Well, it's different."

"That's cryptic. Well, I can't wait to see it. Maybe I'll pop in and bring some sandwiches over for lunch."

"No. I won't be here today," Dorothy said quickly.

"Well, I've contacted everybody who's coming. Marta and

Joseph from *Horticulture* magazine. Edward Leach, director of hybridization, and his new assistant, Peter Eberhardt. The White Flower Farm people can't make it, but the Goetzes can. We'll be nine all together. You think you can handle that?"

"Oh, yes. Yes."

"I told them seven o'clock."

"Yes, dear. Perfect."

"What are you going to wear?"

Dorothy nearly replied "drop cloth." But then stammered, "Uh . . . I'm not sure."

"I don't know either. I wonder if Henke is still so adorable."

Oh God, thought Dorothy. She had forgotten Ginny's crush on the young Dutch tulip breeder. It could be very tiresome. "Now you're single," Ginny chirped.

"Really, Ginny! He's young enough to be my son."

"No, he's not." They always went through this, trying to figure out Henke's age. "He's at least forty. Besides, that doesn't matter," Ginny continued. "Look at these women who go with men half their age."

"Forget it, dear. I'll see you Thursday at seven o'clock. I've got to rush now—my bell is ringing."

"Are you sure you don't want me to come early, help set up, do anything?"

"No . . . no . . . no need."

"Can't I make a dessert, bring wine? I know how you do everything so exquisitely, but can't I help you in some way?"

"No, I can handle it," Dorothy said emphatically.

"Well, I can't wait to see your place and I am already salivating for my first Dorothy Silver dinner in a long time."

She might have to go on salivating, Dorothy thought. It had completely slipped her mind that Henke Viorst, the renowned Dutch bulb grower, the man who had bred the rare black tulip, was coming to Boston from the Netherlands. Five years before, Dorothy and Ira had been in Holland for a cardiology conference which was being held at the same time as

the West Frisian flower show. *Horticulture* magazine had asked
if Dorothy would cover it for them. She and Ira had driven
over to Bovenkarspel on a bright February morning. They had
been touring the exhibit halls for only a few minutes when a
rumor swept the hall that a black tulip had bloomed the night
before at the prestigious Liederman nursery and was being rushed
over for display by its breeder, Henke Viorst. The tulip was a
showstopper and Dorothy's article on Henke and his quest for
the black tulip—her own personal favorite of all the pieces
she had ever written—was not only published in *Horticulture*
but later picked up by the *New York Times.* The article had
been titled "ZWART 0-8-35-79-1: The Quest for the Black
Tulip." The pre-colon part of the title represented the code
name on the stake that had marked the rare bulb. The article read like a hybrid version of *Star Wars* and the Grimm
brothers.

Henke had made two trips to Boston since then. Dorothy
had entertained him on both occasions at rather large parties.
Ginny Harrison had been absolutely smitten by him. But, as
she had generously said to Dorothy, "I was *smat* before I ever
met him. Your article did it."

Poor Ginny was married to the most boring, prosaic man
imaginable. No wonder reading about a handsome Dutchman
who brought rare flowers into bloom at midnight appealed.
Ralph Harrison always reminded Dorothy of the kind of father
one used to find in illustrations for elementary school text-
books—the Basal Reader father. He always wore light gray
suits or, when he was at home, what her own children called
Mr. Rogers sweaters. His hair was like molded plastic and when
he spoke, one expected him to sound like a basal reader. Dorothy had always wondered what Ginny's fantasies might be.
Now she knew. She had in fact provided them. "That one
line," Ginny had said, "where you describe him getting out of
bed to go into the nurseries, shirtless under his jacket!"

The dark prince awakening with the kiss of hybridization.
She wondered what it was about her own life that made Dor-

othy destined to become a vehicle for other people's fantasies. Well, this was no fantasy. Somehow she was going to have to pull off a dinner party for nine tomorrow night. She had agreed to do this months ago. When Ginny called shortly after Ira died and offered to take the whole thing off her hands, she had refused, thinking this would be good for her. She had felt at that time that she eventually would have to entertain, that she would want to pick up her old life style to some extent. By October the condo would be painted and completely furnished and she would be ready to entertain.

She looked around. How differently things had turned out. How had she ever dared to make such projections at that time? Should she rush down now and get John, the condo manager, to summon the boys and move up the furniture? She supposed she should call her butcher. But then again he was not *her* butcher anymore. He was in Lincoln and she had not bought meat from him since moving into town. What would she serve anyhow? She supposed she could go to the supermarket as she did for her own tiny little ladder suppers and see what looked good. And flowers? Oh God! Dyed carnations would never do.

Within half an hour Dorothy was dressed and had a "to do" list in her hand. Her first stop was the basement. She looked in the storage rooms where the buffet, the sideboard, a couch and assorted smaller tables, hutches and chairs crouched in the semi-darkness. It all looked heavy and dark except for the porch furniture. She would send that upstairs. The rest was definitely going to Sophie with the understanding that Peter could have his pick when he got out of the bush and into something beyond a tent. Her next stop was Pier 1 Imports in Cambridge. She bought five-hundred-dollars' worth of wicker furniture. She also purchased cushions to go with them, covered in a bright chintz that went nicely with her jelly bean color scheme. She bought three straw rugs, the kind people had in summer cottages, to go over the areas not covered by the drop cloths. She cursed the BMW and longed for her old station wagon which could have accommodated the entire lot. She stuffed what she could into it with the help of a clerk, while another clerk ran around to the taxi stand to hire a cab to haul the rest.

By one o'clock in the afternoon the furniture was moved in. She had left the drop cloths, the planks on sawhorses and the ladder. As an afterthought she had brought in her stepladder from the kitchen to provide additional seating. Her one real concession to convention had been to place in the dining alcove her glass-top table and chairs that had been on the screened porch in Lincoln. Dorothy was not pleased but felt there was no choice when one was giving a dinner party for nine people. The plank on sawhorses covered with a tablecloth would function as the buffet.

Actually she decided the whole effect of the wicker and old porch furniture, the chintz and the drop cloths was rather delightful. There was the suggestion of a conservatory or perhaps a winter garden. Just as she had finished setting up the new furniture the phone rang. It was Edward Leach from the Arnold Arboretum. Would she like him to bring some flowers for the party? He had some gorgeous ginger in bloom. Would the scent conflict with anything she was serving? Not at all.

She had of course not yet decided what to serve. That was her next step—the supermarket. Usually Dorothy would have gone back in her diary of menus that she had kept for the last twenty years and seen what she had served at various dinner parties in this season. She would then have "designed" from these past menus, all annotated, an exquisite meal tailored to the occasion. In this case it was a dinner in honor of the grower of the first black tulip since the Queen of the Night, which had bloomed in 1955 and was not nearly so black. She was within two blocks of the supermarket when she realized that if she turned left and drove one more block she would be at the Yuppie market, which would be bound to have something very easy for hors d'oeuvres or a first course. After a summer of shortcut cooking she might as well face up to the

fact that long hours of intricate food preparation did not hold
the appeal for her it once did. She had certainly enjoyed the
accolades that went with it all before, but she knew that it
was one thing from her past that she was not going to miss in
the least.

It was going to be a very odd menu. As soon as she walked
into the shop and spotted the black pasta she knew what tack
she would take through this dinner party. She would pre-pre-
pare the dinner in the timeless tradition of Beebie Lipman. It
made infinite sense. She didn't want to be out in the kitchen
all the time. Without Ira and without Mary Jane, her former
cleaning lady, she was helpless. She would now have to be
bartender, cook and server. Of course it would not be a Beebie-type casserole or brisket. No, since the days had fallen
into a true Indian summer the food would be cold. Black pasta
with porcini, smoked Irish salmon, thin-sliced black bread and
assorted stuff from which people could build sandwiches. There
would be bottles of vodka in blocks of ice. She would put the
bottles in empty milk cartons which she would then fill with
water and put in her freezer.

This she did as soon as she returned home from the store.
When the water was half-frozen she would drop two sturdy
mum blossoms in and let them settle in the water surrounding
the vodka bottle. After it was frozen she would tear off the
wax milk carton and the flowers would appear through the ice
crystal blocks. It was not such a bad fate for a blossom, she
thought, not nearly as bad as being squashed flat in a book.
At least the blossom kept its shape and color.

She tried eating her own dinner that evening at the glass-
top table, which she did not find as comfortable as the desk
or the ladder. She wound up carrying her plate and her glass
of wine over to the plank. Ella's last letter stuck out from
under the Jolly book on primate evolution. Dorothy was getting hooked on the whole primate crowd down there and was
quite intrigued by Ella's remarks concerning the immature
mother, Ginger, and Ginger's socially ambitious mother, the

one Ella called Dot. She had scribbled some questions in the
margin of Ella's last letter and decided to write to her now.

> Dear Ella,
> I know that I sound like the pushy, social-climbing
> mother but why won't Dot let Ginger come to tea with
> her highfalutin friends? I mean, if Ginger and Dot are not
> high-ranking, is there not a chance that they could work
> their way up by virtue of association? In one of those
> books you mentioned they spoke of this as being the name
> of the baboon game. If one can procure high rank the ben-
> efits filter down to the offspring.
> Must go now. I am giving a dinner party tomorrow in
> honor of a man who through his manipulations of nature
> has managed to unnaturally select and breed a black tulip.
> He's arriving from Holland and the Boston gardening
> mafia is fete-ing him.
>
> Best always,
> Dorothy

She was not at all tired from her day's activities and decided
to get on with the rest of the preparations she had originally
planned to do in the morning. She had spent countless happy
nights cooking alone in the kitchen during her thirty years of
married life. Now she took very little pleasure in it. It was just
something to get through. She assumed a workmanlike atti-
tude and proceeded with the Cuisinart, using it often where
in the past she would have painstakingly chopped and julienned
by hand.

She had begun night cooking when Ira had been a resident
at Montefiore Hospital in the Bronx. The wives of the resi-
dents had decided to write a cookbook called *The Care and
Feeding of a Resident*. She had agreed to help edit it. She knew
there would be loads of the Beebie-type make-it-now-bake-it-
later casseroles which she countered with her own brand of
easy but offbeat recipes. The one that was ground breaking,

however, and caused *Gourmet* magazine and the *New York Times* to call her to see if they could publish it, was for a cold spaghetti salad.

Dorothy now sauteed the porcini that would go into her pasta salad noire. She could remember the old recipe verbatim—what a relief it had been from those others that began, "Open a can of cream of mushroom soup . . ." Dorothy's recipe began with, "Scream at the kids to finish their vegetables. Tell them about the hungry children in China. Threaten them with scurvy. If none of the above works, boil up a pot of water. Do not throw in child. Throw in half pound of spaghetti. Cook until tender. Refresh under cold water. Put in leftover vegetables from the kids' plates. Toss with any kind of salad dressing, and place in refrigerator with note for husband: 'Eat as is. I don't have a headache.' "

The *New York Times* not only wanted to publish it but had asked her to do a short article including some more of her recipes. As soon as the piece in the *Times* appeared, other publications started calling her to write and her semi-career in food writing took off. She winced at calling it an avocation, although she was never inclined to call it a real job either. Her specialty became the narrow focus piece "Twenty Things You Never Dreamed of Doing with an Olive." She thought of herself as a kind of Tom Wolfe of food journalism. Her favorite type of article involved a bit of historical research. One such piece began, "Long before there were oysters Rockefeller, indeed long before there were Rockefellers as we now know them, there were oysters Cro-Magnon. Thirty-five thousand years ago or thereabouts the first raw bar opened. It seemed to be a rather cataclysmic time for human development. Art, housing and weaponry were all making significant advances in the form of cave paintings, permanent dwellings and the long-awaited hafted blade." The article had gone on to describe how archaeologists had ascertained that indeed oysters were part of the Cro-Magnon diet.

As Dorothy cooked that evening and reflected on her experience as a food writer and eventually a gardening writer, she wondered if this development, too, in some sense had been a corollary. Had it all been a result, an effect of having been asked by the resident wives to help out on the project? All of these women's lives at that time, despite the very real demands of children and husbands, had been rather unformed. The women existed in an adjunctive state. They were coefficients to their husbands' careers, and the husbands in and of themselves could not be thought of as discrete individuals anymore. They had melded mysteriously with their careers at some point between medical school and the extended residencies required for specialization. The individual men the women had married were now part of a web of the pressures of excellence that would turn out top-flight specialists.

This web had nothing to do with living. The women went through pregnancies, births, childhood illnesses, and planned their first real homes and first mortgages alone. They dreamed of the time when they could reclaim their men. When that time finally came they often discovered that they did not know each other. It was as if two strangers were occupying the splendid house on the two-acre lot. Perhaps as they went to buy their first Oriental rug they looked across the tangled design of colors at each other and realized it was not working. He was bored, and she just plain did not recognize this man anymore.

That had not happened to Dorothy and Ira. Despite the adjunctive state in which she had existed in relation to Ira's career, they had always recognized each other. Until now! The thought shocked her. She put down the wooden spoon she had been stirring with. Was that her problem? Would she in her widowhood go unrecognized by Ira? And would she perhaps not know him now? Was this then what it was like to be stranded by nature or history on the margin of a niche— unrecognized by your own and therefore forever alone? If so, the burden to survive seemed rather awesome.

13

"**S**o this, as I am to understand it, Dorothy dear, is your desk—command-central, so to speak." Aside from being boring, Ralph Harrison was patronizing. Dorothy knew that although he was the most staid, conservative man in the world, firmly entrenched in his "piggy" values, as Sophie would call them, he liked to give lip service to what he perceived as "trendy" notions like feminism. He probably would die if Ginny had exhibited the least bit of interest in these notions herself. How did Ginny stand it? Dorothy wondered. And she nearly wished for Ginny's sake that the poor woman could have a tryst with Henke, who was indeed as adorable as ever and seemed younger than ever too.

When Henke was not in his nurseryman overalls but in a suit, he seemed like a stocky little Dutch boy packed into his Sunday best on his way to church. His handsome face had tried to appear sad as he offered his condolences to Dorothy but one felt that he had no more comprehension of death than a young child. His pride over his accomplishments bordered on boastfulness. Yet it was all shot through with this boyish charm. He was one of those people who would always be excused any little excess of pride or enthusiasm because he was almost fatally cute.

Only Ralph seemed concerned with Dorothy's unconventional furniture and accoutrements.

"I think it is a fantastic manipulation of space," Edward Leach said.

"Oh, dear." Dorothy laughed. "Are you going to tell me it makes a statement?" Dorothy was very good at this kind of small talk. "I hate things that make statements that shouldn't— like clothes and furniture, and now they have those talking Coke machines. Only books should."

"Well, my dear, it only makes a statement about light and color and airiness."

"Good. Good," Dorothy replied. She could tell, however, that Ginny clearly felt it made a statement about her emotional state and was worried. She and Ralph would discuss it on the way back to Lincoln. They would nod and agree with each other about their astute perceptions and tomorrow morning there would be a call from Ginny—"to voice our concern." They were not terribly original with language.

The young new assistant of hybridization at the arboretum, Peter Eberhardt, was in an intense discussion with Henke about the Dutch nursery's efforts in the direction of a bright green tulip as well as a deep blue one.

"I understand it's a rather pale sea green, the one you're developing?"

"Oh!" Henke laughed warmly and shook his finger in a mock scolding. "We do not say 'develop.' We say 'create.' " He had corrected Dorothy similarly five years before when she had interviewed him in Holland.

"Dorothy, these are fabulous," Sally Goetz said, biting into a piece of melba toast spread with a mousse pâté.

"I bought it," Dorothy replied.

"Dorothy!" Ginny nearly squealed. "I can't believe it! You actually bought this?"

"Yes, in that gourmet grocery store on the corner of Gloucester."

"Well, not the melba toast," Ginny said. "Dorothy makes the most wonderful melba toast."

"Sorry to disappoint you, Ginny, but I bought that too."

"You're kidding? What's become of you?"

Dorothy laughed. "I don't know, but obviously all those years of making melba toast were for nought; I could have gotten away with this."

"Not necessarily!" Ralph interjected. "I'm not saying this isn't good." He stood by the window poised with a small piece of melba toast in his hand, "but it's not the same as Dorothy's."

"Less distinctive?" Dorothy offered.

"Precisely," he replied.

She was about, indeed, she was sorely tempted, to ask Ralph if he were suggesting that her time would be better spent baking melba toast. He did tend to bring out a caustic streak in her and she should not let it or him get the better of her. Also she had a responsibility to the other guests; she really couldn't let the conversation linger on melba toast. Should she share her latest stock hunch with them? Would it be terribly crude midst these folks devoted to horticulture? No. Everybody except Ralph was good fun and "with it." Henke did have a rather solid Dutch Protestantism about him, but still he loved a laugh. And most of all she was certain that everyone was solidly heterosexual. She would go ahead. As a tactical maneuver around the subject of melba toast, Dorothy introduced that of condoms and their investment potential. Yes, as everyone knew, the Back Bay did have a substantial gay population. "More so than Lincoln," Ginny offered. And Dorothy had noticed in the local pharmacy a very prominent display of condoms which she guessed was because of the AIDS thing and . . .

It was amazing. People pitched right in and the discussion

thrived. Those who had brokers were going to call them the next day. Ralph led the pack on this score and kept muttering to Dorothy throughout the rest of the evening, "Awfully clever, Dor, awfully clever."

Dorothy felt by the end of the evening that the party had been successful, considering that it was her first attempt to entertain since Ira had died.

The guests were all leaving now. Henke, who was staying in a nearby hotel, had walked over on his own and was using her bathroom before he left. They had all said goodnight and now, as Dorothy shut the door, she realized with a sudden sense of discomfort that Henke was no longer in the bathroom but in the living room. She had sensed his presence before she had seen him. Edward Leach had been the last one out the door and as she was turning she had had a strange prescience about Henke's whereabouts. This should not be unsettling, she told herself. On seeing him she exclaimed with some surprise, "Henke! You're still here."

"Just finishing my wine." He had, however, removed his jacket and tie and draped them over the arm of the couch, as one might do if he were inclined toward settling in. "I did not want to say good-bye from the bathroom." He giggled.

This she did not like at all! There was no boyish charm, just a disgusting infantilism that this strapping Dutchman suddenly exuded. "Sit down." He patted the cushion next to him.

Dorothy's eyes widened. His boldness was shocking. Had he had too much to drink? It seemed impossible that this man who studied tulip genealogies, a man who sought out rareness and beauty, who "created" it and not merely developed it, could suddenly become so coarse.

"I really prefer to sit on the ladder," Dorothy answered tersely. He giggled again. Why was he doing this to her? Is this what happened when one's husband or mate died? She felt as if she were being subjected to the sort of biological scenario that might be offered in a primate textbook, or in one of Ella's papers.

Henke, however, would never mention Ira, his death or her widowhood. This she knew. He looked squarely at her with his merry eyes twinkling madly.

"Ginny's husband is quite dull." He said this very lightly, not in a ruminative tone at all, but still smiling and plucking at the cushion of the couch where she had been invited, invited in her own home to sit. The remark was designed to pass time. It was as if Dorothy were supposed to join in this game of waiting for something to happen. As much as she disliked Ralph she would got give Henke the satisfaction of a response. "She," he continued, "is amusing."

"Amusing," Dorothy muttered softly, not trying to disguise the weariness in her voice.

"Yes, but *you* are . . ." He paused and patted the cushion again and smiled.

Dorothy felt sickened by it all—the giggles, the smiles, the pats on the cushion as one might summon a lap dog. Was there an absence so palpable that a vacuum formed around the survivor? Did life then implode to the point of nothing-ness to be filled by leering men, generations younger, in search of some universal teat? Dorothy's outrage swelled within her. How dare he giggle and stroke cushions like buttocks and insult her friends, even the ones she didn't like?

"Henke, I'm very tired. It's time for you to go." She walked over and took his glass quickly from him. He seemed startled. "Up! Up! You have a big day tomorrow, young man. You're addressing the horticultural society and every garden group in the state will be there."

The smile left his face. His blue eyes became vacuous. She spoke to him exactly as a mother would to a dawdling child. And he let her. He let her not only take his glass, put on his jacket and neatly fold his tie and put it in his pocket, but he also let her steer him quite firmly to the door.

She shut it solidly behind him and then sank back against it. The edge of the niche was indeed a trying place to be, even for an old female like herself, beyond reproductive capacities.

14

❧

If it was a burden to survive at the margin of things, there was also a mandate to live coming from all quarters. Some of these quarters struck Dorothy as surprising. There were, of course, her children. But one evening a few days after the dinner party Dorothy came across something she had clipped from the *New York Times* earlier in the month. It was E. B. White's obituary. He had earned three-quarters of a page in the *Times*. Dorothy began reading a letter from White to a friend that had been included in the write-up.

"I have a first-degree heart block, have lost the sight in my right eye because of a degenerated retina, can't wind my wrist watch because my fingers have knuckled under to arthritis, can't tie my shoelaces, am dependent on seven different pills to stay alive, can't remember whether I took the pills or didn't. On the other hand, I am camped out alone, here at Bert Mosher's camps on the shore of Great Pond which I first visited in 1904. I have my fifteen-foot green Old Town canoe with me which I brought over on top of my car. I sat out a

New England boiled dinner this noon by anticipating it with martinis and cheese and crackers." Dorothy guffawed at this point in her reading, took a sip of her coffee and read on. "There is a certain serenity here that heals my spirit, and I can still buy Moxie in a tiny supermarket six miles away. Moxie contains Gentian root which is the path of the good life. This was known in the second century before Christ, and it is a boon to me today."

Dorothy set the clipping on the ladder's bucket rest along with her morning coffee. She was thankful, of course, that she did not have a heart block, a degenerated retina and the other assorted afflictions, but what she envied in him was the bold serenity that gave him the will not just to survive but to live joyfully with his pills, his martinis and his canoe. That kind of style, Dorothy felt, simply took one's breath away. Some people might have read the letter as a sort of ruler-across-the-knuckles scolding to be thankful and not to take health for granted. But for Dorothy the words came as a kind of salute as well as an all-hands-on-deck call to action.

The call, however, came not only from E. B. White's corner. On the morning Dorothy had read his obituary she received another letter from Ella. The first part of the letter was devoted to explaining why she had not written more elaborately in answer to some of Dorothy's questions on history and natural history, as she had promised. She had been occupied by common problems connected with setting up a new field operation and the tasks of introducing a crew of new graduate students to field work. The entire summer had "more or less" focused on teaching field techniques in animal observation and Ella had had little time to focus on her own research— infant abuse and infanticide as related to alloparenting, or aunting behavior.

This seemed an unremittingly depressing topic to Dorothy. She did wish Ella would switch back to sex. If they were going to be writing to each other, she recoiled at the thought of letters strewn with references to murdered baby baboons. Then she had to laugh at Ella's next lines. "I know I'll be accused of being trendy what with Jane Goodall revealing the murderous mothers of Gombe." "Trendy," Dorothy whispered to herself. To think that she had only thought of the word applying to such phenomena as black pasta. How narrow of her. She continued reading.

"It is true that infanticide is quite the issue these days. But I still believe that what happened with the Gombe chimps was out-and-out aberrant behavior"—Good Lord, thought Dorothy. What else could it be?—"and none of the other obvious reasons handed to us by various evolutionary scenarios, be they by sociobiologists or social Darwinists or whatever. That is not to say that I believe that all infanticide is aberrant . . ." This could be an unnerving letter from a potential daughter-in-law, even if it was in the guise of science.

"Did you read the book, I think I mentioned it to you in a letter, the one by Sarah Blaffer Hrdy?" Dorothy was only on page twenty. But there had been something rather off-putting about Ms. Hrdy's insistence on substituting the suffix -ess for -or, as in one chapter where she wrote: "From such female foundresses there may one day originate a new species; Moses becomes Eve." And, in the very first chapter, she spoke of the readers' "own remote ancestresses." Dorothy continued reading Ella's letter.

Your questions on history and chance are wonderful, Dorothy. I only wish the graduate students who are out here could back up enough to begin to gain a perspective that would help them to ask such questions. In any case your questions have given me an opportunity to really back off and reflect. As I have said before, history starts when things screw up. The word "if" functions almost as a verb in history. It opens things up for other things to happen. But when things happen they are always unrepeatable; they never happen the same way twice. But I don't think it has to be big and sweeping and fabulous to be recognizable. To the eye, at the time it is happening, unless it is war, a volcano, etc., it rarely is spectacular in that sense. But then, of course, after the volcano (the "if"), there is the runoff, the historical runoff where the story starts to unfold, to be told; the tale is spun. I'm looking at it right here, right now. The runoff on this savannah.

Let me tell you a story: 25 million years ago or thereabouts there was a dry spell, a change in climate, not just weather. The rain forests shrank, and the savannah expanded. The going got rough for some of our tree-dwelling ancestors, those early apes of the Miocene. Okay now a typical Darwinian scenario will say the stronger, the fittest, etc., made it through this little eye in the evolutionary needle, squeezed through the bottleneck of evolutionary history—pick your metaphor. A strict sociobiologist will say it was all genetically pre-programmed.

But suppose it was this way really. Suppose the stronger ones were indeed the apes that could hang on, literally, in the trees of a shrinking jungle. And the "weak" ones were the ones who got shoved out onto the savannah. They just could not cling and swing as well as the forest bullies, and they got out there and guess what? Through being an isolated breeding population some of the genetic material for erect posture, for standing up, floated to the surface and before you knew it, say five or six million years ago, you had this creature who could stand up. Didn't have a very big brain at all. She didn't stand up because she was especially smart (big brains we know from the fossil record came much later—ask Peter). She stood up because she was a failure in the jungle and got pushed into a marginal situation by what Stephen Jay Gould calls the "contingen-

*cies of history." Now if that's not a crapshoot I don't know
what is. But it's a good yarn too. And it is true docu-
drama.*

*So here I sit in the angled light of the Kindisiu savan-
nah and, like a child or an animal, on one level I am
ignorant of the history that is happening all around me.
But in my grown-up stance, I am like an astronomer who
looks through the telescope at ancient light for clues about
the origins of the universe (also a crapshoot, I might
add—the universe, that is). I look for clues about ancient
primate behavior which might have filtered down through
time. But that is really only a small part of it. I hate this
notion of studying the past for what it tells us about the
present. There is such arrogance in that. I like the past for
what it was—history, irreversible, unique, unrepeatable.*

*There is only grass and wind and sky out here. I like
this much better than being in the jungle. The sky falls
down to meet the earth and history wells up to fill it all,
and natural history I guess is supposed to dig primarily into
the secrets of cause and effect but it doesn't seem to do it
in any predictable fashion, any one-to-one ratios. If anything the very inquiry into the nature of things seems to
confound and deepen the mystery. Here I sit on what was
once 25 million years ago thought of as an "edge," a "failure" by Miocene standards, and if I squint my eyes till
they are just slits and watch the breeze take a tack across
the savannah, the grass seems to turn into a phantom river
and I can imagine that I am back in Nebraska watching
the Niobrara cut across the prairie. It's very nice, this edge
of things.*

*Cheers,
Ella*

So Dorothy could see it. There was Ella sitting on her ample
haunches, her long red hair streaming into a confluence with

the savannah grass. And there was E. B. with his martini and his Old Town canoe. And here was Dorothy on her ladder. If she had let her life become dictated by the logic of a corollary, hadn't she then gone against nature and cheated herself of the chance riches of the crapshoot—or, she supposed, the chance disasters?

15

It had taken Dorothy no time at all to put the dinner party and the unpleasant finish of the evening behind her. When Ginny called, as Dorothy knew she would, to "voice their concern" over Dorothy's "unsettled state" and then went on to jabber about Henke, Dorothy was able to say with great equanimity that she felt he looked rather bloated. That had all happened a few days before. She had had lunch with Ginny to try to ease her concern and show her how normal and settled she felt. Now as the phone rang Dorothy fully expected it to be Ginny but it was not. It was Lacey Concannon. She couldn't believe the Microtron. It had shot up like a rocket. It almost made her nervous. Dorothy would have never taken Lacey for the nervous type. Enjoy it, she advised. They would be cautious and watch things. Mort, her stockbroker, not only knew to keep her posted, but every time she talked to him, which was at least once a week, she reminded him about Microtron. The real reason Lacey had called, however, was to invite Dorothy to a Halloween party.

"A Halloween party? Oh no, Lacey."

"Why not? You don't even have to wear a costume. We are but you don't need to. Come on. It'll be fun. It's down on Lewis Wharf in those condos."

"Halloween's tonight. I'm not really up for going out but why don't you and Bill come over and have a drink first so I can see you in your costumes? Besides, I'm dying to meet Bill."

They looked charming when they showed up at her door. They were dressed as white hunters on an African safari.

"It's all from Expeditions Unlimited," Lacey announced as they walked through the door.

"What's that?" Dorothy asked.

"It's that store over on Boylston, and there's one in Cambridge and Quincy Market too."

"You go in there," Bill said, "looking like two lawyers and you come out looking like Clark Gable and Ava Gardner in *Mogambo*." He touched his safari hat.

Bill was just exactly the kind of man Dorothy wished for Sophie—unself-consciously handsome, with a genuine warmth and nothing driven about him.

"Would you like gin and tonics?" Dorothy asked. "I mean, it seems fitting, doesn't it?"

Three gin and tonics later they were all feeling quite merry. "Oh, my God!" Dorothy exclaimed. "You can't imagine how dashing you both look. I feel as dowdy as the Queen of England." They both assured her she was not. Dorothy raised her hand and rotated it slowly mimicking the queen's manner of waving to crowds. A placid little smile glazed her face. Bill and Lacey became hysterical. "Come with us!" Lacey begged. "Go as the queen. It'll be a riot."

Twenty minutes later Dorothy walked out into the cool October night. "Only on three gin and tonics would I be doing this!" She giggled and adjusted her tin-foil crown. "This is hard to do in white gloves."

"That pocketbook is great. It's so flat. Just like you always see her photographed with."

"How this came into my wardrobe I don't know, never having been a queen. But it's flat because when you're queen you never carry cash or credit cards—which incidentally I don't have with me. So don't ditch me. Oh dear, my toilet paper sash for my medals!"

"Here, let me tape it. I brought the Scotch tape for just such emergencies."

Lacey began fixing the sash of toilet paper that hung diagonally across Dorothy's chest.

"You look great, Dorothy," Bill said.

"Well, if we're really going to carry this off you two must walk three paces behind me."

There were others out that night in costumes. Dorothy waved her hand in the royal salute and held the flat, empty pocketbook with her other hand. Her finances, although not queenly, were awfully good these days. If she should sell some stock, between Reeboks and Microtron alone her cash situation would be impressive. The condoms were behaving rather sluggishly. She nearly laughed out loud at the thought. But still this was a lot more fun than being a queen with pots of money. And to hell with the ruby-red slippers and all that Oz malarkey. She'd take five hundred shares of Reebok at $26\frac{7}{8}$, which had closed today at $45\frac{1}{4}$, anytime. She picked up her pace and walked more briskly in her sensible, low-heeled spectator pumps down the wide sidewalk of Commonwealth Avenue.

16

Dear Dorothy,

I can't answer your questions really. Who knows why Dot is this way? Maybe she's ticked that Fred, her old consort, is now Ginger's friend. Or maybe she feels that Fred is all that Ginger needs right now and that Ginger needs to stay home and become a good mother, as opposed to gallivanting around with her and her "highfalutin" friends, as you call them. Dot sure as hell wants no part of Ginger right now. Dot is cycling at the moment and going at it with all available males. Between her sex life and her social life there is hardly time for Ginger.

In the meantime I do feel that Ginger is learning something from Fred and there is another female, Harriet, who often forages with them. Harriet as far as we know has no children of her own. I've noticed that female baboons are often drawn to other females carrying young infants. Harriet seems to spend quite a bit of time interacting with all the mothers of the five new youngsters—especially with

Ginger and Liberty, the other mother of a black infant.

The other night the four of them made their way to the sleeping cliffs—Ginger, Fred, Harriet and Willy. Willy clung to Ginger's back as they all clambered up the rock face. Midway to the top Fred gave Willy a ride and then switched off with Harriet. They found a good deep shelf with an overhang near the top. Harriet settled down against the cliff, her back to the rock wall, and seemed to snooze instantly. Fred curled up with his back also against the wall and grabbed his toes in both hands. His chin dropped to his chest and he was asleep. Ginger sunk down leaning into Fred. Half asleep, he reached over and patted her knee, then let his hand rest on it. Willy pressed himself in between them somewhere. I stayed there all night.

They did not move until six o'clock the following morning. Willy was up first and began his wake-up routine which involves several tummy pounces—at least three for each adult and a tickling session with Fred. Ginger is starting to participate a little more in the tickling and we are seeing more eye-to-eye contact between her and Willy. So maybe Dot knows what she's doing by leaving her daughter alone and letting her hack out her own brand of domestic bliss and find her mothering instincts, which are there I'm sure. She just needs to discover them. See Trivers, R. L., 1972 Aldine Press, and article by same in Am. Zool, 1974. You can get these at the Museum of Comparative Zoology at Harvard. Just use Ira's card. I'm sure it'll work.

Must dash.

yrs.
Ella

There had actually been three letters from Ella in that morning's mail. One had been mailed five days before and two had been mailed several weeks before. Such was the postal service. Dorothy had not had time to read the other two before leaving for the airport on her flight to Florida to visit Beebie and Gordon. It was time for her obligatory January visit which she always found somewhat less than wonderful and which would be particularly difficult this year without Ira. Although he saw Beebie's shortcomings, Ira had always managed to be the perfect son-in-law, playing golf with Beebie and making himself available for endless informal consultations for all their friends' cardiac problems.

The Lipmans' friends all adored Ira, whereas many of them found Dorothy remote—"always the nose in a book"; "very intellectual." This was not exactly true. She was in fact allergic to the Florida sun, and the water in the swimming pool was kept at a geriatric temperature level, more suitable to treat arthritis than to be genuinely refreshing. She would have gone swimming in the ocean except that she did not cotton to being pulverized by the monster surf. Dorothy hated golf. She hated mah-jongg. And the sun hated her. So she would sit on her parents' balcony reading, in a kind of détente with the state of Florida, wearing a mask of zinc oxide, swathed in light-weight cottons, a wide-brimmed hat on her head.

There had in addition to Ella's letters been one from Peter which begged her not to go to Florida because he knew how she hated it. She should come to Africa. The weather was better and the people more interesting. It was certainly tempt-ing but unthinkable for her to miss visiting her parents. Sophie, too, in an eleventh-hour attempt, had called to dissuade her. "Mom, you're a grownup. You do not have to do this."

"That is precisely why I have to do this. Because I am a grownup and grownups rise above these things. Being a grownup means being a good sport," she had replied.

But Sophie countered, "You don't have to. You were just widowed."

"Look, I can't be explaining everything away with that."
"Why not?" Sophie had pouted. "I worry about you."
"Don't."

Ella did not worry about Dorothy. She was as caught up in the tangled web of baboon life as a TV addict to the afternoon soaps.

> Dear Dorothy,
> At last I think I can safely say that the baboons are habituated to us. They find us all profoundly boring which is just the way it should be. On the other hand for us . . .

So the letter had begun and now Dorothy wondered if by dint of finding Florida and her parents' lives sufficiently boring, perhaps she could habituate to it all for the necessary five days. In this letter Ella described observing an interaction between two male baboons and an infant and a mother:

> Olive and her friend Honest Abe are feeding near one another and Olive's infant Sweet Pea is between them. Another male, Murphy, a non-friend, suddenly appears, stands very still and gives a clear-cut threat by staring at Abe and flashing the white skin above his eyes. Abe, it must be pointed out, is not in consort with Olive, in other words not her sexual partner. That seems to be Pop Eye. In any case Murphy is threatening. Abe picks up Sweet Pea from Olive.

Dorothy was not sure if she really wanted to turn the page and go on. A sense of dread loomed at the bottom edge of the paper and she felt as if she were not simply reading but actually crouched there in the tall grass with Ella watching this savannah soap opera. Slowly, she turned the page.

Abe then nuzzles Sweet Pea and walks slowly about,
back and forth while cuddling the infant, yet never look-
ing at Murphy. The tension within a matter of seconds is
diffused. Murphy loses all interest in Abe, Olive and the
infant and goes off to forage a few meters away.

Dorothy breathed a sigh of relief. No child abuse yet. The
letter went on a bit with Ella's ruminations about platonic
friendships among baboons.

I guess a lot of what I am seeing out here boils down to
concepts of friendships and the dynamics of reciprocity
that underlie these nonsexual relationships. The relation-
ships involve protection and certain economic benefits
(i.e., food sharing). This is all in keeping with some popu-
lar feminist scenarios currently bouncing about. (See Tan-
ner and Zihlman, 1976; Zihlman 1978.) These of course
reject the hunting hypothesis. I too reject this notion of
man-the-mighty-hunter craving meat and women trading
sexual favors for high protein. The old story—he gets
paternal certainty; she gets food (see my recent article, the
one you sent the galleys for).
*   The alternative to this is to put the female hominid, so*
long a bit player in evolutionary scenarios, stage center
with her man. This time it is more or less a co-starring
situation. The female is there as the mighty gatherer. The
first tool is not a weapon but a satchel, or rather a basket,
for the high protein comes from nuts, tubers, roots, etc.
No red meat, please. As Adrieanne Zihlman says—"we
really are what we eat" (see Zihlman, University of Chi-
cago Press, 1978). Evolutionarily speaking I think that she
is probably right about the nuts and tubers, etc., and
woman's role as a gatherer and not in bondage to man-
who-craves meat. And believe me from what is known
about the average hominid brain of 2.5 million years ago,

it couldn't have planned a strategy for bringing home the bacon when it was live on the hoof. Aside from that, meat was simply not an efficient nutritional staple. Too much risk involved in getting it for the amount of calories derived. In terms of cost/benefits it made no sense.

Thus, it is easy now to imagine the little hominid couple walking into the sunset together holding a basket to pick berries. And if the diet was more vegetarian than big game it can also explain a different social organization. However, it still is putting everything in terms of economic reciprocities and posits that all bonds emerged out of such economic exchanges. You can read in any commodity that you want—nuts, meat, sex, paternal certainty, etc.

This might be an insolvable chicken-and-egg question. Which came first, the benefits or the friendships? But I don't think so. And I am beginning to question along with Barbara Smuts (see Smuts, 1981) a strict interpretation based solely on food procurement, be it red meat or nuts. It is not as clear-cut as we might like it to be. We are not entirely what our ancestors ate, as Zihlman suggests.

I think that we began with a capacity for friendship as primates, for sensing mutuality, before we saw the obvious benefits. I do not, however, think that there is one friendship gene as a sociobiologist might believe. I think it has to do with a conglomeration of stuff involved with being a primate—the forward-facing eyes; the placement of the foramen magnum, where the spinal cord enters the skull, lifts the head upward into a more "social" position, if you will, for communication; the greater manipulative power of the hands with their grasping fingers. All this stuff goes into making a more sociable critter. And when I see an old male like Honest Abe being such a good friend to Olive and Sweet Pea, or even some of the spontaneous aunting behavior between females, I cannot help but *think it's not entirely politics here or economic benefits but also something borne from the purer pleasures of companionship.*

The third letter, which was the most recently mailed one, was equally interesting—less philosophy, more nitty-gritty details.

. . . As you probably know [Ella seemed to assume that Dorothy was practically her equal now in primate studies], *forced copulation has only been reported in one wild non-human primate—the orangutan.* [Dorothy did not know whether she should feel relieved or alarmed by the news. Sometimes reading Ella's reports from the field were a little bit like reading Ripley's "Believe It or Not".] *In any case, I have started to notice something quite interesting which has to do with female choice in matters of sex.*

This afternoon I watched Fig, an older resident male in consort with Lulu, being pushed off by Butch in his pursuit of Lulu. Fig is too old to take Butch on and was run off in the early afternoon. By 1300 Butch was ready to begin his campaign for Lulu. He tries to groom her but she moves off to feed. Ten minutes later he begins to mount her but she moves off again. He follows her wheelbarrow style by resting his forefeet on her hind quarters. She swerves quickly and he takes a tumble. But Butch is not easily vanquished. In the next two hours he tries to mount her 37 times. Not only does Lulu continue to resist, but Fig waits patiently nearby observing the whole thing. She occasionally looks his way. Each time she refuses Butch's advances, but she does groom him occasionally. What do you make of all this? I feel that it kind of makes sense. You know females are not just sex objects. They can entertain or exercise choice, let's-be-friends-first type of thing. I can't exactly put it that way in the article

I'm supposed to be doing for Primate Journal, *though, can I?*

Best,
Ella

Well, it was certainly better than infanticide. Dorothy could not help thinking how she herself had folded Henke's tie so neatly, placed it in his pocket and ushered him out her door firmly but gently, in a drawing-room version of this ancient and noble tradition.

On the flight to Florida Dorothy wrote:

> *Dear Ella,*
> *I am glad the* Savannah Courier *does not limit itself or have as its motto "All the News That's Fit to Print." Your letters are better than the* National Enquirer *which I often read in the checkout line at the supermarket—"Woman Gives Birth to Extraterrestrial"; "Man's Dead Wife Leaves Message on Answer Machine"; or my favorite, "Woman with Three Breasts Has Ear for Third Nipple." Re: Lulu, Fig and Butch. There is always the possibility of Fig being a voyeur. Has anything ever been done on voyeurism amongst baboons? Or is this where I can make my mark? (Silver 19—, Harvard University Press). I prefer to think that Fig, in the lingo and tradition of some of our political leaders and their press officers, is being cautiously optimistic about Lulu. I am rooting for him as I am not doing for Mr. Reagan. So for all it's worth tell Fig to hang in there. How old is he? 60 or 70 in human age? I'm all for sexual competence after 60 even if it means having to occasionally wait on the sidelines for the bullies to be rebuffed. Don't read anything into this. I suppose it's hard not to.*
>
>
>
> *Cheers,*
> *Dorothy*
>
>

17

The hard thing about Florida was of course not the sun or the temperature of the water but to resist falling back into the old fantasies, the stories that seven months before, Dorothy had so boldly told her mother were Beebie's tales, not her own. At the time she had declared this she had felt with some surprise the sharp veracity of the words. It was perhaps only a partial truth but now after these seven months, Dorothy had lived with it long enough that she knew precisely which parts of *The Wizard of Oz* did and did not apply. It was indeed her mother's invention to use the story as a theme for her own daughter's life.

There were always old stories, tales and yarns that sapped rather than nurtured, that caged rather than set free, that offered the ultimate paradox: a kind of comfort through discomfort. In truth the old stories finally did become nearly impossible to relinquish for they were too firmly enmeshed with one's being. Psychologists talked of one's "being" in terms of structures and parts; there was always a lot of hype about the personality structure and its complete organization around these negative components. The removal of any one part, even a negative one, supposedly became a risky business, tantamount to removing a support pillar from an arch or dome.

Dorothy felt that basically all psychologists and psychiatrists were simple-minded fools. Their literalness appalled her. They of course tried to disguise it through their elaborate use of metaphor. Hence, all the architectural references and terminology. Basically they tried to spin a very simple tale about things they could never, or had never been able to, prove in their field. They knew this and it drove them to overcompensate through obfuscation. Once one cut through it all these psychiatrists seemed like fundamentalists reading the first nine lines of Genesis.

The only psychiatrist Dorothy had ever really liked or thought profoundly intelligent was Alexandra Hurst, her old friend from Smith. Alex had been a French and Fine Arts major. She had been a very good painter but had terrible allergies and had become increasingly allergic to all varieties of paint. It came as a total shock to Dorothy and her friends when Alex announced that she was applying to medical school.

By the time of their five-year college reunion, Alex was beginning a residency in psychiatry. "I'm not an empiricist at all," she had said blithely. "Oh Ira, I admire you so much," she had gushed. "But that's not for me. Psychiatry is my style. Nothing has been proven!" (She was the most self-effacing person Dorothy had ever known.) "And you know, I can't paint at all anymore. Well, some water colors, but . . ." Dorothy remembered her lowering her voice. "You see, don't tell anyone—I think psychiatry is an art form, not a science. And I'm not allergic to it."

Alex would never speak of structures, but if she had, Dorothy imagined that she might talk of them in the same way Stephen Jay Gould had in his essays. Dorothy had followed Ella's advice and picked up some books and articles by the evolutionary biologist. Writing about the spandrels of Saint Mark's Basilica in Venice, he had said that those tapering, historical triangles had been thought of as being there to provide space in which mosaicists could arrange their elaborate designs. Gould suggested that people had forgotten the real starting point, the "architectural constraint," which dictated the simple fact that to support a quadripartite dome one needs arches, and each quadrant will flow into its supporting arch via the constraint, the pathway of the spandrel. The spandrel, as a by-product to its support duties, provided doodling space for great Italian mosaicists.

Was this not, Dorothy wondered, analogous to the old stories and yarns with which families became enmeshed? People began with the "paintings," the old stories that hovered in the spandrels of the family, and these in turn came to be thought of as indispensable components of the structure. These yarns, like the paintings, were only decorative art arising as by-products of the architecture. Such decoration was in a sense the corollary of the spandrels, the gratuitous effect of the proposition of the architectural constraint but nonetheless unnecessary and unproven. Decorative garlands. Other stories could fill the space and did not by any means define or inspire the entire structure.

And so Dorothy was sure that her friend Alexandra Hurst, mindful of the real structure, the architectural pathways and constraints, would gently distinguish between the functions of support and the decoration. And thus urge the mosaicist toward a new story of her own making while offering reassurances that the old structure would not crumble in the process.

Dorothy would proceed in this manner, mindful of the integrity of the structure but bold and subtle in her new designs. She had no need to go about this business with stridency or any of the obstreperous fanaticism of her younger counterparts. She was, after all, fifty-two years old—and if those fifty-two years counted for anything in Dorothy's mind, they had given her a measure of style. It did not matter if Beebie knew or did not know what was happening, and if Dorothy had her way her mother would not know. Dorothy the mosaicist would try and conceal the new design. It would be a reversed pentimento. Instead of the first sketch lying discarded under the finished work, the new painting would be concealed under the temperas of the old design. It would appear that all was normal. She would arrive in Florida cheerful with the same goals as always: to have a visit and fix her parents some really nice food that had not been assembled and frozen two weeks before. Some nice fresh food. Her father especially seemed to enjoy her cooking. She had never really chafed in the bridle of being the dutiful daughter.

"We're playing a second Charleston . . . agreed . . . sure . . . what a kong! . . . She's got a pung . . . is she going to curtsy the wall? . . . Red dragon? . . . Bams . . . Did you count that chow? . . . of course, Ruth, I'm not that blind."

A woman named Rose leaned toward Beebie who was playing the East Wind position. "Oh boy, what is it, a chow coming up?"

"What bamboo 5-6-7, ground that kong, Sylvia. . . . What . . . Dot or a crack. No bams."

There was the click of the tiles and the oddly pictorial language that floated out through the sliding screen door to the balcony where Dorothy now sat in her lounge chair which she had provisioned as one might a life raft. It had become for her a kind of buffer. Acceptable and not in the least offensive, it insulated her to a pleasant degree but gave her a certain accessibility to the life that flowed around her.

The schedule in Florida was a simple one. Beebie rose at 6:00 to be ready to tee off at 7:30 and play her eighteen holes in the cool of the morning. Gordon joined her for the first nine and then returned to the condo to take Dorothy grocery shopping for fresh fish or whatever else was planned for the day's meals. By 1:30 the mah-jongg game was under way. Normally the game rotated among the players' homes. But since Dorothy was visiting and happy to make all sorts of pastries, cakes and fruit platters for the dieters, they met three times that week at Beebie's. In spite of their sympathies for the new widow and the excessive praise for her delicious food which helped them wend their way through an afternoon devoted to an ancient Chinese game, Dorothy did need a buffer. She felt comfortable in her little life raft under her mask of zinc oxide, swathed in a gauzy tunic and with her straw hat battened down with a huge white scarf in the stiff breeze.

"How can you bear that wind?"

"Is that the South Wind calling?" Dorothy replied cheerfully to Ruth. The women laughed at Dorothy's little pun.

"Yes, you'll get blown away."

"No, no. I'm well anchored," she called back and took a reef in her *Wall Street Journal*, pleating it in much the same manner that people riding subways fold newspapers for maximum readability when jammed into a tight space. The space here, however, was filled not with people but with hot, humid wind. Dorothy had decided that there was no such thing as a crisp breeze in Florida. When the wind blew, it blew in heavy hot sheets of air. The wind was really just an inconvenience. The element that disturbed her more was what they referred to on the weather reports as the "gray factor." It apparently had something to do with haze and cloud coverage that turned everything gray. What Dorothy disliked most about Florida was its monochromatic quality—and it seemed to be the definitive, the essential element of the Florida east coast.

The sea, uninterrupted by islands and never blue, met beaches straight and unvarying that were fringed by condos of precast concrete painted pale sand colors occupied by gray people. The gray factor was then neither fog nor smog but instead functioned like some optical filter through which sunlight could deliver its full strength but not its precious white light which might shatter the monochromatic essence into the spectrum of color. Such was the physics of Florida.

Dorothy glanced in at the Four Winds. Beebie played East, Ruth South, Rose West and Sylvia North. Except for Beebie they all came from New York—Long Island. Their language seemed overloaded with vowels, huge deep holes into which consonants vanished without a trace. Entire words were swallowed into vowels. *N'Yowk. Quoters. Hort attacks.* But there was never much talk aside from that which applied to the game. One woman was thin—Sylvia. Beebie had a slightly padded look to her robustness but was far from heavy. The other two, Ruth and Rose, were definitely heavy. They spread over their chairs but were kept from slovenliness by proper foundation undergarments.

They dressed expensively. As a result they appeared massive rather than fat. They all adored Dorothy's "girlish" figure and "natural" hair. But they would never dream of leaving behind their dyes, rinses, hair lacquers and industrial-strength elastic undergarments. This natural look was not for them. This was derring-do and offered a chasm not to be breached, a voyage into uncharted waters. "She's so natural," they said of her. They would never directly address a compliment to her, but rather to her mother. When she had greeted them today they had raved about her creamy Indian cloth tunic. "Oh would'ja look at this . . . Is she not adoable in that, Beebie? Oh Gawd, so natural . . . She looks like Gandhi . . . No, no, the lady . . . the English lady . . . his goil friend . . . what a movie . . . she's much prettier . . . Didja see that movie . . . gawjus scenery but a little too much already. Too long . . . Such a natural beauty. See, no stomach. That's why she can wear that . . . Where'd you get it? . . . Oh yeah, Expeditions Unlimited . . . My grandchildren love that place . . . Yeah . . . And you say the stock's good too? I'll tell Harry." Ruth pinched Dorothy's cheeks as she spoke "Ya see, Rose—

that's bone structure. That shiksa Richard married, no bone structure. And that's what they're suppose to have. Gawd! So plain that Lorraine. It rhymes—plain Lorraine."

Poor Lorraine, thought Dorothy. She went back to reading her newspaper as the women continued to play. She inhaled sharply. Expeditions Unlimited had skyrocketed. There must be a takeover pending. She would call Mort. God, she'd done well. It was really unbelievable. Since May her earnings in paper profits were nearing $100,000. In October she had sold the sailboat *Ventricle* for $42,500. With the cash she had bought fifteen hundred shares of Expeditions Unlimited at $10 a share. They were now up to 23⅞.

She had visited the Expeditions store after Lacey and Bill had told her about it. She had actually hoped to find some clothes for Florida and she had. But she also found a very imaginative, well-run outfit absolutely thronged with not just teenagers, but middle agers. Earlier in the month she had sold the Microtron and cleaned up tidily. She had then bought some more of the Expeditions stock. Allayor, the condom company that Dorothy had recommended at her dinner party, was on the move again too.

She thought of all those nice little packages with their nice soft graphics that appealed to instincts of health and hygiene and responsible sex, rather than the macho stuff on the other prophylactic packages. In comparison these looked like Hallmark cards. Dorothy had noticed them at precisely the right time. Ten days later there had been articles in the *New York Times*, the *Wall Street Journal* and *Time* magazine about safe sex and women's choices. The stock had shot up. The Allayor had actually preceded the Schlumberger move, but she had always felt that it was the Schlumberger that had marked the beginning. She had bought only a few shares of the Allayor and although the timing had been fortuitous, Dorothy had also felt it to be just a very flukey coincidence.

The Schlumberger she had sold out of a kind of stubbornness that seemed to involve declaring her independence from Sophie in matters of financial planning. She had come home from her trip to New York slightly annoyed with all of Sophie's advice and counsel, but the stubbornness paid off handsomely and gave her cash to really do something for better reasons. She liked what she was buying now. There was no more sec-ond-guessing about the Japanese. She infinitely preferred these safari clothes, the condoms, and, yes, she would buy back some oil stock when the price came down and perhaps get some silver as a hedge against inflation if the price was right. She began calculating her positions and profits. She could glimpse in her sunglasses the reflection of her own eye, sly with figures, and it caught her by surprise. She nearly laughed aloud.

Again, just like Dorothy's first moves on the stock market, it had all seemed so flukey. In the pocket of the seat in front of her on the flight back to Boston was an old *Down East* magazine. What drew her eye to it was the color of the sky on the cover picture—a clarion blue that seemed to announce fresh winds and no gray factor. There might be fog, of course, that perhaps would swirl in, tangy with salt and mystery, and transform landscape and the sea. Nothing like the monochro-matic filter, however.

She took the magazine out of the pocket and feasted her eyes on the blue, the curved shoreline of the cove and the hummock of lupine leaning away from the breeze. The gray factor, the sheets of hot humid wind, crept right out of her. The picture was a veritable tonic after five days of filial torpor in Florida. She turned immediately to the real estate listings in the back of the magazine and on the second page found the ad. "Gray shingled saltbox waterfront cottage on Shag Island, Penobscot Bay, Maine. Three bedrooms, woodstove, deck and porch. Occupies prime location on East Point. Spectacular view with 900 ft. shore frontage, deep water anchorage.

Charming. $100,000." A realtor was listed with a telephone number in Camden.

Less than a week earlier she had read the ad. Now Dorothy sat bundled inside the cabin of the *Sea Queen,* the mailboat out of Rockland that delivered people and parcels to Shag Island, North Haven, Vinalhaven and Islesboro. Dorothy, Mrs. Pond, the real estate agent, an older man in sea boots and a young mother with an infant and a small child were the only passengers.

The sea turned choppy as they rounded the point and came out from under the lee of Rockland. Dorothy felt slightly queasy at first but sucked hard on a mint and pressed her face against the glass. The prow of the boat rose and fell with a great crushing sound and Dorothy concentrated on the wings of spray cast up as it plowed through the sea. The water was dark green, almost black. The wind was blowing a hard twenty-five knots and peeled the tops off the breaking waves in great arabesques of foam.

Her queasiness seemed to steal away as she felt her excitement increase. The notion that she might actually be purchasing a house in this wild and wind-spun place, that one of these islands pounded by the sea might provide a home, even if only a summer home, thrilled her. The thrumming noise of the engine and the crash of the sea precluded normal conversation, but the other passengers and the captain occasionally exchanged a piece of information, mostly about the weather, loudly in the chopped cadences of Down East.

"Harbor's got more ice than seen in a long time . . . you know it comes when it blows from the North so steady . . . Blew southeast last week . . . not t'enuff to do much."

"Robert's boy goin t'school on the mainland next year. . . ."

"Ayuh."

"Can't keep school open . . . not 'nuff kids for the state to send a teacher."

"Like over at Frenchboro . . ."

"Tink scallopin' this winter?"

"Ayuh."

"Too bad he cain't get a job cap'n'ing like his brother down in Florida."

"Gotta hang 'round Northeast to pick up them jobs."

"S'pose so."

"Jimmy got hung up in fog off Isle au Haut . . . come in all a sudden . . . nasty place to be. It'd been blowing southeast all that week . . . That's when he was out."

"Fog can pile up thick as mud round there."

When they came into the Fox Island Thoroughfare the sea flattened. Dorothy asked the captain if she might go on deck. "If you kin take the cold. Stay aft, though."

She did. Mrs. Pond came out for a few minutes but declared it too cold. "That wind still has a bite in it," she said as she turned to go inside again. A welcome bite, Dorothy thought, a breeze to chase away any remnant of Florida's thick, humid winds and blow out the miasma of the gray factor. A gull shrieked and pressed itself against the pale blue sky, then melted into a cloud bank. As the *Sea Queen* turned toward Shag Island, Dorothy could see the harbor clogged with ice. Captain Beal had mentioned the ice when they had left Rockland, but Dorothy had not expected this much. The *Sea Queen* had already made the trip once that day and seemed totally unperturbed by the icy maze as the captain proceeded to steer her through the dark water ribbons that opened pathways through the floes. The wind sliced against Dorothy's cheek. Her nose was stinging. She turned up the collar of her sheep-lined coat. The sun burst out suddenly and the harbor glared with a crystalline ferocity.

The village nestled at the end of the harbor, cozy and protected. But if she squinted hard and made her eyes just slits,
filtering out almost everything except sunlight and ice, it could
have been the Arctic. And perhaps, she mused, if someone
had been squinting back she might have appeared to them to
be Roald Amundsen or Robert Peary dodging the pack ice,
and about to name a new sea.

"It's good you wore those boots," Mrs. Pond said as they
disembarked at the town dock. "Cecil Weed, the caretaker,
can only drive us so far. It's a quarter mile in to the cottage
from the road—a blessing in the summer, of course; less convenient in the winter. . . . Ah, there's Cecil now."

A tall man in a heavy parka and watch cap waved as he
drove up to the dock. Dorothy was introduced and sat between
Cecil and Mrs. Pond in the pickup truck. The ride promised
to be short; the island was only three miles long and a mile
and a half wide. Within the bay the island lay on a northeast-
southwest axis. The first thing she had done after reading the
ad in Down East was to go to a chandlery in South Boston,
one that Ira had frequented but she had never even visited,
and purchase a chart of Penobscot Bay. On a larger-scale
quadrangle map the realtor had sent, she had been able to
pinpoint the location of East Point and was pleased to note
that it resembled in shape the wing tip of a bird.

The entire island for that matter appeared in its contours
like a bird in flight, the tail tapering off to the west, a head
ducked southwest. This particular day, Dorothy thought, it
was a bird flying into a near gale, on another day perhaps it
rode the summer thermals and on still another it might be
reaching on the northwest wind, the clearing wind, the opposite of the wind Cecil was now telling her about.

"Oh, this wind now will back round to southeast by t'night.
Bring in the fog and some rain. Make everything a mess. That'll
loosen the bowels." Mrs. Pond gave Cecil a cold stare. He
coughed slightly, realizing too late that his weather report,

although on target for accuracy, might be missing the mark in other ways. "Well," he cleared his throat, "anyhow, as I was saying things'll be churnin' for a while. Then the northwest wind'll come through and clear it all out."

That was what people here talked about, Dorothy realized—weather, in the most visceral terms. Weather was the main character, the star player, unpredictable, petulant, unnerving and arrogant. She liked it.

At the juncture between the East Point road and the main road Dorothy noticed a house absolutely swallowed in drifts of snow. A junk car stared hollow-eyed out of a drift, and what looked like TV antennae rose from another drift. A pathway had been tunneled in the general direction of the front door and an abandoned barrel-style washing machine, capped with snow, stood sentry at the entrance of the path.

"What's that?" asked Dorothy.

"The Macchias's," Cecil said. "Kindest folks in the world but they live in a junk heap. Don't seem to bother them at all."

"How do they ever get in and out?" Dorothy asked.

"Burrow!" Cecil laughed.

The small cottage they had come to see clung to the rocks like a limpet. Dorothy could tell that Mrs. Pond desperately wished that the wind could have been blowing from the other direction, as torrents of snow, mixed with the wet air, dashed sharp and slanting against the living room windowpanes which Cecil had unshuttered, giving Dorothy a perfect view of the gale driving in from the northeast.

"Great Seal Head and Little Seal and Parker's Island, Bent and Cat." Mrs. Pond tried her best to give a picture of the missing parts—the islands, channels, thoroughfares and lighthouses. Dorothy could see the beam of the lighthouse. The whole scene looked not unlike one of those trapped in a little plastic dome containing water and "snow" dots swirling about a snowman, or a Christmas tree or sometimes a lighthouse. To make the blizzard rage one shook the dome. The snowflakes outside the cottage were not nearly so perfect as those in a dome, nor was the scene so serenely pristine. Snow and sleet lashed the air and great ragged dark clouds raced across the sky. It was spectacular. The windows rattled and shook, but the house seemed tight against it.

"Built on ledge. Everything at this end is," Cecil said.

"Good septic system, though," offered Mrs. Pond.

"Lord knows where they found a place to put it!" Cecil commented.

"Well, they did," Mrs. Pond replied. There was a definite snap in her voice. Cecil realized, again too late, that perhaps his comment was not exactly the thing to be said to a prospective buyer. He tried what Dorothy sensed to be a midcourse correction that backfired, with her help.

"There's a real good well here, too."

"I hope not too close to the septic system," Dorothy said.

"No! No!" both Cecil and Mrs. Pond chorused.

Dorothy had a hard time worrying about wells and septic systems when confronted with the charms of a cobbled fireplace that looked perfect for a miniature Teddy Roosevelt, and a kitchen with a black wood-burning stove and an eating end that made no pretenses about being a half-baked dining room called a "bay" or an "alcove." It was just the end of the kitchen which hung right over the water and was supported by pylons driven into granite.

"Now what view is this?" she asked, looking out a window by the dining table.

"Well, straight out you see there's a narrow channel. And on the other side of that channel—that's Back Island. No one lives on it. That's straight east, but looking that way." Mrs. Pond pointed slightly to the left. "That is northeast. See, there's the light."

The bedrooms were cozy with window seats and slanted ceilings. They were all painted white, with the woodwork in a dove gray, as were the wide, old floorboards except those in the master bedroom which were clear Georgia pine and had been left unpainted.

"She's leaving the beds." They were nice beds, old-fashioned iron ones with brass knobbed posts suitable for nuns or ship captains. "But now for the best!" Mrs. Pond said, swelling with anticipation.

"What might that be?" Dorothy asked.

"The porch. The 'sunset porch,' they call it."

A door off the kitchen led out to the sunset porch. There was also access from the living room. Dorothy had caught a glimpse of it before and wondered why Mrs. Pond had not shown it to her then. Obviously it was to be the *pièce de résistance,* shown as the climax of the tour with the object of clinching the deal. Cecil unlocked the door. Mrs. Pond led Dorothy through. "You see," said Mrs. Pond, "it's designed to look like a ship's hull."

The walls, shingled on the outside, ship-lathed and painted white on the inside, bowed to the floor like an inverted ship's hull. Framed in the arch was a view out over the wide channel called the Western Way. The land, naturally terraced by granite ledges, stepped down to the sea. The ledges themselves were for the most part bare of the snow, which had collected in drifts between them. "Good space for a garden between those ledges," Cecil said. "They had a small vegetable garden, but you could do more if you had a mind to. There'd be room between those ledges for things to grow all the way down to the shore."

Over the snow in the swales between the ledges, Dorothy saw a garden hover with drifts of sea lavender and frosty mounds of artemisia and lamb's ear and soft explosions of heather. It would be bright with pinks and cool with periwinkle blues and silver, colors that would catch the fog and the dew and the light of the moon as well as the brightness of the sun. And it would all grow over, between and against the granite ledges.

Dorothy imagined that this could be an enchanted spot, a perch from which to watch the night sky, the rising moon, the transit of the stars. One could have drinks and dinner on the porch, and then have breakfast at the eating end of the kitchen, looking east. Of course if the weather was really clear, the rocky point just beyond, where the dock had been pulled out, would give a spectacular view at dawn.

Yes, one could sit on this wing tip of a bird in this shingled, salt-washed cottage and follow the moon and the stars and the sun about the house and see the water from three sides. If this was the margin of a niche, it seemed to Dorothy the center of the universe.

She wrote out a check for forty thousand dollars and got a mortgage for the remaining sixty thousand at $10\frac{1}{4}$ percent. There was no need to tie up all that cash. She had always felt that real estate was a hedge against inflation, but it was a moot point in this case. She knew she would never be tempted to sell this cottage. For the sake of prudence she should get herself a real hedge, one that she would have no qualms about parting with. So she bought herself 5,000 ounces of silver at $6.50 an ounce. In another cautious move she followed Mort's suggestion and bought a chunk of Digital and some more Gillette. If she did well with these she might put some of her profits toward something called Charme shops, an over-the-counter stock that specialized in moderately priced clothes for large-sized women. America might be obsessed with thinness, but there were a lot of large ladies in Florida as well as in Maine.

18

"**C**ongrats." If there was one word Dorothy loathed, that was it—that raspy truncation of an otherwise perfectly decent word. Instead of a festive accolade, the suggestion of laurel wreaths and celebratory fireworks conjured up by the whole, real word, this "congrats" business sounded like handfuls of grain or corn kernels being scattered—chicken feed.

She should not complain, however, because this scrap of a word had been sent by none other than Ella and was the only hearty, unquestioning approval she had received in regard to the purchase of the Shag Island house. Everyone else had been terribly cautious in their endorsements. "Well, I suppose if that's what you want," Gordon had said. "You got forty-two thousand for the boat, right?" "Right," Dorothy had answered and had resisted elaborating how she had played that money into substantially more on the market.

"But Maine!" Beebie had said. "That's so far north and all those rocks and there's lots of fog, isn't there?" She might have been describing a lunar landscape.

Sophie was interested solely in how Dorothy had financed
it. And for the first time Dorothy revealed her stock market
maneuverings to Sophie in elaborate detail. She began by saying, "Well, dear, do you remember when you told me to hang
on to the Schlumberger . . . well, I didn't." And she continued on through Reeboks, Expeditions Unlimited and Allayor,
culminating with the Japanese Ministry of Trade.

"No shit" was Sophie's stunned response. Dorothy did feel
that had Sophie not been so nonplussed by her market report,
she would have shown more enthusiasm for the Shag Island
house, but all she seemed to be able to focus on was the prop-
erty as another dazzling investment of Dorothy's.

Peter responded to the news in a rather tedious letter that
dwelled upon issues such as "the needs of a widowed woman
of your age." It was filled with words like "assert" and "independence" and phrases like "establishing one's own personal
space." It was the same style of language, that banal claptrap
that Ella had used with her when she had talked about the
therapeutic effect of anger. God, she had hoped that Peter
could ward off some of this. True, she had come to like Ella,
but there were still certain things about Ella's style that she
found very annoying. There was no doubt in Dorothy's mind
that Ella was much more original in her language and observations of baboons and theories of history and evolution than
when speaking about people and psychology.

It was clear to Dorothy, however, that Peter viewed the
Shag Island house as a simple countermeasure to the condo—
a gesture of sorts, and she read the letter with a building sense
of dread that he might actually use the word "gesture." It was
no such thing. The Shag house was exactly what she wanted.
So it had come to her as a total shock when she opened Ella's
letter a week after receiving Peter's. The "congrats" blared
out. Ella didn't say anything about her "needs" or personal
space, nor did she talk about it as a financial investment. She
simply asked all about the house and what it looked like, how

close it was to the water, whether there was enough room for Peter and her to come and visit. Dorothy should please send a picture.

Ella had written in that letter that she had once been in Maine—"ten days of fog but that's my kind of lousy weather." And then, of course, she went on to report the continuing saga of Dot and Honest Abe, Murphy, Pop Eye, Ginger, Fred and Willy. Dorothy only had time to skim the rest of the letter because Halsey Winthrop was due by at any moment. He was off to Patagonia for trout fishing. There was no doubt about it, Halsey was one of those folks whose life could be described as having a certain panache. To be able even to report such a piece of information as she had just done on the phone with Ginny added a flourish to one's own life.

Because of Halsey's visit Dorothy was able to avoid a tedious evening with Ginny and Ralph. She had tried very hard of late to confine her social engagements with the Harrisons to lunches with Ginny. Ralph had become insufferable in his concern for what she knew he considered her aberrant lifestyle. The Shag Island house had capped it. The Harrisons thought she had absolutely cracked. Ralph's comment: "It could be worse. You could have bought something in Provincetown." But, if Dorothy insisted on Maine, why not Northeast Harbor or Vinalhaven or North Haven or Shadow Harbor? Dorothy did not mention that Halsey was actually going to Patagonia via Shadow Harbor to check on his mother's house and that Betsy, the mother, insisted that Dorothy, of whom she was quite fond, take her pick from "scads" of stuff in the barn she no longer had use for.

Dorothy and Halsey had planned to drive up together in Dorothy's car with a U-haul trailer stuffed with her first load of things for the Shag Island house. Cecil Weed would meet them in Rockland and take the contents on to Shag. Dorothy would proceed with Halsey to Shadow Harbor to pick through his mother's stuff. Then Halsey and Dorothy would go on to

Shag. He was anxious to see the house and had offered help to get things ready for summer.

First, though, Halsey was to come to Boston, and Dorothy looked forward to this. Halsey always stayed at the Ritz and usually had the most delightful kind of business to attend to, and it had become his habit to include Dorothy. His "business" seemed to Dorothy to belong to that extinct species of nineteenth-century wealthy gentlemen scholars. He came on yearly visits to Boston to purchase rare books, Oriental rugs and marine paintings. Dorothy usually tagged along. There would be lunch at the Ritz and the chance to touch leather volumes with creamy pages of soft vellum often edged in gold and to look at some fine art.

Dorothy and Halsey now stood in the dim, dust-filtered light of a musty emporium of antiquarian and rare secondhand books on Charles Street. The proprietor, a Mr. Beasley, had come out to help Halsey. Beasley was a man of undetermined age who shared a yellowish pallor with his books. She had come to think of this pallor in terms of a kind of bibliographic photosynthesis, a phenomenon that turns white to yellow and drains the color from cloth covers so that in time nothing was ever its true color. She liked to imagine that Beasley's cells in some way had been adapted to turn dust and dimness into chemical energy. Dorothy could not imagine how else he could survive. She could not envision him outside, or eating.

She had accompanied Halsey to the shop on several occasions in the past but Beasley never seemed to remember her. It did not disturb her in the least; he simply had no memory for faces, only for books and, of course, a few long-standing favorite clients like Halsey. Most of his dealings with these clients were through the mail, except of course for the Arabs. "They don't write," Mr. Beasley was telling them now. "They send agents in to purchase. Anything English, of course. They are particularly fond of early Anglo-Saxon and Middle English— Chaucer, Beowulf, you know."

"No John Donne?" Halsey chuckled. Mr. Beasley laughed
too. His laugh had a creaky quality to it that was almost indistinguishable to Dorothy's ears from the sounds of the wooden
floors as he walked to his office to fetch something to show
Halsey. When he returned he handed Halsey a faded red cloth-
covered book and whispered in his low, velvety voice, "Scrib-
ners 1883."

"*Love Letters of Thomas Carlyle and Jane Welsh.* Splendid!"
Halsey exclaimed.

"Well, to make up for the unfortunate mangling of the
Jewsbury diaries."

"Not your fault, Beasley. Editors do nasty things to diaries."

"Who's Jewsbury? And how was she or he mangled?" Dorothy asked after the waiter had set down her Pimm's on the
rocks with a slice of cucumber. Only in the Ritz Carleton
dining room did Dorothy ever drink Pimm's.

"Novelist and bosom buddy of Carlyle's wife, Jane Welsh.
It had always been suspected that the Carlyle marriage was
never consummated."

"Really?" Dorothy's eyes widened.

"Yes."

"Well, I can't imagine that the love letters would be so
great."

"Love letters for the most part happen before marriage, my
dear, unless of course the husband goes off to war or something. It's precisely because the marriage remained unconsummated that the letters are so interesting. I know that people
will quibble that this is not a valid way to do any kind of
critical interpretive work. But hang it! This is just for my library
and my own enjoyment."

"And where does the mangling of Jewsbury come into all
this?"

"Jane Welsh confided in her. There have been all sorts of

allusions in biographies on Thomas Carlyle to a kind of sexual détente between the two. Quotes from friends, you know, making delicate statements about his being 'one of those persons who ought not to have married' or references to the marriage being not a 'true' one but rather one of 'companionship.' "

"Good Lord."

"Yes, well, for all ostensible purposes Jane seemed fine enough. She played a lot of shuttlecocks apparently, read voraciously and took care of Carlyle and the household. It was her mind that had attracted him originally. If it could have been a fabulous intellectual relationship, that would have compensated somewhat for sex perhaps."

"Perhaps not," Dorothy said.

"In any case," Halsey continued, "he wouldn't let her participate to any degree in his intellectual life after they were married. In one of his letters he paints what he obviously believes is a dreamy little portrait of connubial bliss, referring to his wife as being on her side of the household having faithfully completed her household duties, while he will have written his 'allotted pages.' They then will meet at the end of the day over what I believe he describes as a 'frugal meal with happy and proud hearts.' "

"Oh yecch!" muttered Dorothy over her Pimm's.

"No. I'm afraid that Jane Welsh Carlyle was not that happy or proud and she suffered in not quite complete silence."

"Is this where Miss Jewsbury comes in?"

"Yes. There was a description that I saw in the original Jewsbury diary, the unmangled one, which described how Miss Jewsbury had summoned James Anthony Froude to her deathbed to describe a scene that Jane had told her about. The morning after their wedding, when Carlyle, 'engorged with rage,' raced from the bedroom into a flower garden and proceeded to tear it apart."

"Really!"

Halsey then explained that it was a watered-down version

in Froude's book, "but the diary told it straight, except the one Beasley got me which had been edited."

Dorothy half listened to him as he described the private library in Hertfordshire where he had seen the original Jews-bury diary. She was gazing over the dining room. Outside the weather was bleak, a sleety March rain. Inside, of course, the Ritz had a weather unto itself. The pale yellow walls and crystal chandeliers created an eternal high-pressure system of gold-spun light and airiness. The table flowers were always the same at the Ritz—whites, yellows and a touch of something blue. The yellow picked up on the walls and the gilt trim of the room. The blue provided contrast and offered, she felt, a reference to sea and sky.

Within the dining room there was a whole world, ordered and serene. It was like the fifteenth-century painting she remembered from her art history course, a vision of the universe of Dante. It was a contained universe. An inflated Earth was of course at the center, and around it the sun and other lesser bodies rotated like gnats around a light bulb. But at the very center of the swollen sphere of Earth was Florence with the Brunelleschi dome of the cathedral looming large.

The Ritz Carleton had that same sort of belief about itself, not so much in terms of its placement within the universe but rather of its power to enclose and encompass a superior world within. This was the presumption it shared with fifteenth-century Florence. Rome might be the eternal city but Florence was the complete universe.

Dorothy drew these analogies as she listened to Halsey's spirited discourse on an unconsummated marriage of another century. She looked about as she listened to this odd tale and wondered what kinds of détentes or peculiar marriages had been fashioned within the lives of the other people in this room. Hadn't she herself, within her own life and marriage until recently, been in a kind of détente?

The people in the dining room always interested Dorothy

more than those in the grill or bar because they seemed to be a kind unto themselves. In the grill business people met for breakfast and lunch meetings. It was largely a publishing crowd. Within a three- or four-block radius around the public gardens and the common were Little, Brown, Houghton Mifflin and the Atlantic Monthly Press. In the evening in the Ritz bar one might see a "personality." "Personality" was a word Dorothy hated even more than "congrats." Used this way it suggested that only people like Barbara Walters, Ted Kennedy or William Buckley had personality. But all of the people in the dining room had a timelessness about them, and Dorothy never failed to be struck by the notion that these impeccably tailored or acceptably frayed men and women could have come straight out of some nineteenth-century drawing room from Jane Austen's Highgate or George Eliot's Middlemarch. Here in the gold-spun air it was still a little universe where, as Jane Austen said in *Emma*, not having money was all right, but not having manners was unforgivable.

"Dorothy!" Halsey was leaning across the table.

"Oh, Halsey. I'm sorry," she said, realizing that her attention had wandered and he had just asked her a question.

"You want to know what I'm going to do there all summer? Well, you know, summer things—garden, bum sailboat rides." She laughed. "I was just thinking right now actually that I might reread Jane Austen. You know, it always reminds me of Jane Austen when I come here."

"That's just my point, dear," Halsey said, leaning forward again and looking over his reading glasses. "I'm afraid Shag Island won't remind you of that. I do worry about you on a place like Shag. It is isolated."

"There are summer people there."

"Yes, but Shadow Harbor . . . I mean, it's rather more . . ." He gestured toward the other diners.

"They read Jane Austen at Shadow Harbor?" Dorothy deadpanned.

"No." Halsey chuckled. "Hardly, but there is a very nice community. I know it's no business of mine and that you've already bought the house. I'm sure it's charming but . . . you know, I worry."

Dear Halsey. He was an incurable romantic. Dorothy leaned over and put her hand on his. "Halsey! Halsey!" She patted his hand and sighed. "Your Shadow Harbor." He grimaced as she spoke. "You know then what I am going to say?"

"Dorothy, the world isn't that way anymore."

"Legally it's not. You're right. But Halsey, you can bet that islands are the last to change, and summer island communities are islands within islands, if there can be such things. Just because your mother has always loved me, and loved Ira, and even though she is the duchess of Shadow Harbor . . ."

Halsey waved his hand in a dismissive gesture. "I'm way out of line, dear. Forget what I just said. But I don't think you're entirely right about Shadow Harbor."

"Of course you don't think I'm right. I would be disappointed in you if you did."

"I don't know what that's supposed to mean. Want another Pimm's?" He was signaling the waiter.

"No, thank you."

He ordered another martini for himself and drank it as an accompaniment to his salmon.

"Halsey, did I tell you that I went to the Frick a few months ago when I was visiting Sophie in New York, and I've decided I don't like the Boucher portrait of the little wife anymore?"

"Now, I don't quite remember the Boucher. I do remember that you didn't like the Polish rider and it was proven a fake."

"Yes, well, guess what? I do like that one now—the fake."

That evening Dorothy reread Ella's letter. On the second page, after the "congrats" and the inquiries about the Shag Island house, Ella wrote:

Guess who's back on the scene? None other than the durable Fig. Lulu, as you might recall in my last letter, finally succumbed to Butch's advances and has not been in consort with Fig for a month or so. Well, the other day we observed Fig within twenty meters of where Lulu and Butch were copulating. He was watching them patiently and not coming any closer than twenty meters. It has been noted that female baboons end their copulations with quite a flourish. In a typical withdrawal response the female runs away a few steps or she might in a real burst of energy dash up to 100 meters away (Smuts, 1984, Aldine Press). Smuts reports that she once saw a female who had just copulated on a cliff edge jettison right off it at the time of withdrawal! There seems to be this compelling need to get away quickly. No afterplay here. Hamilton and Arrowood (1978, Science magazine—you can get a copy with Ira's card at the MCZ) suggest that this is part of the female design, a kind of advertising campaign, the objective being to promote competition amongst males for sexual favors and may the highest-ranking male win.

In any case Lulu in consort with Butch had always, until Fig showed up again, confined her withdrawal to a few little steps or a short dash. But when Fig reappeared she really cranked it up quite a bit. For three consecutive days Fig was observing them and each day Lulu's withdrawal got wilder. The third day she actually crashed into a higher-ranking female. A real faux pas! Also during copulation she became more noisy. It is typical for the female before the male dismounts to do what I refer to as the three P's—puffing, pursing of lips and pouting. The female will then begin a series of low-pitched grunts that can be heard up to 200 or 300 meters away. It is a kind of prelude to the advertising campaign. Well, you could have heard Lulu a mile away. All this of course seemed aimed at Fig. But Fig has thus far made no move. He is higher ranking than Butch but Butch is younger and stronger and rising fast. What's one to make of all this?

Other developments: Ginger and Fred are having to deal with a newcomer to the troop, a certain Marcus. I, along with others (Smuts, Altmann, etc.), have said for years that females initiate and pursue relationships that go far beyond the sexual act. I knew that females exercise choice in matters of sex, but I am beginning now to see more clearly some of the political implications of it. The most recent example of this makes me a bit hesitant for other reasons.

Troop #8, the one we are observing, is a medium-size troop. The other day we followed them to a high plain where they spent the night in a stand of fever trees near Troop #5. Peaches, a cycling female with a handsomely swollen bottom, who had been copulating vigorously with a variety of males (middle to high ranking), wandered over to the edge of Troop #8 directly across from the other troop and sat staring for several minutes. She then got up and began sashaying across the space separating the two groups. She had her sights set on a certain male, the one we have since named Marcus. When she had attracted his attention, she turned, looked over her shoulder and presented her flaming rear end and began backing up toward him. She turned away, looked, turned again and began backing up. She kept up this little ritual for some time.

Needless to say, Marcus's gaze was riveted on her rear and when she was within five meters he made a "come hither" face with the concomitant chin pull. The come hither face plus the chin pull is the male reciprocal signal. In short it says, I read you loud and clear now move those buns over here for a closer look and feel. Of course as soon as Marcus made this face Peaches skittered away. She then stopped short, looked back over her shoulder and began

the whole thing again—sashaying, backing up, presenting,
etc. etc. Each time she got closer.

The third time Marcus reached for her hips and lip-
smacked but she scooted away. Peaches continued to play
him flawlessly. He was soon totally obsessed with her she-
nanigans and in his efforts to get close and touch her was a
pathetic sight indeed. He would almost have her and then
she would give him the slip. He would be left sitting there
stunned, lips smacking, penis erect, hands outstretched
but no hips between them. But then when he least
expected it she rushed directly toward him, and with split-
second timing peeled off in the direction of her own troop.
It worked like magic. He followed right after her. She
bounded for the middle of the troop. He stopped, looked
around, realized where he was and then looked back at
Troop #5. There were several cycling females in his new
troop whom he chased about.

He finally did copulate with Peaches. She could have
cared less. Her work was done—getting him into the
troop. He consorted with several of the cycling females for
the first week, but now seems to be very interested in Ginger, who is not cycling, having recently given birth to
Willy. Fred, who is always very protective of Willy, was
forced yesterday to pick up Willy (much like Honest Abe
did with Sweet Pea when Murphy threatened). Ginger
isn't even that high ranking. Marcus had his pick of several high-ranking cycling females. So we can't quite figure
this out, as he seems to be becoming increasingly obsessed
with Ginger. Ginger isn't keen on it. Fred less so. So that
is all the news from the savannah for now.

yrs.
Ella

19

❦

Over one hundred years of conspicuous consumption,"
Halsey said, looking about the barn. He was perched on a
massive claw-footed Victorian table.

"It's never conspicuous the way you folks do it," Dorothy
replied.

"You mean WASPS."

"Well, old money. Who bought that?" Dorothy asked. "The
thing you're sitting on."

"Oh, this probably came down through Aunt Todie. She
had god-awful taste."

"Everyone did at a certain time—collecting all that hideous
Victoriana. That's why your mother is so amazing. Everything
of hers is beautiful." She looked about the barn. It was full of
priceless old wicker, the kind that Boston dealers would kill
for.

"Well, pick what you want. Those were my instructions."

"It's too kind of her. Really, I feel odd."

"Don't. There aren't any heirs. Or at least none that she

likes, other than me, of course, and I'll get the whole she-bang." By "the whole shebang" he meant Wind's Way, the lovely, sprawling, shingled cottage that commanded a spectacular view over the Fox Island Thoroughfare. "And I'm no good at running yard sales."

"Halsey, you don't sell stuff like this at yard sales. You have an auction and get someone up from Sotheby's in New York or Phillips in Boston."

"See, you know that and I don't."

"Don't play the rube. Remember that two days ago I spent a morning and afternoon with you looking at marine paintings and rare books. You know about these things."

"Okay, how about that cherry trestle table there?"

"Oh, it's lovely but it's too big. I can't seem to impress upon you how small this place is."

"Well, there's the wicker. That should fit and it's light. We'll have no trouble getting it over on the mailboat."

"Yes. Yes. I do love the wicker. I think actually that love-seat would go quite nicely." She pointed toward the piece. It was handwoven, amber-colored wicker. The border was painted dusty green with a soft pink piping.

"There's an easy chair, ottoman and table to match. It's yours."

"Good Lord!" Dorothy was delighted. People paid thousands for this kind of wicker. And if they couldn't find the old stuff they paid handsomely to have new wicker made into instant heirlooms by oiling and staining.

It took two trips on the mailboat for there was another set of wicker, a white one more coarsely woven and not nearly so old, that Dorothy realized would be perfect for the sunset porch. What could be better for viewing sunsets and an ascending moon than a rocker? There were two. There were also wicker plant stands, some Chinese cachepots, an entire box filled with Irish linens, tablecloths with lovely fretwork that almost mirrored the geometry in the wicker furniture. The linens were in perfect condition and Dorothy imagined them covering tables like poured cream.

It did not take long to install the furniture. By afternoon of the following day Dorothy had put a first coat of white paint on the kitchen cabinets which had been a brackish green.

The ledges had melted out of the snow and from the kitchen window Dorothy could see Halsey in foul weather gear down on the shore inspecting the pier and float. She cranked open the window and called down to him but her voice was no match for the wind. She put on her slicker and boots and headed down for the shore. It was a sloppy wet wind.

"Come on in, for God's sake. It's a mess out here," she called.

"Your pier and float are in very good shape. That one drum might need replacing. That's all, though. I'll talk to your man Cecil about it."

"Fine, but come in. It's time for a drink."

They walked up the ledges. They were black and slick. Dorothy slipped a little and felt Halsey's hand lightly on her elbow. "Good God, don't break your leg."

"You'd have to shoot me."

It was not what one would call a bold assault, although uncorking the proffered champagne did add a percussive note to it all. Dorothy had just come out from the kitchen to the living room where Halsey had poked the fire into new vigor. She was carrying a tray with a bottle of vodka, vermouth and a bowl of ice and was just about to apologize for the old jelly jars they were going to have to use for glasses. Halsey, his back to her and bent over in what she assumed to be fire-tending duties, suddenly stood and turned around with a bottle of champagne in his hand—very good champagne.

"I put it in down by the shore to chill when we arrived."

"Oh Halsey, how dear! What a nice way to celebrate a new

home. I hope you don't mind the jelly glasses."

"Not at all. I can't believe we couldn't find any crystal in the barn at Wind's Way."

"Well, I wasn't looking."

"I was." There was something so matter-of-fact in his tone that it almost startled Dorothy.

"Oh, you were?"

"Yes," he said, uncorking the bottle and pouring into the two jelly jars. "Shall we sit down?"

They each sat in the amber-colored wicker easy chairs in front of the fireplace. Halsey put the bottle on the table between them. "You see, my charming Dorothy." He picked up her hand in a companionable way and gave it a squeeze. "I believe we should—how should I put it?—get married."

"Married!" Dorothy gasped.

"Yes. Does that shock you?"

Dorothy set down her jar and nodded.

Halsey continued. "Well, you're speechless now, but this might shock you even more—I have always loved you, desired you." *Desired!* Dorothy barely had time to contemplate the word before Halsey shocked her again. "And hell, there are three bedrooms here. One's filled with furniture. I know the second is quite comfortable, but what would be even more comfortable would be to be with you!"

"Comfortable?" Dorothy said in a small voice. Good Lord, she thought. She would have expected a little more of the troubadour from Halsey. As it was, with this blunt, head-on strategy, he hardly seemed to accord her the canniness or the cunning of a trout in still water. There was a kaleidoscopic turning and flashing of thoughts in her mind before she even could try to muster a response. Was it possible that Halsey was trying to follow the old biblical injunction, in a strange way needless to say, of marrying the "brother's" wife? It all seemed quite grim to Dorothy. She could almost conjure up images of "allotted pages" and "frugal meals." She knew that was a mean exaggeration on her part. But what about the business of the bedroom being more comfortable with her? For heaven's sake, even old Peaches with her strategies for bringing Marcus into the troop seemed to find more than just comfort in her first copulations. Suppose . . . Dorothy could hardly bear the thought and began to chuckle.

"Is it that funny, Dorothy?"

"No! No! It's not that . . . oh, God . . ." And she began to laugh again. How could she ever explain about Ella and the the picture that was now in her mind of herself, in the venerable tradition of her baboon "ancestresses," flying off the small deck outside the bedroom, over the ledges and into Penobscot Bay in withdrawal response? Now you see her! Now you don't!

"Am I to take this as a rejection?" Halsey said, pouring them both some more champagne.

"Don't use that word," Dorothy said and reached for Halsey's hand. She had composed herself by willfully banning all images of baboons. She looked directly at him. He had that reddish blond hair that would never go really gray but just become duller with perhaps a few gray touches. His eyes were a soft hazel color. He had that rugged elegance befitting gentlemen explorers, the ones who preferred harsh climates, most likely Polar adventurers who perhaps had Aleut or Inuit mistresses—for comfort and warmth when the pack ice came in early and they were trapped in Melville or Frobisher Bay, or wherever.

"Dorothy, I find this cottage charming."

"You mean you're not trying to rescue me from the isolation of Shag Island?"

"By no means. I'd be happy to spend my summers here, and falls. I'm going on part-time at Yale, taking early retirement in a few years. I don't want you to change your life for me."

"But *I've* changed."

"Yes. I'm sure all widows, newly widowed women must go through tremendous changes."

"No. I don't mean that. I am very different from the person I ever imagined myself to be—ever!" Halsey opened his eyes wide over the half-glasses he was wearing.

"I don't quite understand it myself," she went on. She realized that for Halsey, marriage to her was indeed a corollary act for unproven reasons, be they comfort or some skewed version of biblical law or whatever.

"Did I ever tell you," she said, "that I have had the feeling that as good a marriage as Ira and I had, and two great kids, perhaps we should have never married?"

"What in the hell are you talking about? You were great together. Do you know how envious I always was of you both for three decades? And don't call me a romantic."

Dorothy leaned back and smiled at him, still holding his hand. "You know I will. But let me tell you something more romantic."

"What's that?"

"Suppose Ira and I hadn't married. And suppose that instead I had gone to the Art Students League."

"Did you want to go there? I never knew that."

"Well, not many did, dear. That was my problem back then. I was too subtle for words. In any case, suppose I had gone to the Art Students League and got myself a little apartment in Greenwich Village."

"Bleecker Street."

"Oh, I always sort of liked Bank Street. And it would have been a little cramped place, and Ira would have come to visit me and we would have had this torrid affair."

"Oh God, on Indian print bedcovers."

"No, dear, wrong period. That's what college kids have now. Have you been seeing undergraduate dorm rooms?"

"Dorothy!"

"Just teasing. Anyway, no Indian print bedspreads but maybe I would have had one of those paneled screens to get undressed behind and throw my clothes over. I would have had to get better underwear."

"And I suppose Ira would have put some Cole Porter on the record player."

"Oh yes. Now, you're getting into the spirit." Dorothy laughed.

"But then would you ever have gotten married?"

"I guess not."

"But why not?"

"But why did I?"

Halsey's face fell. He pushed his reading glasses up on his forehead. He looked utterly dumbfounded, like a child who had heard a perverse telling of a favorite fairy tale. Mother Goose had turned into a hard-nosed, mean old biddy. A troubadour had just given a Bronx cheer, a trout had gone belly up in the middle of the fight. Halsey was staring at her in utter dismay as a child might stare when he got the final, undisputed word on Santa Claus.

Dorothy felt bad, of course, having to introduce Halsey to such cool realities. She felt certain that nobody had ever spoken this way with him. Halsey had his roles in life. These were not roles that were affected by, or imposed from, the outside. He was not an actor who "assumed" a character. He was a genuine character in his own right, with a variety of facets. But these facets, because Halsey was so stylized in his attitudes, became more than mere aspects of a personality. They were in fact roles, in the best and most active sense of the word. He was a professor of medieval literature. He was the only son of an old-money New England family. He, if anyone, brought the Word from the somewhat dank but still hallowed past into what he regarded as the oxymoronic present, with its glitzy veneer and tarnished values. Few brought the Word to Halsey. Not his mother, not his students and certainly never the occasional girlfriends who were often the embodiment of the paradox. Dismayed as he was by Dorothy, he listened carefully.

They had dinner, finished off the champagne and talked late into the night. They talked as only the closest of friends can talk, with the ellipses of unfinished sentences and long silences.

"Imagine that . . . ," Halsey sighed when Dorothy told him about Ella's work on the savannah. "Pre-*logos*."

"Quite *pre*."

"From that to *La chanson de Roland.*"

"Well . . . eventually."

And then there was a long silence and Dorothy watched Halsey's eyes become dreamy as he contemplated a world with ears that had never heard the words, the cadences, of *The Canterbury Tales* or *La chanson de Roland* or whatever it was that he was imagining.

"Would you like to go back millions of years, if only for a day, to listen?" Dorothy asked.

"Yes. How'd you guess?"

"Because maybe you think they had their own Chansons de Something?"

They both laughed. "Well," Dorothy continued, "if I were Merlin I would do for you what he did for Arthur when he turned him into a hawk for a spell so he could spend the night in the falconry."

"You'd turn me into a baboon or a chimp, eh?"

She laughed. He picked up her hand and squeezed it playfully. "You know, that's precisely what you are, a Merlin— part alchemist, part witch, teacher, parent."

Dorothy felt shamed. Hadn't she just turned an image of a golden marriage into dross? But she knew within her that this was how Halsey was most comfortable thinking about her—a Merlin, a wizard and thank heavens not a Jane Welsh Carlyle or a Peaches. So let it be. It was certainly a darn sight better

than being a Dorothy Gale. Instead of being buffeted by the
maverick winds, she conjured them.

They kissed each other goodnight and went to their own
rooms. Dorothy watched the night from her bedroom window. It was an eventful sky, blasted by the light of a full moon
and streaked with gale-torn clouds. She had cracked her window a bit so she could smell the wet tang of the high neap
tides that surged below. She fell asleep, her face cold and dewy
from the breath of the sea.

It was the stillness that woke Dorothy before the dawn. The
moon had slipped away. The clouds stole out with it, and the
wind had died to a whisper. Dorothy woke at that hour or so
before dawn when the skin of the night grows thin and a few
stars shine through—like the eyes of the new day, she used to
tell her children. She propped herself up a bit so she could
watch the slow transformation. The night began to dissolve
into gray. Then the faintest of pinks stole into the gray, tinge-
ing it slightly blue and making the sky appear for a brief moment
the same color as a baby's eyelids. To watch the sky of a new
day was like watching a dreaming baby, monitoring its every
flicker as it floated up toward consciousness from the milky
tranquility of sleep.

Halsey took the mailboat back to Rockland where he caught
a flight to Boston and on to connecting points for Patagonia.
Before he left he presented Dorothy with a "Merlin stick." It
was a piece of driftwood, a crook of sorts, silvered and smoothed
by wind and sea, a perfect walking stick for the ascents and
descents over the ledges between the house and the shore.
She kept it by the door.

The three days Dorothy had planned to spend extended
into a week. It was not simply that there was so much to do,
but so much to explore and to plan. Every day she seemed to
make a wonderful discovery. That first morning after Halsey

left she had gone down to the shore to try out the place she suspected might be a good early morning coffee spot. When she first came and decided to purchase the house, it had been too foggy to see those rocks. The previous few days with Halsey, the rain had precluded much exploring. But this morning was dry and the wind and sea were calm. When she took her coffee down she had discovered a natural ramp of pink granite sliding gently into the sea, perfect for swimming.

Just at the top of the rocks below her own bedroom window was what she guessed to be a flowerbed. It was covered with a layer of seaweed mulch. The former owners of the house had been particularly diligent about mulching the few beds they did maintain. She peeked under the mulch and tried to see what might be coming up. It was too early to tell. Shag Island's spring was far behind Boston's.

Two mornings after Halsey had departed, Cecil arrived unexpectedly with a load of topsoil and promises of more for some of the patches between the ledges which held hope as rock gardens. Dorothy had decided against lots of vegetables and limited herself to some herbs, lettuce and beans. Cecil's grandson, however, was going to build her a cold frame for tomatoes.

By the afternoon of her third day on Shag, Dorothy realized she had not planned enough food for a fourth day. Cecil again arrived, this time with a roller, paintbrush and more paint. "You call in your grocery order to Doug's in Rockland and it'll come over on the mailboat tomorrow with the rest of the paint you ordered from Agway. In the meantime Clare Macchias down the road picks crab. She was pickin' this morning I think. You can get a box from her, and anything else you need, come on down to our house. Agnes has got two refrigerators full t' burstin.' "

"Clare Macchias—that's the family with the washing machine in the yard?"

"Her kitchen's as neat and clean as anything." Cecil chopped the air with his hand for emphasis.

Dorothy picked her way through a labyrinth of lobster traps, motor scooters and abandoned household appliances. There was an old rowboat filled with dirt and a burnt-out TV set. At the front door of the house, an arched trellis was being torn at by very healthy looking vines of climbing roses. Dorothy knocked and the whole cottage seemed to shudder. She could see a television going inside but nobody was watching it. She knocked again, wondering if anyone was at home. A baby, naked but carrying a clean diaper, toddled out into the kitchen from a back room and stared through the window at Dorothy. Then a little girl of four or five ran out, saw Dorothy and yelled "Grandma!" A short fat woman in her mid-forties bustled into the kitchen. She carried another baby under her arm. She smiled with a diaper pin in her teeth and waved at Dorothy as she came toward the door.

Cecil was right. Clare Macchias's kitchen was immaculate and so was Clare. Cheerfully she rattled on about the babies who seemed to be crawling out from every nook and cranny. "I won't let them out 'til end of April. Just too darn much mud. I won't have 'em trackin' in here. My daughters think I'm mean as anything. But if they dump the kids on me, it's my rules, and I won't have mud in the house. I've already had to give four baths today—without mud. That one there"—she pointed to a little girl, the naked one who was carrying her diaper—"had to have two already today because she was a naughty little thing." Clare bent over and squeezed the little girl's cheeks. "Tell the lady what you did . . . go on, tell her." The little girl remained silent. "She got into the last of the raspberry jam. And your grandfather's going to be mad because I put that up specially for him. But look at this, will you?"

Clare, with one baby still under her arm, reached up to a shelf. "Here!" she said, handing a color Polaroid picture of the child smeared with the jam. "I just love taking snaps. Film's expensive, though."

There seemed to be hundreds of snapshots all over the kitchen. Two bulletin boards were full and numerous frames held several pictures each.

As Dorothy was leaving Clare's with a half-pound box of crabmeat, she could not help but comment on the rowboat filled with dirt. Just as the immaculate kitchen seemed a remarkable contrast, so the boat seemed to be a small oasis of order in the disastrous chaos of the front yard. Dorothy noticed that the dirt had been trowled and string guidelines were neatly set up from bow to stern except where the television set was.

"I see you must plant this, Mrs. Macchias," Dorothy called back over her shoulder as she walked down the implied path.

"Oh, I sure do. Getting ready to put in seeds in 'nother couple of weeks. It's more protected. I can get a jump on things. I already got my tuberous begonias in. I plant them in the TV set. Just a minute, I'll get you a snap of it." She ran back in the door and came out with a picture which she thrust in front of Dorothy. "Arthur says that it's the only burnt-out TV that still has living color!" Dorothy looked at the picture. A dozen or more bright, velvety begonias in oranges and pinks and yellows crowded out of the frame where the picture tube had once been. In the rest of the boat there were neat little rows of lettuce and what looked like carrot tops.

"Well, my goodness," said Dorothy. "Who would have thought?"

"Ayuh. Pretty nice, isn't it? And see here." She pointed to the rabbit ears of the antennae. "I grow my sweet peas around them—perfect for that. I want to get another pair. Arthur says next thing I'll be doing is growing stuff in a satellite dish." She laughed raucously at this. Then suddenly she wheeled

around. "Get into that house, Krystle Lorraine! You know
better than that!" The little girl scampered inside. "You'd think
that they'd learn by now that they can't sneak up on me. It's
one of the things that comes from being a mother. After six
kids you learn to see from the back of your head—I tell you!"
she said, shaking a finger toward the rowboat. "Antennae and
satellite dishes don't have a thing on me." She paused and
turned toward Dorothy. "Same with you, I bet, dear. You got
children?"

"Yes. Two. Grown up."

"Any grandchildren?"

"No. Not yet."

"Not yet? I was a grandmother at thirty-two. I'm forty now.
It's just perfect. Perfect age to be a grandmother. Fifteen,
though—that's a rotten age to be a mother. . . . Well, I won't
keep you."

Dorothy felt that with the slightest encouragement Clare
Macchias would have kept her. She had even started to say
something about the weather, which on Shag Island was never
simply a conversation filler but often led to very involved dis-
cussions about mailboat schedules, fishing tragedies and the
tourist season. Cecil Weed's wife, Agnes, a lovely lady who
was the church organist and choir director, kept a journal in
which she wrote every day—mostly about the weather. When
Dorothy had gone down the previous day for milk she had
found Agnes writing at her kitchen table. It had been unsea-
sonably warm that day so Agnes went back in her diary to
check what the weather had been like on the same day the
year before. She had kept the diary, she told Dorothy, since
she was first married. Had she ever missed a day? Dorothy
asked. Once, the day she was operated on—her hysterectomy.
Dorothy was amazed. What discipline! It wasn't any such thing,
Agnes commented. When she had married Cecil, which she
was careful to point out was a marriage of real choice, not like
most on the island with the bride five months pregnant, she

did not want a day of her marriage to go unremembered, so
she took to writing them down—"every day accounted for."

Dorothy ate an early dinner of crabmeat salad on the sunset
porch. It was chilly but she had bundled herself up and dragged
out one of the wicker rockers. She watched the sun sink like
a big, slightly squashed pomegranate behind some distant
islands. She thought about Clare Macchias and then about
Agnes Weed. "Every day accounted for." Presumably Agnes
could look up a date twenty years ago, read the weather and
know precisely what was going on with Cecil and herself and
their marriage. Whereas the days of Dorothy's marriage were
indistinguishable and in a sense unaccountable.

She had a kind of starting date: the ring, the condom. The
actual wedding mushed together in her mind in the May–June
swirl of final exams and graduation. She had an ending date:
when they, rather Al Fischer, called and told her that Ira had
collapsed. That was as far as Dorothy could get in reliving that
horrible day—Al's voice saying the word *collapsed*. Even though
she had sensed the truth, she had imagined that there was still
room to turn things around if she did not panic. She brain-
washed herself into a kind of trance which had never shat-
tered even after she arrived at the hospital.

Now she wished that she remembered the days in between
the start and the finish and the weather of those days. Dorothy
imagined that she could talk like so many others about the
decent climate of her marriage, but could she remember the
daily weather of it?

20

Dear Dorothy,

Well, an update on the Ginger, Fred, Marcus situation.
For a while there I thought we, or rather they, were off
the hook. It seems as though Harriet had started to cycle
again and Marcus showed interest. Ozzie, Harriet's former
consort and friend (he's also a friend of Peaches—one of
your all-round good guy sociable baboon types), was most
accommodating. Ozzie and Harriet and Fred and Ginger
often forage together and could not have been ignorant to
the mounting tension between Ginger, Fred and Marcus.
Ozzie on occasion even took on some protective duties
with little Willy.

We are all quite worried about little Willy. I'll get into
that later. In any case it almost seemed planned on Ozzie
and Harriet's part. Harriet began cycling. Her bottom
became quite bright. She pranced. She danced in front of
Marcus just as he was about to begin his morning vigil of
Fred and Ginger and Willy. Ozzie came in and began play-

ing with Willy while studiously ignoring Harriet's behavior. Marcus began lip smacking, really getting into the
sexual swing of things. Harriet lured him over a hillock
toward a grove of giant fever trees several meters away.
They were there for over 24 hours. A real savannah love-
fest. And then guess what? The next afternoon Marcus is
back to resume the vigil. This time Fred is again forced to
pick up Willy to use as a buffer. Ginger is becoming
increasingly "glazed," for lack of a better word. She seems
to be withdrawing into herself more and more. Less eye
contact with Willy. Fred has taken on almost all the child
care. She rarely grooms Willy or Fred now and yet she is
not submitting to Marcus. Although Marcus is not exactly
asking directly. He is just like this weird presence and he
seems to enjoy that kind of power.

Male aggression toward females is certainly not rare. It
usually happens between nonfriends in feeding contexts.
For example, Butch and Dot the other day: Butch was
feeding about 15 meters away from where Dot was. He
suddenly noticed her, rushed in and opened up a gaping
wound on her flank.

Sometimes it is not just feeding contexts but some sort
of redirected aggression on the part of the males to save
face. The females' male friends are good at protecting
them against this kind of stuff. With Marcus, however,
none of this seems to apply exactly or make sense. He has
copulated with a number of females and we think impregnated at least two in the troop of higher rank. Although
paternal certainty is one of the big problems with studying
these primates, he has done his male duty in terms of
seeing that his genes get a little play in this troop. Why
then does he persist in hanging around with Fred, Ginger
and Willy?

On the lighter side, did you see that they printed my
letter to that dumb ass who wrote to Anthropology Journal

defending Desmond Morris—where has this guy been for the last twenty years? In any case the letter was really in reference to a very good article that Sonya James has written on pair bonding or lack of it in early hominids.

The guy who wrote the letter, a certain Richard Melquist, feels that there is an "unnatural bias" creeping into anthropology, particularly primatology, because of the recent "insurgence" of women in the field. He then goes on and of course defends the good old hearth, home, pair-bonded Mom and apple pie. He winds up with that great myth about Homo sapiens inventing the missionary position, "thus achieving an intimacy heretofore unknown in the animal kingdom" which he claims is the cornerstone of hearth, home, etc.

As you know from those last galleys you sent me for my article in Natural History, we did not invent this position at all. The honor, if any, can most likely be claimed by the pygmy chimpanzee. (See me: Scientific American, July 1980, Animal Behavior, June '82, Science '82—my bibliography runs rather long in this area.) Anyway Ned Lambert, the editor, says there's never been such an out-pouring of letters to the editor. He's sending me copies. They are running 99% in my favor.

Peter and I meet in Nairobi in two weeks. Your trip to Maine sounded great.

Best,
Ella

May 1

Dear Halsey,
Tried to reach you to thank you for the Jane Austen. Your housekeeper said you were "still fishin.' " Mr. Beas-

ley sent the books to me wrapped in an old Herald Trav-
eler—*1948! Two lovely volumes,* Sense and Sensibility
and Pride and Prejudice. *They both have beautiful amber
cloth covers and Mr. Beasley has advised me, in a crimped
handwriting that one might imagine would belong to a
mouse, if a mouse could write, that if I feel "compelled" to
clean the books' covers I should do so with a teaspoon of
baking soda and one-quarter teaspoon of vinegar mixed
with liquid Ivory. Do you suppose that is how he bathes
himself??*

*Your mother sent me a darling note chastising me for
not taking more stuff from the barn. Everything here is
doing fine. I went up to Shag in April and did more fixing
up, more topsoiling and loaming 'tween the ledges and
plan to go up tomorrow, for a week mid-May and then in
June for the summer.*

*I want to go to New York sometime this month to see
Sophie. She was here in March. She's seeing a nice fellow
and I would like to meet him. He's hung around for a
while, at least in comparison to some of the others Sophie
has been involved with. All I know is that his name is
Fitzsimmons and he's in international investment banking
and goes to Italy quite a bit.*

*Oh, by the way, if I ever get to exercise my Merlin-ish
powers I shall turn you into a pygmy chimpanzee. According to Ella Voight (my sort-of-daughter-in-law) they, and
not we Homo sapiens, invented the missionary position
and, not for this reason necessarily but for several others
too, they are the premier candidates for being our most
direct nonhuman primate ancestors. So the chances are
that the roots of* La chanson de Roland *shall be found
there as opposed to elsewhere.*

Cheers,
Dorothy

May 3, Shag Island

Dear Ella,

I raced right over to the MCZ. I'm a regular now. They don't even ask for Ira's card. Anyhow I got both issues of Anthropology Journal *so I could read his letter and your reply. One should always be suspect of people who use words like "heretofore" but what a tedious soul that man is! Let us pity Mrs. Melquist, if there is one, for having to endure the missionary position with him. I thought your response was just super. It showed gentle* [Dorothy nearly wrote "surprisingly gentle"] *restraint and eloquence. I particularly liked the bit where you talk about what really might be achieved with all that intimacy derived from the missionary position. . . .*

Dorothy reread the part of Ella's published letter that she had Xeroxed. "If indeed the missionary position, as you say, has helped us achieve an intimacy unknown in the animal kingdom and if indeed it is within this "shroud of intimacy" that the "sacred exchange," as you call it, occurs between man the hunter with his bounty of meat and woman, the sexual satiator and guardian of the favors, is it not also possible that within these darkest and most intimate moments of the night that a woman might share her dreams along with her favors, and among those dreams might be the one of better understanding our primate origins and thus the desire to become a primatologist?"

Dorothy picked up her pen and finished the letter.

That is very classy, my dear.
Yours,
Dorothy

21

She had seen them coming down the road. But of course, she could not really see who was in the car. What she saw was a bright green thing rolling toward Clare Macchias's house where she had just purchased some crabmeat. The car, an old Porsche, seemed even smaller under its burden of a roof rack piled nearly four feet high with gear. The interior of the car was filled to the ceiling with what looked like rolled carpets, duffel bags and baskets. The car for all intents and purposes appeared driverless.

"It's the Starbucks!" Clare exclaimed. "Your neighbors."

"Oh! I haven't met them yet," Dorothy replied. She had seen their sign, a seagull printed on a piece of driftwood with their name pointing in to their driveway. "Are there two of them in there?" Dorothy asked as she watched the car approach.

"Yeah, they're kind of small folks and they stuff that little car to the brim."

Suddenly, just as the Porsche was passing by, a freckled arm shot out of the passenger window. "Hi, Clare! Can't stop now. See you later."

"That's Chowdie."

"Chowdie?"

"Yes. Mrs. Starbuck. They've been coming here for years from Connecticut. They come now to plant their garden and then they'll be back for the summer sometime in June. Lots of folks do that. Old Mrs. Bancroft is here now planting her garden. Then she'll go back to Philadelphia and come back up in July."

"Cecil tells me the Starbucks have no plumbing or electricity."

"It's true! Can you believe it! They love living like that. They are at least seventy years old and the feistiest things you ever saw."

Dorothy watched the car move down the road slowly, like an overloaded burro down a steep narrow path.

The Starbucks were Dorothy's nearest neighbors and although the house was obscured by a thick screen of spruce, she could see part of their beach while working on the lower ledges of her garden. Dorothy was up early but Chowdie was up earlier. Somewhere within that Porsche along with all the other gear the Starbucks had stuffed a dachshund. As Dorothy walked toward the coffee-drinking rock the morning after their arrival, she heard the dog running up and down along the beach yapping at something. The something was Chowdie swimming furiously between a rock and a buoy about one hundred feet offshore. She paused midway and turned and yelled. "Minnie! Stop that barking this minute."

Dorothy could see the woman's rubber-capped head bobbing as she managed to tread water while shaking a scolding finger at her dog. "Minnie, stop it! This is ridiculous." She suddenly caught sight of Dorothy. "Oh, Mrs. Silver," she called, waving her hand now in greeting while still treading water, "we've been meaning to come over and say hello. Welcome to East Point."

The dog kept barking. "Oh, Minnie! Honestly! Don't worry. She only does this the first day. She gets absolutely panicky when she sees me swimming. But I promise she will not be waking you up every morning when I swim."

Chowdie had now started toward shore. She did the breast-stroke as she continued to talk to Dorothy while occasionally interrupting the conversation to soothe Minnie. "Mama's coming, you little nut. She's really a very obedient dog. She was a star pupil in doggy obedience school, but they didn't cover this."

Dorothy wondered how they could have covered swimming in frigid Maine water.

Chowdie clambered up on a rock below the ledge where Dorothy was standing. Minnie came scampering down. Chowdie Starbuck was a sight to behold as she stood there dripping in battered old sneakers, presumably to protect her feet from the barnacles, a pair of old plaid shorts and a T-shirt. She pulled off her bathing cap as Dorothy walked down toward her.

"Isn't this an absurd bathing costume? My old suit finally fell apart and I dread the thought of having to search for an old lady bathing suit. You know, we of the wrinkled thighs have to find suits with skirts. I suppose I'll have to go to Camden. All these new suits are cut up to the armpits."

She had scooped up the dog. "See, Mama's back safe and sound." She held the dog close to her face and nuzzled it. Dorothy thought she saw her chew briefly but affectionately on the dog's ear. "Well it's so nice to meet you." She tucked the wriggling sausage under one arm and extended her other to shake hands. She was a tiny freckled lady with white hair cut in a Dutch bob. "And this is Minnie, or Minerva—yes. She's terribly smart for a dachshund. Well, dachshunds are fairly intelligent but nothing, of course, compared to standard poodles. We used to have standard poodles. They're great for sailing but they don't fit into kayaks."

Dorothy was trying to figure out just how these canines were used on boats—as crew or ballast. "Kayaks?" They certainly couldn't paddle. She was having a hard time following the conversation. Not only did Chowdie talk in a rapid-fire style but she was at the same time towel-drying her damp hair. So Dorothy found herself standing in front of this small wet lady whose head was shaking violently under a towel while she held a squirming dachshund.

Chowdie Starbuck never, Dorothy would come to realize, did only one thing at a time. She talked and dried her hair, or she would swim and talk, or stir a pot on her stove and read or needlepoint and listen to a cassette player with conversational Greek lessons. Now she stopped rubbing her head briefly and looked out from under the towel. "Yes, kayaks. You know, a dachshund's hull shape, so to speak, conforms nicely to a kayak. Minnie just loves going. Don't you, baby?" She nuzzled the dog. "Mrs. Silver . . ."

"Dorothy, please." She had learned so much about Chowdie in such a short time that it seemed incredible that they were not yet on a first-name basis.

"And I'm Chowdie. My real name is Charlotte, and don't ask me how they got Chowdie out of Charlotte. Some little kid probably mangled it at some point and it came out Chowdie which makes no sense at all." She was now pulling at Minnie's mouth and examining the dog's teeth. "Minnie, hold still. You've got something between your teeth. Good gracious! We'll have to get one of Daddy's toothpicks.

"No, everyone thinks my name has something to do with eating chowder. You know, they imagine that I loved eating chowder or something when I was a kid. I do love chowder but it was never an obsession to the point I had to be named after a fish soup. Good Lord!" She laughed and set Minerva down, then picked up a stick of driftwood and hurled it across the ledges. "Go fetch!" Minerva scooted off after the stick. "Faster!" Chowdie cried. "She needs exercise. You have to be very careful about weight and exercise with these dachshunds.

You know, they develop terrible back problems in their old age. No, I don't know why I was named Chowdie . . . Good dog, good dog."

Minerva had dutifully deposited the stick at her mistress's feet. "Okay, again. Here we go!" She threw the stick again. "Go, Minnie! Go! Faster! She's really quite lazy. She much prefers kayaking. We do all the paddling. But our marine operations aren't in gear yet. That's what Andy's going to be doing all day. Why don't you come over for a drink tonight about five?" Minnie was now scampering back. "Gads! They are the most absurdly designed dogs. I think Mark Twain said that dachshunds really should have about a dozen little legs running along underneath their torso." She laughed. "Well, see you at five."

"Yes. Yes. That will be nice," Dorothy said. She watched as Chowdie neatly climbed the steep rocky shore toward her house. She moved swiftly, her small body perfectly balanced. She knew each rocky niche and tree root for foot and hand holds. The dog looked clumsy and ridiculous. At the top Chowdie stood and looked down while giving her head another rub with the towel. "Come on, Minnie. Come on, baby. You can do it. Four legs will do you fine. Mr. Twain was just kidding. Come on. Don't be insulted." She turned and called back to Dorothy, who was still standing on the shore. "I think I hurt her feelings. As I was saying they're quite smart and that means sensitive. Yes, baby, you are a lovely, low, sweet machine, just like Daddy's Porsche. Yes, you sweet sausage. Come along now."

All day while Dorothy worked in her garden above and between the ledges, she saw and heard the Starbucks setting up their "marine operations." Andy appeared to be about seventy-five. Like two nimble elves they clambered over the rocks with ropes and paraphernalia to be either sunk or floated for anchoring and hauling various craft. They were rowing in and out of the shore, setting moorings and retrieval lines for dinghies, toggling buoys, putting in floats and docks. Around one in the afternoon she saw them sitting on a rock drinking beer and eating something.

At three o'clock in the afternoon, at dead low tide, she saw Chowdie in what looked like men's drawers, high boots and a shirt going out with a bucket to harvest mussels. Andy called down to her from a cliff to ask where she wanted the bush beans planted this year. Dorothy had never seen such calorie burning in her life. The Starbucks made Beebie seem phlegmatic.

A few minutes before five, Dorothy started down the pine path through the woods toward the Starbucks. As she approached the back of the house, behind a screen of birches she saw a wooden stand on which stood a ceramic bowl and a Japanese water dipper. A small mirror was propped against the edge of the stand and a towel hung on a tree limb behind it. This she realized must be their "dressing room." Until that moment she had almost forgotten about the lack of plumbing and electricity. Smooth black stones paved a short path to the back door. Along the edge of the stone path the ground was covered with moss and bunchberry. There were clumps of wild irises for accent and in a hollowed-out log, gray-green with lichen, violets grew. It was all artfully done. The transition from the woods to the house landscape was seamless. The plants in and around the house were all wildflowers. Many, Dorothy guessed, had been brought in from the fringes of various beaches, bogs and glades as well as the woods of Shag and other islands in the bay. There was a sense of these growing things having been lured here rather than transplanted.

"Welcome!"

At that instant Minnie charged out of the back screen door. "Oh, Minnie! No! No! Bad dog. Get out of that columbine. Gads, I've been trying to get that going for three years now.

If it survives Minnie, we know it will endure."

"Oh, I think it all looks wonderful," Dorothy said. "I was just admiring everything so. These black stones are the love-liest."

"Oh yes. They are beautiful. We get them over at Loon Island. We go in the kayak two or three times a year to haul them."

"My wife's going to kill me hauling rocks from Loon to Shag," a voice from the kitchen called. Andy Starbuck appeared holding a martini shaker. He was just slightly taller than his wife and had a fringe of fine gray hair that reminded Dorothy of a bird's nest, a not particularly well made one. His bald head was as mottled as a lichen-covered rock with freckles and age spots.

"Gads, Andy! You've cut your head again."

"Where?" he said, patting his scalp.

"In the back. Keep shaking those martinis. I'll get the first-aid kit. Oh, this is Dorothy Silver."

"Hello, Dorothy, sorry to greet you this way. Come on in. I'll get you a drink."

"Why don't you ever wear a hat, Andy?" Chowdie was say-ing as she ran through the kitchen to get the first-aid kit. "You know," she called from another room, "he gets those skin can-cers. So he should wear a hat all the time."

"Not indoors, Chowdie."

"No, dear, you should wear a helmet inside." Chowdie had returned and proceeded to clean the scrape and put on a bandage while Andy mixed the martinis. Dorothy silently marveled. They were truly ambidextrous from their brains to their tongues to their hands. Andy poured all the martinis as Chowdie dressed the wound and explained the peculiar wonders of living with-out electricity.

"As you know, everybody thinks we're absolutely nuts for not having the amenities."

"Not nuts—weird, weirdos," Andy said. "That's what Cecil's

granddaughter told me last summer."

"I suppose we are," Chowdie continued. "If anybody'd seen us last night turning our refrigerator upside down."

"What?" Dorothy said.

"Yes. You see we have a gas-run refrigerator and sometimes it refuses to start up when we get here. Cecil Weed was the one who told us the trick of turning it upside down. Don't ask me how it works but it does. That's why we're having martinis tonight—to celebrate our first three trays of ice cubes. Usually we just have rum or wine because we can take those at room temperature. Don't feel obliged to have a martini, Dorothy."

Minnie was now jumping wildly at Andy's knees. "Oh dear," said Chowdie. "She's concerned about Daddy's bashed head."

"No. No she's not! She's feeling obliged to have a martini."

"Don't you dare, Andy!"

"Oh, just a little."

"Andy, that dog's not used to martinis." Dorothy was just about to ask what Minnie's usual drink was when Chowdie said, "she likes sherry, but we're out. A little bit of sherry goes a long way with Minnie. But martinis are terrible for her. She always has bad dreams and tummy problems and I get stuck with taking her out in the middle of the night. You never do, Andy. You never did when we had babies, either. You know it's so wonderful nowadays. I have two daughters-in-law and my goodness do they have those husbands trained. They change diapers and get up in the middle of the night with the babies."

"Oh, I know," Andy said as they made their way into the living room. "I'm so untrainable. You're going to have to send me to doggy obedience school. Take a seat, Dorothy."

It was an enchanting room. The clear pine caught the light of the kerosene lamps which enveloped everything in a rich honey-colored glow. Bright Peruvian woven rugs in burning oranges and vermilions covered the floor. The view was west toward the Camden Hills. And when the sun slipped away dark purple shadows seeped out of the granite ledges, stole over the land and began to fill the room. Andy lit the wick on another kerosene lamp and moved it near them. Chowdie was needlepointing. "Dear me, I forgot to ask you, Dorothy. Do you have to go to the bathroom? People are hesitant sometimes, you know. But we have the most charming outhouse."

"You have no idea, of course," Andy said, "how many bad jokes there are about folks like me—retired urologists who have outhouses."

Dorothy had not been hesitant; she had merely not thought of it. The time had passed quickly and pleasantly, although the conversation was rather fragmented. The Starbucks were constantly interrupting each other's narratives with some practical detail.

"Our oldest son, Ken, he's an investment banker—keeps us solvent," Andy said.

"Oh, Andy, they're coming the last week in July. We must get a new mattress for that bed. The mice wreaked havoc with it."

"As with your bathing suit."

"Andy!"

"Ate the crotch right out of Chowdie's bathing suit!"

Andy chuckled. "Our other son, Patrick, is a lawyer. Keeps us out of jail."

They had not given the dog a martini but had managed to find some sherry and poured a tiny cup for Minnie. "Good for her," Andy said.

"Exercise is better," Chowdie said. "She was absolutely waddling today when I tried to play fetch with her. She's getting fat."

"She is not fat," said Andy, reaching for a yardstick that was propped against the wall. "Tell her that, Minnie." He began poking her gently with the yardstick. "That is not fat. That is all muscle."

So it went. They had insisted that Dorothy stay for dinner—mussel soup. Before it was served Dorothy did go to "the little house," as Chowdie referred to the outhouse. It was a two-holer and as charming as Chowdie had said. Hanging on the wall were a few Sierra Club photographs of seals on rocks and one of a lighthouse. Across from the hole that Dorothy used was a photograph of the famous white-pebble Ryoanji gardens of Kyoto. In a corner was a bucket of lime and one of ashes with small shovels. A notecard above each bucket indicated that this was the hygienic alternative to flushing. Dorothy was impressed. It was the most elegant outhouse she had ever been in.

When she returned the soup was ready to serve.

"Yes," Chowdie said, passing the pilot crackers, "everyone thinks we're nuts, or weirdos, as Cecil's granddaughter says, for living this way. No telephone, that long path to carry everything down, cooking on a wood-burning stove, pumping water from a well. But it all seems to work for us. We actually stay quite clean. Did you see our solar shower hanging up in the trees?" She paused. "The kids worry, though."

"Worry?" Dorothy asked.

"They don't worry about us keeping clean, Chowdie." Andy laughed.

"No. You're right. They worry about us dying," Chowdie said cheerfully.

"Dying?" Dorothy said, looking up from her soup.

"Dying without a telephone," said Andy. "Not something to be done at this end of the twentieth century."

"Yes, the idea being if one of us keels over the other one will have to run up that long path, to your house or the nearest phone," Chowdie offered.

"And if the phone call is made," Andy continued, "and the volunteer fire department comes—they are also the ambulance service on the island—they won't be able to drive down the path."

"So our kids want us to put in a driveway and a phone, but Andy won't cut the trees. They are lovely trees."

"Yes," said Andy emphatically. "Let them drag me up over the path. Or if it's high tide they can float me out round the point to the town landing."

"Well," said Chowdie, busily crumbling a cracker into her soup, "we have it all written out in our living wills—no extreme measures."

"That means phones and driveways," Andy chuckled.

"You're a recent widow aren't you, Dorothy?"

"Yes. My husband dropped dead of a heart attack in the middle of the public gardens. Phones all over the place, an intern within twenty feet and Mass General Hospital four blocks away."

"So there you go!" Chowdie slapped the table.

Dorothy had a feeling that a description of Ira's death would be going out in a letter to Chowdie's sons directly.

The evening at the Starbucks had been so nice, but now as she returned to her own cottage she was filled with thoughts of death and unfinished lives. In a few days it would be a year since Ira's death. The air was chilly. She did not feel like going to bed. She remembered a bottle of brandy that Halsey had left. She poured some into a quilted jelly jar and put on a heavy sweater. A three-quarter moon was in the arch of the sunset porch. She sipped her brandy and thought. She tried to imagine what she and Ira might have been like as an older couple, mid-seventies, in their "twilight years." It, of course, would have never been a twilight lit with kerosene lamps. They had discussed death in the somber, responsible way that middle-age people do—in terms of money, estate planning and the decision of either opting for cremation or buying a plot. And there were, of course, the no-extreme-measure clauses.

They had discussed death but they had never really contemplated it, as Chowdie and Andy had, and they had never really talked about retirement. Would they, however, really have wound up in Florida? In his profession Ira had dealt with death

constantly. How often had he come home irascible after having had to deal with "next of kin" who had flown in from
Seattle and had not seen Uncle So-and-So for years and had
no notion of how he wanted to wind up "the whole messy
business." That was always how Ira had referred to death—a
messy business. "And believe me," he would add, "I'm in the
neatest part of it—cardiology, not oncology. But it's messy no
matter how you cut it."

So they had, as so many of their friends and colleagues, set
down the details of death. There was a certain smugness about
it all. Death might be messy but they were not going to make
it a mess for others. There would be no bumbling next of kin
to foul up the doctors. They would be clever about the finish.

Of course, it was easy to be clever and smug and business-
like when one was in one's late forties, early fifties. With all
their concrete plans, they were reducing death to a new kind
of abstraction. It was nothing like Chowdie and Andy who,
despite their living wills, had actually envisioned the moment
of demise, yet not planned it in the way one could with the
legal buttressing of wills and the purchase of cemetery plots.
There could be no plans in that sense for the likes of the
Starbucks. It would be a seat-of-the-pants kind of thing—will
Chowdie run up the path to call the ambulance? Or would
Andy say, "What's the rush? Let me die here. Hold my head
up so I can see the bay and the islands swimming like schools
of fish across the sunset. And for Christ's sake, don't tear up
the path with a goddamn fire truck. I don't want to hear a
siren blasting. I want to hear the water on the rocks and maybe
the whistle buoy off Dog Island. Now please shut up, Chowdie."

It hadn't been that way with Ira. It had been sterile and
silent with the white noise of a hospital death. Everyone had
known his or her part, including Dorothy. It had been quick
and painless and for that reason alone it had been considered
"wonderful," a death to be envied, one that had inconve-

nienced no one. However, there had been no preceding twilight burnished with the light of kerosene lamps. And if there
had been a twilight, she supposed it would have bounced off
the smooth surface of the Charles River to the tungsten sheen
of their condo. After the details had been set in terms of living
wills and estate planning, there had been no time to grow
romantic again at Church Tower. Dorothy no longer needed
to ask how she and Ira had missed so entirely on this last
installment of their married life, Church Tower. The question
now was not why Church Tower, but would Ira have come to
East Point, Shag Island? She thought she knew the answer,
although it did not matter anymore. Besides, was there anything worse than a widow second-guessing a deceased husband? She was here now. Here and alone.

So much that came to the island came by accident, blown
by wind and currents, Dorothy reflected. This time, though,
she had not been borne by some maverick wind. This time
she had chosen. She had never thought of herself as being
unfree or unliberated during her marriage. So now she was not
heady with sensations of newfound freedom. She felt instead
the weight of a new kind of mass which in turn gave her a
direction, a velocity. She had acquired enough mass and
momentum to move in chosen directions. Although it felt
good, she could hardly say she was drenched in euphoria, since
she now realized that for the majority of her previous fifty-two
years she had passed through life as some kind of flotsam, bobbing about in the eddies of other people's lives.

Dorothy rocked herself in the wicker chair and watched the
moon swing into the sky. It was a clear night. She leaned her
head back. Could she actually see the Pleiades, those star-
flung daughters of Atlas? A dim cluster of stars seemed to pul-
sate in the sky. Monica had once tried to explain to Dorothy
that the phenomenon of night was the proof of the universe's
pudding. It was a hard-to-follow story, suggesting that the universe, that total celestial cosmos, although expanding, had a

kind of proper mass. Monica would use words like *isotropic, homogeneous, matter-dominated,* and her voice would remain quite calm with that tinge of English coolness she had acquired from living there for over three decades. Then her voice would begin to rise and become more animated. An old Midwestern strain would twang in as she spoke of the possibility of multiple universes and the applicability of Q.E.D. theory for more proofs of more universal pudding.

Dorothy could not even begin to imagine multiple universes, and she marveled that she had as a close friend one who could visualize such things so fearlessly. This universe, the one with the skin and the days and the nights seemed as cozy as an old shoe compared to Monica's imaginings. For Dorothy it was a universe where science and myth had happy collisions, where it was as easy to imagine the gaseous beginnings of a star's life as to envision the celestial trajectories and metamorphoses of Atlas's daughters. She could imagine both phenomena. She could imagine Electra, Maia, Alcyon, Sterope, Merope, Celaeno, and the seventh one whose name she always forgot—Taygeta! She could conceive of them up there, just a star's throw away from Ira.

She felt herself blush now, as she admitted to herself for the first time that indeed when she thought about Ira she imagined him "up there" on a cloud. She did stop short of wings, but he wore an open-necked shirt and scrub pants.

However, if she contemplated the stars in terms of mythology or science, what interested her more was the physics of her own newly acquired mass. This did not lend itself to cosmic or stellar comparisons. If there were any metaphoric elements to this new state, they were earthbound, and even then Dorothy tended to be modest in her assessments. The Starbucks, metaphorically, seemed to be pure New England granite.

She looked up at the moon, that huge luminous rock, reeling the tides in and out. It was difficult to think of herself in lithic terms. What came to mind instead were those battered spruce trees she saw on her walks along the shoreline around East Point. Often those conifers, unlike deciduous trees, did not probe downward in their growth, but instead the roots of the spruce and the pines crept out just below the surface of the ground to provide a spread of support. It was for this reason that Dorothy so often saw these trees growing practically on the granite so close to the sea on islands like Shag that had been left with the thin soils from the scourings of the last glaciation. In life the trees were mysterious and elegant. Their pointed green-black tops often pierced through the layers of fog to hover between earth and sky, detached like some separate celestial forest.

There were, of course, risks in growing so close to the edge. The shore was torn with the wreckage of upended trees; winter gales had not broken the trunks but their roots had been pulled from the ground instead. The tree became equally beautiful in death. Gorgeous wrecks turned paisley with lichen, hoary with moss, their bark decaying, they became havens for new life. The island spruce represented a complicated mixture of life and death, of resistance and yielding, of rooting and upheaval that for Dorothy had a certain clear resonance.

Unable to sleep, Dorothy rose several hours after midnight and went out into the night. The moon was nearly down but in its vanishing light she saw a shadow moving against the rocks, descending toward the water. Then she heard the jingle of a dog's collar and realized that the figure was Chowdie, stark naked and followed by Minnie. Minnie seemed as ordinary as a frumpy housewife, but Chowdie, tiny and bare and white in the failing light of the moon, appeared like a nocturnal animal as she moved across the rocks and slipped into the cold water to swim. Dorothy watched, transfixed. Would she be transformed into a seal, a septuagenarian mermaid? The next time she saw Chowdie barefoot, she must check for webbing between the toes. She watched as Chowdie turned in the water and whispered some inaudible words to Minnie, who was keeping a nervous vigil on the rocks. She swam for several minutes and then climbed out again and started up the rocks toward her cottage.

Clear morning light vaporized projections about Chowdie. Now she stood in front of Dorothy in thong sandals, introducing a delicate wisp of a woman who leaned lightly on a cane. "This is one of my dearest friends, Dorothy, Elsie Bancroft, up to plant her garden, too. She, however, is the premier gardener of the island."

Elsie nodded and smiled and inclined her head a bit toward Chowdie, as if she could not quite hear her.

"You're on my bad side, Chowdie."

"I said that you're the premier gardener of Shag."

"Oh, nonsense. I didn't need to hear that. I thought you were saying something about our new neighbor. Hi, I'm Elsie and I am slightly deaf. My batteries are down on my hearing aid so you'll have to scream. I love what you're doing here." She gestured toward the artemisia and the heathers. "They'll be nice colors in the fog."

There was something startling about Elsie Bancroft's voice. It was a deep, rich contralto that welled up from inside this very fragile, thin body, a body that appeared as if it would need a good anchor in any kind of wind. Elsie was over ninety but her voice belonged to someone much younger, physically heartier and possibly of a different sex. "Yes," Dorothy said. "I like those soft blues and pinks too. Although around the back door there seem to be a few brighter colors—yellows and oranges, which is nice too."

"Ah, yes," said Elsie. "I remember that from when the Hays owned it. Myra had put in some black-eyed susans."

"Oh, is that what I can expect? I do like them."

"Come 'round, dear." Elsie motioned with her cane. "I'll show you what you have to look forward to."

Elsie led the way. She moved boldly although somewhat stiffly.

"Ah, yes," she said. "Now right there will be your black-eyed susans. You can see their fuzzy little leaves coming up now." She waved her cane over the spot. "Always reminded me of goats' ears, those leaves. Now over there, I believe, Myra had some delphiniums. Did the slugs get them? Nope, there they are. You really have to ride slug patrol around here until mid-July. Beer doesn't work. Get Slugetta—ha ha! Catchy!"

There was something absolutely mesmerizing about the woman's voice. It was so commanding but with no hint of smugness or false authority. She remembered every flower the previous owners and the ones before them had planted. Dorothy was invited up for tea that afternoon and to collect a supply of Slugetta to "hold the creeps at bay."

The front porch of Elsie Bancroft's house projected like the prow of a ship over a vast green lawn that swept down the north side of the Fox Island Thoroughfare. Elsie had met Dorothy at the beginning of the drive with her housekeeper and companion, Letha Hardy, a sister-in-law of Agnes Weed. She had insisted first on taking her on a tour of the gardens. There was a small cutting garden that Dorothy could imagine in another month would be adrift with clouds of snapdragons and varieties of poppies. For the most part, however, the gardens were quiet, contemplative designs using rocks, mosses and ferns. There were secret pools that one came upon, flashing with a few goldfish and afloat with water lilies. "Letha," Elsie said, "you must get your grandson to catch me some more frogs. There's not enough croaking going on here." They followed stepping stones around a small pool.

"What's this?" Dorothy asked. Straight ahead along the path an enormous piece of driftwood reared like a silver dragon.

"That's my sculpture garden. All driftwood. That fellow there," she indicated the large piece directly ahead, "was the last piece of driftwood my husband got for me before he died. He and our captain, Tinker Dow, would sail over to Pickering

Island. There are two points on the weather side of that island that driftwood fetches up on. Magnificent stuff. Tinker would take the chain saw and two beefy nephews of his for these operations. It was a hard business. But they'd go every summer for me. Of course, now we've sold the boat and Tinker's got such bad arthritis he can hardly move. A lot of this driftwood is really quite rotten now. So I doubt if in another few years we'll have much left. Nothing lasts forever. But I figure you just let it go. Ashes to ashes. This soil will be terrifically rich from it."

"It's wonderful," Dorothy said. From a distance the mass of driftwood appeared like a silver forest, but as they entered it became a menagerie of forms—small dinosaurs, leaping dolphins and rearing horses.

"It's my private zoo," Elsie said as if reading Dorothy's thoughts. "Here's Moby Dick!" Elsie tapped a white whale-shaped piece the size of a small rowboat. The wood had fractured into a crooked smile in just the place where a whale's mouth would have been and there was even an eye above it. Elsie sat down on its back. After a minute or so she rose. "Time for tea," she announced suddenly and led the way to the house.

They sat on the porch. Letha soon came out carrying a tray bearing at least fifteen pounds of Georgian silver, complete with all the most elaborate and intricate paraphernalia for tea service.

"I keep telling her she needn't use all this gear." The words came disembodied from the shadows of the chair. It was an enormous fan-back chair and within it there was a hat and under the hat there was Elsie, as small as a parakeet, a deep-voiced one, in an enormous cage. The low-angled sunlight slashed the porch and Dorothy peered into the cool shadows of the wicker cave as she listened to the voice. When Elsie leaned forward the straw hat with an open-work brim cast a lattice of sunlight and shadow across her face. Her body seemed to melt away under the thin cotton dress printed with forget-me-nots. The cane hung from one of the arms of the chair.

"I like to use this stuff," Letha said. "It's like playing dolls or something." She giggled.

"Take a load off your feet, dear," Elsie said to Letha.

Letha plopped down into a wicker chair next to Elsie. She was a woman of about sixty. Her short, thick, pink, freckled legs rose like cones from the white anklets. She wore running shoes which Dorothy commented on.

"She keeps me running." Letha chuckled as Elsie poured the tea.

"She won't let me walk is the problem," Elsie replied.

"You heard me say that, Mrs. Bancroft?" Letha asked, surprised.

"Yes. I put a new battery in my hearing aid. I found one in that tiny drawer in the vanity." Then she added, "We're totally battery-operated around here. I've got a pacemaker."

"Me, too!" Letha added cheerfully. "Tell her about your hips."

"Well, they're not battery-operated." Elsie laughed. "Just replaced."

"But with what? Tell her that."

"Titanium. The whole shebang." Elsie patted the arm of the chair firmly for emphasis.

"Same stuff my grandson has in his new lobster boat. Titanium—he has it for something. His prop or something in the diesel. I heard him talking about it the other day and I said—'Titanium! That's what they put in Mrs. Bancroft just last November'—and he says it's the most durable stuff on Earth. And I say, 'Well, 'course, I wouldn't expect nothing else for Mrs. Bancroft.' "

Elsie laughed. The deep, rich rumble shook her thin shoulders. "I suppose I should have the other one updated."

"The other hip?" Dorothy asked.

"Yes, I had that one done several years ago before they used these exotic new things—probably just some cheap alloy in there. It's okay now, but for durability." Her flinty blue-gray eyes danced, and she looked at Dorothy sharply. "I'm ninety-two and I still think about durability. Living around all these rocks does it to you. If you think about it at all, you're either cowed by the geological time scale or challenged by it. Don't get me wrong. It's not immortality I'm after, just good materials. Suppose this hip starts to go, 'Ol' Rightie' I call it, the one they did in 1970. Should I creep around on this nickel-plated stuff just because I might only have another year or two? My great grandson calls me the Bionic Grandma."

"Well, look at his grandma!" Letha said.

"Little Elsie? Yes, she had a facelift. I thought that was crazy. But then again they think I'm crazy even contemplating a new right hip. But basically it comes down to what makes you feel good about yourself, I suppose, and honestly, Letha, don't you think little Elsie's a changed person since she got her face winched in? Much more cheerful."

"Yeah, except she can't smile now at all. Everything's so tight."

The conversation shifted to local news—lobstering, ferry schedules, new babies, when various summer people would be arriving. The Portchesters were always on the island by the Fourth of July, the Harrises rarely before the first of August. Mrs. Harris hates sailing; Mr. Harris is always looking for a crew. Jimmy Eaton caught eighteen Mako sharks off Mount Desert Light, about twenty miles out, last week.

"I don't like shark, Mrs. B. Do you like it? They say you can't tell the difference."

"I don't think I've ever eaten it, Letha."

"You might have. Something they try to pass off shark for scallops."

"No! How do they do that?"

"Punchouts." They got this thing like a giant paper punch and they just punch out scallop-shaped pieces."

"Oh dear!" sighed Elsie. "My palate's not bionic yet. I'd like to think that I could still taste the difference. Besides I think it's best to have a truce with sharks. This is a case where I don't want to pick on something my own size or bigger. Real scallops are definitely smaller." Elsie laughed.

"Cows are bigger—you eat beef, don't you?" Letha asked.

"Yes, you have a point. You should have been a lawyer, Letha. Well, I don't want to eat something that might eat me."

"Cows won't do that," Letha replied.

There was a slight lapse in the conversation. Dorothy felt that there were probably not many such lapses between Letha and Elsie. Ordinarily it was the kind of silent space that might have been padded out with talk about the weather—often a kind of hamburger filler in terms of conversation, except perhaps on a Maine island. Elsie leaned forward toward Dorothy very deliberately. She took her cane from the arm of the chair and rapped sharply on the porch floor with it in a manner identical to an old-fashioned schoolmarm calling her class to order or a student to account. The diamonds of sunlight that poured through the brim of the hat slid across her fine-boned face. "My dear," she said, "tell me something. It always interests me . . ." She paused. Dorothy could not imagine what would follow. She had a feeling it would be something terribly personal. It was. "If you," Elsie began in a conspiratorial whisper, "could do anything at all in the world, what would you most like to do?"

Dorothy was taken aback completely. Then Elsie Bancroft leaned closer to her and peered directly at her. "I'll tell you what I would do." There was not a trace of a smile. "I would skate the canals of Holland—from one end to the other!"

The afternoon tea culminated in Letha being dispatched to dig up some of the lady's mantle for Dorothy to take home along with a bag of Slugetta. Dorothy had said good-bye and was walking across the lawn with her carton of plants and poison when she heard a low, rich voice coming from behind like chimes in the wind. She turned and saw Elsie on the porch, her cotton dress fluttering in the breeze. She was jabbing the sky with her cane as she spoke. "Dorothy, do not hesitate to chasten the lady's mantle. It can get awfully exuberant. It is not given to the rampages of calendula but be careful. Don't worry about thinning it out or even ripping it out. Good luck. See you in July!" As she waved her cane in a gesture of good-bye, leaning over the rail of the porch, she appeared like an animated figurehead jutting out across a green sea.

22

The principal reason Dorothy had not stayed in Maine for the rest of May was so she could make a quick trip to New York to visit Sophie, hoping to meet her new man Rob Fitzsimmons. The name alone conjured up wonderful images in Dorothy's mind. All of Sophie's previous men seemed to have names like Larry or Gary, singularly unmusical names attached to uninspiring men, as far as Dorothy was concerned. Of course there was no reason to think that this Rob would be any more dashing than the others. He shared the same profession—money, investment banking. They were all equally dull, no matter what the players' names were. Very few of these men had hobbies or interests beyond money. They were tethered to their phones, and "dating," if the word was still used, was confined to "civilian dinners" as Sophie called them, which meant those few meals that were not devoted to making deals. There was the occasional stolen weekend, but even those hours were apparently laced with phone calls. So Dorothy was disappointed but not surprised when she arrived in New York and Sophie told her that Rob had been called to Rome. "Well, not really *called.*" She laughed. "But, you know, the deal ripened a lot faster than he had anticipated and he just had to go."

"Oh dear!" Dorothy replied. "I had so looked forward to meeting him. I thought I'd take you out someplace really nice. We can still do that, of course."

Dorothy was not one to pry, at least not directly, into her children's affairs. She tried to gather as much information as she could by indirect routes. This required much patience and restraint when dealing with the likes of Sophie, who played her cards extremely close to her chest. Peter, by comparison, was virtually an open book. Sophie had first mentioned Rob in October. When Dorothy called on a Sunday evening in February, the doorbell rang while Sophie was on the phone. She had turned away from the receiver and asked Rob to ring them in. So Dorothy had been able to ascertain that not only had Rob hung in for several months, but he even seemed to have settled in comfortably for a leisurely Sunday. He was not living there. That she would have heard about.

In April when Dorothy called up one evening, Rob answered the phone. He had been absolutely charming to her, but what had endeared him most to her was his obvious embarrassment that Sophie was in the shower. He had not actually told her this. Dorothy had guessed it as she heard Sophie say, "It's my Mom? Wait a second while I grab a towel." Dorothy on her end felt she could hear Rob blushing long-distance as Sophie, still damp and swathed in her terrycloth robe, came to the phone. This Dorothy found quite enchanting. She immediately preferred Rob to Ella, and felt terribly guilty about that.

Despite the disappointment of not meeting the blushing banker, Dorothy was assured by Sophie that there was a definite possibility of their visiting her in Maine. Perhaps it was her imagination but Dorothy thought she sensed a subtle change in Sophie. There seemed to be something slightly more yielding in her. Whatever it was, it was an illusive thing and it would have been much too simple to say that Sophie was in love. Dorothy was not at all sure whether Sophie would ever be in love in the traditional sense. But who was she to speculate on such matters—she of the corollaries, the little proofs, the Venn diagrams and the rubber garlands of love and marriage?

When she returned to Church Tower she was faced with the happy chores of closing up the condo for the summer—forwarding mail, cleaning out the refrigerator and packing up the last boxes of things to take to Maine. She had so much to look forward to. She did wish Elsie Bancroft would be returning sooner, but the Starbucks would be there and the garden would be unfurling its colors. There would be slugs to patrol, lady's mantle to chasten, more Jane Austen to read—Halsey had now sent her *Northanger Abbey* from his London book dealer. This would be a summer to relish. She was caught in mid-synapse, somewhere between relish and regret, when she started to think, "too bad Ira isn't . . ."

It was of course the impulse of a still-fresh widow, but it was skewed in passage at the point of jumping off from axon to dendrite and it came out instead, "not that bad. He would have preferred the Vineyard and *Ventricle.*"

Dorothy was chilled by the thought she had just allowed herself. She got a tumbler and poured herself a half-inch of Scotch and sat down on her ladder. There was no denying it. Shag Island had become the watershed between the Dorothy of the past and the Dorothy of the present. It was a watershed not only between the two tenses of Dorothy's life but between Dorothy as she was now and Ira as she knew him to be. It was a moot point in her mind that Ira was dead and that she was alive, for she imagined their spirits divided and draining into separate rivers.

Then there was this terrible loneliness that came upon her. It was not simply the loneliness of bereavement but that of being essentially a single spirit and realizing that this single-ness had not been imposed by death, but had been an unreal-ized condition throughout her marriage. She had never in that sense truly been conjoined, and this made her desperately sad as she thought of their lives, their two spirits so divergent. This was the loneliness of the separate river, the waters that would never flow into the same sea.

There was a little litany that had begun to tap somewhere in Dorothy's brain recently. Although there were only frag-ments, the words and the rhythms had become familiar. Too often since she had bought the Shag Island house she had had to repeat them, the phrases that reminded her that it no longer mattered what would have been or what Ira would have liked. Now she had chosen and there was not exactly regret over her previous life, but there was doubt. If she could not resolve the doubt she must chase it away, vanquish it, forget it, with this little litany which in its shabby essence spoke of nothing more than spilt milk and carrying on.

In the next morning's mail there were two letters, one from Monica and one from Ella. She read Monica's first as she was not quite ready for Ella's latest installment of the Savannah Simian Soaps.

> Dear Dorothy,
> Great news! Can you stand a visit to your Shag Island estate come August? There's a conference in New York (N.Y. Academy of Science) on this business about the missing universe—in case you didn't know it, this is the hot topic today amongst some of us. 90% of the universe seems to be missing ["seems to be!" Dorothy whispered to herself as she read on]. "The Missing Mass" they call it or "The Illusive Dark Matter." Anyhow Walter Freddles at Princeton and I have been working long-distance on a

paper about this for the past two years and it seems that
we have been summoned to do our little song and dance
in N.Y. I call it the Dark Halo Two Step.

The Halo refers to the dark matter which supplies gravitational force needed for galactic stability. Anyhow the
conference is July 29–30. I could make it up to Maine by
August 1.

Rupert will not be accompanying me. He still hates
physicists in large groups, and has opted to be bashed
about in Lord Glynnbourne's million-dollar yacht in the
Round Britain Race. The girls are between, starting or finishing affairs. And they are all doing the activities that are
concomitant with those states—e.g., at a fat farm (shap-
ing up for the next round), on long weekends or in shrinks'
offices. What a silly batch we've raised. But they are sweet
things, very dear really, and not a drug addict or an anor-
exic among them, which is a rarity today. How are your
own supercharged offspring?

I am fairly flexible in my dates. If you want me a day or
two later or pre-conference I can arrange it. This'll be
such fun. Write soon.

Love,
Monica

Dorothy was thrilled with the prospect of her visit and wrote
her that afternoon.

Dear Monica,
I'm so excited! Of course, Aug. 1 is perfect. Good grief,
how come 90% of the universe is missing? This is unsettling. Who misplaced it? God? This sounds like Alzheimer's on a cosmic scale. My goodness, I do love the
language of you physicists—Dark Halos! Get me one. I
sometimes think my galactic stability is slightly a-wobble.
Don't worry. I'm really doing quite fine. The Shag Island

house has been a wonderful tonic. Even this dumb condo seems much more palatable now. I'm busy scheming and plotting gardens for up there. It's not going to be anything elaborate. An island has a way of immediately letting you know what works and what doesn't. You don't scheme as much as follow obvious leads.

I leave Boston tomorrow for Maine for the duration of the summer. I met some awfully nice people on Shag when I was up there earlier planting and fixing up. My nearest neighbors are unbelievable. They are in their early seventies and live in this rustic Zen cabin with no electricity or plumbing. The woman swims like a seal. The man is dear, a retired urologist with an outhouse—does that strike you as weird? There is another very elderly lady with whom I have absolutely fallen in love. I can't wait to take you to tea at her house. She has had two hip replacements and harbors a dream of skating the canals of Holland. Did I tell you that in the past eight months I've had one proposition and one proposal? Not bad for a postmenopausal bag of bones!

Love,
Dorothy

She then read Ella's letter, which she planned to answer on Shag.

Dear Dorothy,
Things are rather status quo here on the Ginger, Fred, Willy and Marcus front. Ginger has not grown any worse really, in terms of her detachment from Willy, but it is hard to hope for an improvement with Marcus still maintaining his ominous vigil. Fred does seem a little tired from his double-duty child-care chores. He is not all that young after all, and Willy is—well, I can't tell. It's very

hard when you compare him to what he was a few months ago. He certainly has lost a lot of his playfulness. If I were a mother I'd be worried.

What do I mean if I were a mother! I am not a mother and I am worried. Don't ever believe any of that horse-shit (pardon me, Dorothy, but I had to say it) about dis-passionate scientists. It's simply not true. Scientists have passions that make poets look like wimps. It's our blessing and our curse. How do you think things like the Piltdown Man hoax occurred? Simply because passionate White Anglo You-know-whats wanted the first human ancestor to be British even if it were an apeman.

My best hope now is that through some hormonal quirk Ginger could resume cycling and become impregnated by Marcus. It wouldn't have to be that much of a quirk. Some female baboons have resumed fairly early after birth—probably not this early, but I can hope.

(Two hours later) Bad news: a field assistant, Marcie, has just come in from some night observation work and reports that Marcus has now extended his vigil into an actual night watch. He slept on the same cliff site as Ginger, Fred and Willy on a shelf not three meters away. And get this! Marcie said that she had a clear view as it was a full moon and that Marcus never slept. He just watched Willy all night long. This is really getting bad.

I am going to have to go into Marui for supplies. The crew is getting mutinous about my flourless bread. I man-aged to pulverize my finger the other day instead of the mealy-mealy. Seems that a hyena ran off with our grinder and I had to use the hitch from the truck. Thanks for the shirts from Expeditions Unlimited. Peter likes his too. No, they weren't too cute. They're very comfortable. Keep *your fingers crossed for Willy.*

Best,
Ella

Dorothy pushed up her reading glasses. It was amazing but the last line did unnerve her. Ella, in the course of six months, had succeeded in dragging Dorothy close, too close, to the heart of this little drama being played out amongst nonhumans eight thousand miles away. She had not as yet lost sleep over Ginger, Fred and Willy but she was concerned that Ella seemed so disturbed. Odd! she thought. Just a year ago she had reared like a hissing cobra and spat the worst invectives, at least the worst in her book, at Ella. She had fired off those two little words, "young lady," that become so venomous when linked in anger, and then she had proceeded to vent her thoughts concerning such obnoxious concepts as "therapeutic anger."

When one really wanted to demonstrate a kind of outrageous disdain and natural superiority, the ultimate insult for a female was to call her a young lady, which when translated came down to desexualized female-minor-without-power-or-reason. She had done that to Ella. And—who knew?—she might do it again. It had been distance and not proximity that had forged this bond between them. Right now she was feeling lousy about poor Ella out there on the savannah moping over a neglected baboon infant. But suppose Ella were here with her five pounds of frizzled red hair, galumphing about with her pendulous boobs and making pronouncements about Oriental rugs and therapeutic anger? Dorothy might be tempted to call her a young lady again. She might shoot her, for all she knew! Good Lord, didn't she already prefer Sophie's beau, with whom she had only chatted briefly on the phone?

The telephone rang. It was Lacey Concannon catching Dorothy before she left for Maine. Could she drop by after work? "I've got a great stock tip for you. I can't talk about it over the phone. It's a little weird. But I sure do owe you a few."

"A little weird?" Dorothy asked. "Is it over the counter?"

"Nope. It's not on anything yet. I'll tell you about it when I come."

"Sounds interesting."

"Well, as I said, it is a little bit weird."

"Orbital burial," Lacey said, setting down her glass on the coffee table.

"And they call it 'Yonder'?" Dorothy asked, opening the blue folder that had a white cometlike streak embossed on its cover.

"Yeah. I actually kind of like the name."

"It is rather snappy," Dorothy said, putting on her reading glasses to look over the prospectus. "Has a ring to it—a distant one."

"Well, you can see why I was rather reluctant to bring this to you, especially right now just a year after Ira's death, but Bill said . . ."

"Oh no," Dorothy interrupted, "don't worry about that. We scattered Ira's ashes off the Vineyard. As a matter of fact it was a rather humorous experience."

"Humorous?" Lacey repeated.

"Well," Dorothy said, taking off her glasses and rubbing her eyes. "Would you believe that we couldn't get the boat out of reverse? We kept backing around in circles—an orbital water burial, I guess. Lord! I hope that doesn't happen to them. What are they using here for transport?" She looked at the black-and-white photo of a rocket.

Lacey leaned over. "See, that's just the carrier. Then it jettisons and the part with the payload goes on."

"Yes," said Dorothy, pointing to a paragraph midway down the page. "Says here that with each launch they can carry the remains of some five thousand individuals. Goodness! That's the payload?"

"They have a special technique for reducing the ashes into a smaller than normal amount so they fit into the capsule. There's a picture on the next page."

Dorothy turned the page. There was a closeup of a man's hand holding a capsule between his thumb and index finger. On the capsule there was an inscription and a cross.

"With the stars." Dorothy read the inscription. "Sort of sounds like dinner at the Brown Derby, or I guess it's Spago's now, where you see all the movie actors and actresses. I wonder if they'd put a Star of David on the capsule for Jewish ashes?"

Lacey tried not to appear startled but somehow it was clear that she had not quite anticipated this kind of response.

Dorothy was reading in a low, mumbly voice. "Says here that the capsules will be placed in an orbit in the Van Allen Belts. Where the hell are those—or rather where in the heavens are those?" Dorothy chuckled. "I just got finished writing a letter to my friend Monica Morton-Jessup today, very old childhood friend, who's a physicist in England. I'll put a P.S. on the envelope and ask her where the Van Allen Belts are." Dorothy closed the folder. "So Bill thinks this orbital burial might be a winner?"

"Yeah, but listen, I'm not sure. I just wanted you to know about it. I mean if it would do one-tenth as well as the semiconductors and the Expeditions Unlimited, it would be fantastic."

"It's going for a dollar a share?"

"Yeah."

Dorothy sank back in the chair and pushed an ice cube around with her finger. "Well, I don't know, Lacey."

"Oh listen, I understand. If you're not comfortable with it. . . ."

"It's not that. I've bought a lot of weird things this year—

semiconductors, for me that's weird, and Expeditions, not to mention the whole condom thing. I felt a little bad about that—profiting off AIDS. By the way the stock's down right now but I had dinner with Jack Cohen and his wife the other evening. He's a cardiac surgeon at MGH. He says there's really going to be a problem for surgeons in particular and health care workers in general with this AIDS thing and that hospital supply outfits have got to start beefing up all the protective gear—rubber gloves, that stuff. There's a company, Rub-Co, that's doing a lot of R and D. They just bought Bio-Mem which does stuff with membrane technologies and I've asked Mort, my broker, to check it out."

"See, I came to give a tip," Lacey said, "and I get one instead."

"No. No. I'm not sure it's anything either."

"It's better than ashes in the Van Allen Belts."

"It all seems rather death-oriented, doesn't it?" Dorothy sighed. "At least it's not United Technologies."

"Oh yeah, Bill has some of that."

"Well, they're supplying the hardware for Star Wars. And that I won't be a part of. Tell Bill to dump it, or I'll tell him— I don't want you to botch your relationship. This administration, honestly, it's the pits as they say. I'm so proud though, of my alma mater. They decided not to give Nancy Reagan an honorary degree. In the words of the lady herself they 'just said no.' "

"So you want to pass on this orbital thing for now?" Lacey asked, getting up to leave.

"For now, I think." Dorothy leaned back in the wicker sofa and took a sip of her drink. "Why don't you and Bill come visit me in Maine? I can needle him about United Technologies."

"Sounds like fun but we've taken a house on Nantucket for three weeks in August and timewise that's all we have."

"Oh dear," Dorothy said as they got up to walk to the door.

"Well, I better give you a kiss because I won't be able to see you until Yonder—timewise, that is."

"When do you plan on coming back?"

"End of September, early October. I'll probably be all out of shape from not going to the health club."

"Well, we'll meet in the steam room in October, then."

"Better than the Van Allen Belts," replied Dorothy.

"Dorothy!" Lacey exclaimed.

23

"What do you mean, Elsie Bancroft is not coming back? Did she die?"

"No." Chowdie Starbuck had just clambered up on a rock from swimming. She was taking off her bathing cap. She had a piece of shock cord tied around her wrist which she took off and tied around her damp hair. "My hair's gotten too long. I have to do this so I can keep it off my face. No, she certainly did not die. I think she's as fit as ever. At least that's what Letha feels. It's those wretched children of hers. Well, in particular, little Elsie and that husband, Dick. Dick actually is more palatable than Elsie. How such a lovely lady as Elsie Bancroft could have produced such a nasty little weasel of a daughter I'll never know."

"What happened? Why's she not coming back?"

"Well, her hip began giving her some trouble. So she checked herself into the hospital and by God had it replaced. This is her third hip replacement. Little Elsie and Dick were against the operation and they said if she insisted on having it she would have to recuperate at home in Philadelphia and not come up until the end of the summer. Well, Junior Eaton's daughter works over at the Norumbega Inn in Camden and says there are rooms reserved there for Elsie and a nurse. Then guess who arrived on the island yesterday with loads of gear?"

"Little Elsie?"

"Yes, and Dick. They've been salivating for that house for years. And you can bet that they are going to entrench themselves and not get out. Letha, of course, is heartbroken. She lives for the summers and taking care of Mrs. B. I don't know why Dick and little Elsie want to come to Shag, really. They're much more Shadow Harbor types. They have Elsie's house here, I suppose that's it. I don't think Dick's ever made much money on his own. It's mostly Bancroft money."

"Oh dear! I can't stand it. I adored that woman. I was so looking forward to seeing her."

"We all were. But it's Letha who is beside herself. You know her husband, Ebert, is . . . well, he's had a drinking problem and I think that Letha just lived for her summers with Elsie. Gads! It's just too awful. Imagine trying to recuperate in hot old Philadelphia and then being held hostage at the Norumbega Inn."

"Why don't they at least use Letha as her companion over there?"

"I don't know. I suppose they think she might hatch some conspiracy to come back. You know that's not a bad idea! Spring her!"

The exile of Elsie Bancroft seemed to dominate much of the island conversation. Cecil Weed reported that Letha was in a bad way. "After all, thirty-five years she's taken care of Mrs. B. As you might know, Letha's husband has had a drinking problem over the years. It seems to do both of them a world of good to get away from each other in the summer. Now he's drinking again and Letha's got nowhere to go."

When Dorothy went to the post office later that morning,

the town pier was covered with boxes of geranium plants. There must have been nearly two hundred of the plants in bright reds and deep coral pinks. Burt Grindle, the captain of the *Sea Queen,* was unloading still more. He looked up at Dorothy.

"Mornin', Miz. Silver. Need any geraniums?"

"Are you going into the business, Burt?" Dorothy asked.

"Nope. Little Elsie and Dick Askwith ordered them up for the big house. You know they've kinda taken over up there."

"So I hear."

"Yeah—bit of a shame. They're nice folks but we all miss Mrs. B."

Although she had seen Mrs. Bancroft's gardens only briefly, it was hard for Dorothy to imagine all of these violently colored plants finding a place in Elsie's subtle scheme of things there.

On her way home she stopped at Clare Macchias's for crabmeat. On this mid-June day a thousand climbing white roses in full bloom had a stranglehold on the tiny house. There was barely a shingle or a window visible on the front side. The TV set in the rowboat was ablaze with tuberous begonias and the TV antennae were entwined with sweet pea vines. The lettuce was up, so were the radishes. Behind the rowboat was a new addition—a Coke cooler connected to the house by a power line. The cooler was thrumming away. A little girl came out and climbed up on a stool by the cooler and opened the lid.

"A Coke so early?" Dorothy asked cheerfully. The little girl, who was about six, gave Dorothy a wilting look, opened the lid and pulled out a live lobster.

"Goodness!" Dorothy exclaimed.

The child smiled at her. "I tricked you, didn't I?"

"You certainly did. Is your grandma home?"

"Yes."

Dorothy followed the child up the path.

"Sherrilyn, git that lobster out of here."

The child had gone through the screen door and let it slam behind her leaving Dorothy outside.

"There's a lady outside, Grandma."

"Well, for heaven's sake, bring her in. I'm on the phone. And take that lobster out. You're going to wear them out playing with them like that."

"I just want to show it to Vonnie."

"She don't need no lobster in her crib—Come on in!" Clare called toward the door. Dorothy walked in to find her on the telephone. "Okay, Mrs. Askwith—that'll be eight pounds of crabmeat for Thursday night. Then Sunday you'll be wanting lobsters for ten. Now do you want Myra to make up those little midget quiches. Yes, ma'am, she's still baking this year. No, she's not pregnant. She's done gone and got her tubes tied, thank God. Yes'm, I still do the pies and cakes and she does bread and all the other stuff, the hors d'oeuvres food you know . . . okay . . . okay . . . yes'm . . . you bet. Bye now."

Clare hung up the phone and looked straight at Dorothy, shook her head and blew a mouthful of air out through her lips until they vibrated wetly.

"Oh do that again, Grandma." The little girl had returned from delivering the lobster to the cooler, but Clare ignored her.

"They're back," Clare said. "Don't git me wrong. The Askwiths are nice enough people. Whenever they're here visiting Mrs. B. or before she gets here they entertain a lot. But she's awfully finicky and this summer I guess she's here for the whole time. Seems they've taken over for good over there. I don't know how I'm going to get enough crabmeat for them by Thursday. Arthur isn't going lobstering on Wednesday so . . . oh well, you don't have to stand here and listen to all this. What can I do for you?"

It seemed that everywhere Dorothy went she was hearing about Elsie and Dick Askwith and that in some fundamental way the Askwiths had upset the ecology of the island. She thought of the scores of geraniums on the pier. Where would they fit into a landscape of silver driftwood and Oriental calm? She thought of Letha with no summer break from her alcoholic husband and finally she thought about Clare worrying about enough crabmeat for what must be a substantial cocktail party.

24

Dear Dorothy,
   You little shit! Tantalizing me with your references to a
proposition and a proposal and then putting on a P.S.
about the Van Allen Belts. They are, for your information, two donut-shaped belts in the magnetosphere of the
Earth. Charged particles from the solar wind are trapped
there. So how 'bout that? Okay, I showed you mine, now
you show me yours. Who proposed marriage and who proposed getting laid? I suppose you'll make me wait until I
get to Maine to hear it all. Listen sweetums, just remember that when I did it the first time with that fellow from
Harvard it was really coitus interruptus just so I could
rush back to Northampton and tell you every lurid detail.
I want every lurid detail when I arrive on Shag
Island. Looks like August first is the date. So see you
soon.

                                        Love,
                                        Monica

Dear Monica,

To further tantalize you. The proposition was not all that lurid but it did involve a black tulip.

I am enclosing the ferry schedule from Rockland to Shag Island. You can catch a plane to Rockland out of Boston. Call me as soon as you get to New York. Maybe I should come there and hear your paper. Are Dark Halos anything like black tulips?

Love,
Dorothy

By the end of June, life had fallen into the pleasant cadences of summer for Dorothy. She was up at dawn and, unless it was raining, down on the rocky point with her Merlin stick and first mug of coffee. She could look straight east as the sun rose. Occasionally on a flat, calm morning she would see the sleek dark head of a seal break through the surface. Once she saw two dolphins swimming. They were no more than seventy-five feet off the point proceeding on a course toward Back Island. Their dorsal fins rose and dipped in a nearly circular pattern through the water so it seemed as if they might actually be rolling under the water on a kind of Ferris wheel.

Dorothy loved these first moments of the morning. She felt as though she were the first person on the continent to see the new day. There was a feeling of ownership about a day when one climbed into it from the earliest hours and perched on the easternmost rock and watched the sun rise on the rim of the ocean. Her mind felt peaceful yet alert, keen to the new light and to sensations of the most transitory nature.

By the time she finished her coffee and was making her way around the shore on the long route back to her cottage, she would see Chowdie descending for her morning swim followed by Minnie. The unspoken protocol seemed to be that they would wave to each other but never call out a greeting so as not to fracture the milky tranquility of the morning. Even

Minnie had fallen in with this procedure. Although she still fretted some over her mistress's swimming, she seemed even to walk in a manner designed to reduce the jangling of her collar tags.

Dorothy always chose to walk back the long way so she could see what the night tides brought to her beach. She would rinse her mug in the sea water and look for things—the perfect sea urchin shell, complete, pale green with its radiations of bumpy lines, a piece of sea glass, a sand dollar. She kept these sea things in a speckled pie dish on her dining table. Years before she had watched her children pick up countless crab claws and shells and pieces of driftwood and sea glass from New England beaches. She marveled at how they never seemed to tire of picking up the same kind of objects. At the time, she had wondered why. Once she thought that it was the repetition that fascinated the children. Just as they loved to hear the same nursery rhymes over and over and just as the old fairy tales filled with repetitive phrases and cadences had held them spellbound, so it had seemed to be with the things they found on the beach. Now she realized that it was not the sameness at all that they sought. It was quite the reverse. Each shell, each piece of glass or crab claw differed slightly and the children delighted in these differences and were urged on like taxonomists dedicated to assembling a collection that showed the most subtle variation within a range of form. Because they were children with no prejudices, no categories, no notions of quintessential character or essences, they became enchanted by the sheer variation from which life was made. Now she too had fallen prey to the mesmerizing task of combing the beach to find, to collect, and to attest to that diversity at the heart of life. She let the bits pile up in the speckled pie plate and later in the morning, with her second mug of coffee and cereal, she would turn the pieces over and over and again wonder about the forces and pressures that made each piece what it was.

After breakfast she worked in her garden while the earth was still damp and soft. She grew easy things for the most part, the kind she had become dismissive about during her twenty-five years of gardening in Lincoln, things that gave quick color and because of pliant stems could keep a truce with the wind. She wanted nothing that she had to coax along or baby. She was finished with bribing children or flowers.

She often swam after gardening, not as far or for as long as Chowdie and she did not really enjoy it. What she did love was lying out flat on the rocks after swimming. She liked the feel of the hot granite directly against her. She had found a particular slab of rock that conformed nicely to the angles of her body. She had even found a stone headrest which she had rolled over to the spot where she lay. When she draped it with a towel it supported her head nicely, and when she braced one foot against another rock her stone chaise longue suited her perfectly for reading. She still took great care with the sun but her skin did not seem nearly as allergic in Maine. She wondered if it were possible that the ozone layer was thicker here.

In a heavy plastic bag she brought the copy of *Pride and Prejudice* that Halsey had sent her and after her swim she would begin to read. Then growing drowsy in the sunshine she would start to imagine what Mrs. Bennet would make of the likes of Sophie, or Ella for that matter.

This particular morning, however, she did not grow drowsy. She had just finished reading the scene where Darcy first proposes to Elizabeth Bennet, truly one of the most astonishing proposals in literature. Jane Austen, of course, was master of the literary proposal. She had no match. This particular scene was like a high-wire act—lives and feelings were in such precarious balance that one had to hold one's breath while reading. Darcy had just confessed his true feelings for Elizabeth while simultaneously detailing his own sense of her inferiority and the concomitant family obstacles to such a union. Elizabeth, not impervious to "such a man's affection," holding true to her course, delivers one of the most eloquently indignant speeches in nineteenth-century literature.

Dorothy reread the scene. Was it possible that she had first read this scene in the same semester of college that Ira had proposed? She cringed again as she remembered Ira's proposal, and then became upset with herself. Would she have preferred that kind of arrogance to what she now had come to think of as the "double ring" ceremony of their engagement—the diamond and the condom? She held her left hand up. The diamond sparkled fiercely in the sunlight. Was it not all perhaps, from Darcy to Ira, variations in arrogance? She just had not had the chutzpah of an Elizabeth Bennet. Could she have transposed that wonderful speech of Miss Bennet's to fit what she now believed was her own true character, the one that might have gone to art school, taken an apartment on Bank Street and undressed behind paneled screens?

"In such cases as this, Ira, I believe it is the established mode to express a sense of obligation for the sentiments avowed—to wit, your high regard for me as attested by the offering of an engagement ring. We need not marry in order to enjoy the less lofty aspects of our attraction. So let's just hang up the honorable intentions and get on with the baser things. The ring, after all and in itself, becomes a coarse symbol of a soulless convention when presented in tandem as t'were with the prophylactic. It indeed becomes a kind of prophylactic itself." Oh, wasn't she clever with this kind of thing? Too bad she hadn't thought of it at the time.

"Yoo hoo!" The cry warbled from the rock ledge above where Dorothy lay. She sat up and turned around. A woman stood at the edge. She wore a short, stiff dress that was a blaze of tropical flowers. "Elsie Askwith here. We haven't officially met but Mummy told me all about you. She was just enchanted. Dick and I want to know if you'd come for cocktails next Tuesday? The Starbucks are coming. We'd love to have you."

Dorothy had picked up her Merlin stick and started to climb up the rocks. "Don't disturb yourself," Elsie called. "Can you come?"

"Well, yes. How kind. Yes I shall."

At the post office later that morning Dorothy ran into Chowdie.

"You're going to the Askwiths?" Chowdie asked in a low voice.

"Yes. I guess so."

"Well, we are too. I feel quite hypocritical but Andy says it's an island and islands aren't big enough for grudges. I intend, however, to see what's going on over there." She said this in an almost conspiratorial whisper. Perhaps Chowdie was planning to reinstall Mrs. Bancroft. They were standing outside the post office as a rather shabby Mercedes pulled up. "Oh, for heaven's sake, it's Jane Portchester," exclaimed Chowdie. An elegantly weather-beaten lady of about sixty-five stepped out of the car. She was rangy and tanned and wore a straw hat which appeared as though it had been chewed by mice.

Chowdie quickly introduced Dorothy. Jane came from Pride's Crossing in Massachusetts. Her family had been coming to Shag Island for over one hundred years and they "holed up," as Jane put it, over on Rich's cove—generations of them. There was not a house along the cove road that was owned by anyone other than a Portchester or a Kimball. They were all related.

"You heard about Elsie Bancroft?" Jane asked Chowdie. Chowdie clamped her mouth shut and nodded. "You going to cocktails over there?"

"Yes. What can you do?"

"I know." Jane nodded. "It's an island."

"Hi, Grandma," a small child with white-blond hair called out.

"Oh, Steffi," Jane replied, "come right over here."

"Is this Steffi?" Chowdie asked. "My goodness, you've shot up."

Jane Portchester was now bending over the child. "Let me kiss you. I can tell you haven't been swimming yet. No salt."

"I have. . . . Me too. . . ." Other voices began calling and three or four equally blond children were crushing around Jane Portchester. "Lick me, Grandma . . . lick me . . . lick me . . ."

"Oh you're quite salty . . . Ummm, tastes good . . . water's not so cold as last year this time."

Dorothy said good-bye. There had been a letter from Ella in that morning's mail, the first in ages. She was eager to read it, but now as she sat down at her dining table, she was almost frightened to open it. Suppose something had happened to little Willy? Odd but she felt closer to Willy than to any of those salt angel children she had just encountered in the village.

The news was about the same. There were no dramatic changes except, Dorothy suddenly realized, in the way Ella was reporting on the foursome. Gone was her previously chatty style, replaced now by simple, terse statements, and there was no more speculation as before concerning what Ella hoped might be the outcome of Ginger's resumption of cycles or the simple possibility of Marcus leaving. The deteriorating state of affairs was communicated with a cool detachment, and it was hard to believe that the writer of the letter was the same Ella who had written just weeks before about the notion of objective scientists as horseshit.

Ella now wrote of "increased whimpering . . . loss of appetite, little play," in describing Willy. "We are seeing, from both mother and child, demonstrations of some bizarre motor behavior of the repetitive type often associated with autism in humans—ceaseless rocking, tapping of self with hands. This kind of monotonous repetition seems to disengage the animal temporarily from his surroundings and allows for a total withdrawal from the social and physical world. It is a matter of some concern that although the mother indulges in it only sporadically, the child has picked up on it and is engaging in this kind of behavior more and more. Willy's leg now is almost bald from hair pulling. He spends hours pulling on it. This is of course not considered a grooming behavior as its intention here is neither to . . ."

Dorothy threw down the letter. Good Lord! she thought. After eight months of exchanging letters she did not need this textbook explanation of grooming. What had happened to her ebullient, irreverent Ella who had even said in one letter that it was such a relief to write to Dorothy after writing in field notebooks all day long and lecturing graduate students? How had she put it? Gossiping about baboons had given her as much insight as observing them. Well, Dorothy was simply going to have to stop writing if Ella did this to her. What was all this "we" business? She didn't say "I" once in this letter. No news about Peter, no news about the promiscuous Peaches or the social-climbing Dot, and she had not even asked how Dorothy was doing in Maine.

Dorothy did not really relish continuing a correspondence with Ella if it was going to be carried on in the monotone of a lab report. There was something depressing about the letter, which had nothing to do with poor little Willy who was now referred to as "the infant," or Ginger, who was called "the mother." Instead it stemmed from the change in Ella's style of writing. Dorothy did not like the change and she found herself focusing on it more than on what was happening to the players in the strange savannah tale. For the past four weeks when she had not heard from Ella she had been terribly anxious about the little baboon family. Perhaps she had been too flip in her last letter. After Ella had reported that Marcus had taken up the nighttime vigil, Dorothy had written that she would pray to whatever "baboon gods" look out for such things as hormonal change. It was facetious, but after all these months of writing she trusted that Ella would know that she was truly concerned.

Every day that a letter had not come she became more convinced that the worst had happened. She had even rehearsed hearing those written words in her head, but the words she read now she had not rehearsed and they were not welcome. After all, Dorothy reasoned, Ella and she could hardly be said to have a natural affinity. Had it been dislike at first sight? But because Dorothy was such a "good egg," as Ira always said, she had made an effort and she felt that she had forged as much of a bond as possible with someone with whom she had precious little in common. She would not even have tried to forge such a bond save for the fact that her son and this woman were in love.

Now with Sophie's man, Rob Fitzsimmons, it was entirely different. It was quite clear in their very brief phone conversation that he and Dorothy would hit it off immediately. There was that instantaneous feeling of having much in common. Dorothy did not like to use the word *background*, for it was generally an offensive term that bordered on racism, and besides it was rather silly to speak of background, she supposed, when it was a case of her two Jewish children being involved with gentile lovers. This was America, the melting pot, and what her kids had come up with in terms of partners, for now at least, was pot luck in the American tradition. But she did have a feeling based on her phone conversation with Rob that within the melting pot the Silvers and the Fitzsimmonses had melted or smelted within closer range of one another than the Silvers and the Voights.

There was still something essentially foreign about Ella. She was not simply rural, she was from a land in that region that has no real name but is spoken of in terms of river boundaries. And Dorothy knew virtually nothing of Ella's family. Ella never mentioned a father or a mother. Peter perhaps had said once that the father was dead, but it was as if Ella's family was as vague and ill-defined as that region from which she came.

At 3:30 in the morning Dorothy awoke exhausted from her own dreams. Her night's sleep had been scored with fragmented images. In one the nincompoop wife from the Boucher portrait suddenly began to turn furry, her face flattening. *"You know, she is such a good egg, Dorothy."* It was both Ira's and Halsey's voice together talking about the woman in the portrait.

"But you don't understand," Dorothy had answered in her dream. *"That little baby baboon is dying and I can't find Ella. Ella will be so upset. And I don't know what to do."*

"You can't intervene with science, Dorothy. This is a study of creatures in the wild."

"Oh, horseshit! Where's Ella? Ella is the only one who understands what's happening."

"Waa . . . a, waa." It was the whimpering of a baby. Dorothy reached down to pick up the little baboon but it floated away like a helium balloon.

"Catch your baby!" Dorothy screamed at the furry mother, but she was back in the portrait smiling inanely as the room filled with sun-blond children. Where was Ella? Where was Willy? Please God, she prayed in her dream.

Then she woke up. Her nightgown was soaked with perspiration. It had seemed too real, especially the terror of not being able to find Ella or Willy. It was that horrible gripping fear that every parent has known when he or she imagines a child lost or in danger. She got up and went to the window. The fog had rolled in so thick that it had sucked the blackness out of the night and filled the air with a milky opaqueness. She put on a sweater and walked out to the sunset porch. The arches framed nothing. She sat down and rocked a bit. She did not think about the dream. She thought about Ella and the letter. She felt ashamed of her impatience. She must write back to Ella soon. She must get her back on the track, or certainly off this track. If Ella wanted to write letters that were like field notes that was one thing, but Dorothy did not have to follow suit.

25

By morning the wind had shifted to southeast and brought with it a warm sea smell, dank and full of the resonances of distant water. Dorothy liked it. The fog wrapped around the cottage. She built a fire and baked an apple pie just so she could smell its fragrance. All afternoon the kitchen and living room were aswirl with the scent of the sea mixed with that of cinnamon and apples and burning wood.

When she became too hot she walked down to the shore. The fog was still thick. Chowdie was swimming. "Get your bathing suit on," she called. "The water is wonderful." So Dorothy returned to her house to change clothes and in a few minutes was swimming with Chowdie. The fog had thickened and she and Chowdie could lose sight of each other within a few strokes.

"We need miners' hats instead of bathing caps." Chowdie laughed.

"Where's Andy?"

"Sleeping, natch. There's only two things that Andy likes

to do in the fog—kayak and sleep. We went kayaking this morning."

After swimming, Dorothy invited Chowdie in for pie. They demolished nearly half of it. That evening was the Askwiths' party.

If it hadn't been for the fog, Dorothy would have noticed sooner, but it was not until she was directly under the prow of the porch that she looked up and saw the fringe of red and pink geraniums hanging in window boxes off every rail. She sighed as she remembered the clean lines of the porch, graceful as those of a clipper ship, and the figure of Elsie leaning against the rail, exhorting her to chasten the lady's mantle. She had a fleeting moment in which her resolve to go in wavered. Then she squared her shoulders and went up the steps. In the end, she was quite glad she had come. Except for the hosts, the people were all quite nice. Little Elsie and Dickie were almost as obnoxious as she had heard and, indeed, she did wonder how a person as lovely as Elsie Bancroft could have produced such an affected and totally charmless daughter. Elsie and Dick were either exceedingly stupid or so deep in the euphoria of being the lords of the manor that they did very little to conceal it. Dickie spoke with great enthusiasm of his intended renovations, which included his and Elsie's plans to take out the driftwood garden and substitute it with a gazebo and a flagpole.

"I've always fancied a gazebo! I'm just sick of getting eaten by mosquitoes," Little Elsie said. "We would have screened in the balcony porch but that would have cost a fortune. . . ."

"Well, Mummy insisted on the operation. Dickie and I were dead set against it, as was her internist."

For the life of her, Dorothy could not figure out why a woman pushing sixty felt it necessary to refer to her own mother, in anyplace other than direct address, as "Mummy."

"Those orthopedic surgeons—I don't trust them," Dickie broke in. "This guy, Rosenthal was his name. . ."

Dorothy felt something clench inside her. She started to wander off toward the bar. Through a partially opened door she could see into the pantry. Slumped on a stool was Letha.

"Letha! How are you doing?"

"So-so," she said. Then there was a flicker of recognition in her eye. "Oh, you're the lady who was here for tea."

"Yes. Dorothy Silver."

"Of course. I remember you. Mrs. B. took to you so." She sighed. "Guess you heard."

"Letha, dear, I think we need another platter of those mushroom things. Use that black lacquer tray, the one Mummy got in Java."

"Mummy would shit a brick if she saw what's going on here," Letha muttered under her breath.

"Letha! Letha! Thank God I found you." Chowdie Starbuck came running into the pantry. "Oh hi, Dorothy. Letha, what's the news on Mrs. B.?"

"She writes me that she's fine. She thinks she's coming in August. They haven't told her about the Norumbega yet."

"Can you beat that!" Chowdie slapped the counter. "Listen, we can't talk here. I'll be in touch. What's that dress you're wearing? It looks like a nurse's outfit."

"It's a uniform. Little Elsie has them in all sizes for the help. We all have to wear them."

"You're kidding?" Chowdie's mouth dropped. "Who the hell does she think she is? By the way, Dorothy," she said, not waiting for an answer, "Porty Portchester says it was your husband who did his triple bypass. He wants to meet you. He's out there by the crabmeat."

That evening Dorothy wrote to Ella.

Dear Ella,

Troop #8 is not the only primate group worthy of observation. The Shag Island troop is quite fascinating.

We don't number them here. There is just the native troop and the summer troop.

I was of course very upset to hear the report on little Willy and Ginger, et al. We also have a very distressing situation here. What do baboons do about aging members of the troop? I think I might have written to you about the lovely old lady I met here in May, Elsie Bancroft. Would you believe that her children have turned her out of her own house—all under the guise of health reasons? People are pretty upset. They all prefer the high-ranking old female to her offspring. Her daughter and the son-in-law are insufferable. They are really the only unpleasant folk I've met so far.

This dislodging is causing reverberations. Letha Hardy, Mrs. Bancroft's longtime helper and companion, is looking absolutely doleful. She apparently lived for her summers with Mrs. B., as she calls her. She is now forced to wear a uniform and carry around platters of what I call very "goyische" hors d'oeuvres. [Dorothy could not imagine that anyone from Niobrara County, Nebraska, would know the word, so she footnoted it. Goyische: Gentile-like.] *Anyhow the daughter and her husband have now taken over the house and I was invited to a cocktail party which was quite nice if one discounted the host and hostess.*

I met an old patient of Ira's. A Mr. Portchester. There are hundreds of this family on the island. Many of them are very portly. His wife, however, is not. She's quite handsome and has that lean, lined, scoured look of certain New England women. One thinks, of course, of Katharine Hepburn. Jane Portchester is very skinny and tall. So I think of her as Stringbean and I think of him as Porky, although everyone calls him Porty. Porty is a bit much for me to say. But I guess I shall have to, as I can hardly call him Porky to his face. Stringbean wears a straw hat and drives a beat-up Mercedes—her "island car." They have scads of white-blond, sun-streaked, salt-stained grandchil-

dren whom Stringbean licks each day to make sure they've been swimming.

Ira did a triple bypass on Porky. Porky "adored" Ira and told me how upset he was over his death. "So fit," he said. "So thin," he then muttered, patting his own paunch. I felt sorry for him really. I am sure he was actually wondering why, despite all the odds, he was still standing there eating crabmeat, which he shouldn't have been eating, and his lean doctor was dead. I could read it all in his face. I nearly said it was "disheartening"—can you believe it? A very bad pun that could have caused an on-the-spot coronary.

There was another very interesting lady, a certain Rosie Daniels Kimball. She looks like one of yours, Ella. A tiny little monkey of a thing with a truly simian grace. She was dressed in these wonderfully voluminous thin pants and a tunic. She told me they were made out of parachute material. She's an environmental artist—whatever that is. If chimps had a fairy queen she'd be it. She apparently is related to the Portchesters but is nothing like them. She does not live along the cove road where they all live, but has what Chowdie Starbuck describes as a very weird house that is a cross between a tepee and a geodesic dome on Eagle Point. According to Chowdie she had a very close relationship with Buckminster Fuller. She's an awfully nice lady and was most interested in your and Peter's work. I do have so much to brag about with the three of you!

We've had fog for two days now. But it doesn't really stop me. Please keep writing. It was rather long between your last two letters. And I am concerned about Ginger, Fred and Willy. Also I miss all the others—Lulu, Fig, Butch, Peaches. Dear Lulu, is she still so exuberant in her withdrawals from intercourse?

Best,
Dorothy

She reread the letter. She wondered if it sounded too forced, too jolly. All that stuff about the Shag Island troop, was it too obvious? She had not put so much into a letter since the ones she had written to Peter twenty years before, when he first went to overnight camp and had written homesick letters that ended with such phrases as "if you love me come and get me," and his favorite signoff, "love with tears, your son Peter." In one he had even allowed as to how the previous night it had been very cold and his teardrops had turned to ice crystals. Oh God, she had poured herself into those letters feeling that she was literally pulling him through every day of the three weeks at Camp Quinnapoxet. It was a much more difficult letter to write than the one to Ella because when she had written Peter as a youngster, she had to be very careful not to give too many details of home life for fear it would make him even more homesick. Nor could she report that Sophie was loving camp and had won all sorts of awards. Little did she dream that twenty years later she would be writing to try and bolster Peter's girlfriend's spirits. She supposed that was what the intention of these letters was, when one really got right down to it. She had concluded that Ella was depressed over the Ginger, Fred, Willy and Marcus situation and was retreating behind a shield of scientific detachment. It was as simple as that. It probably happened all the time. Hadn't Ella said that in their passions scientists made poets look like wimps? She did wonder if she were the only person writing to Ella. Peter wrote to her obviously. She wondered if perhaps he had noticed the change in her tone. But did Ella have any blood relatives who wrote to her in care of the Kyo Ranch on the Kisimui Preserve in Kenya?

The fog hung on for several days. Dorothy got into the habit of listening to the marine forecasts. She now thought in terms of fronts and depressions and systems, rather than mere rain-showers and temperature and humidity readings. Andy Starbuck was a weather nut and when he came over to help fix a leaky faucet with a wrench and a spare gasket, he described the low pressure system in which they were caught so vividly that it became a landscape unto itself. It was not merely a depression. It was "a dimple trapped between two slow-moving systems." He spoke of "vast convections to the north and south," of "locked fronts." He finished fixing the faucet and slipped the wrench into his pocket.

"There you go! Nothing like a urologist for plumbing." He chuckled as he went out the door. Cecil Weed came by later the same day to fix a plank in Dorothy's pier. Over a cup of coffee Cecil also talked about the weather. His metaphor differed. "Got a phlegmy situation here," he said, looking out Dorothy's window. "You just kind of wish the whole place would cough and clear out its tubes. Agnes looked in her diary. You know, last summer we only had eight days' fog all told between Memorial Day and Labor Day."

"How is Agnes?"

"Fine. Fine. Worried, of course, about Letha. They're goin' up to Bar Harbor for a day next week. Thought it might perk up Letha a bit."

"Now, you do some caretaking for Mrs. Bancroft, don't you, Cecil?" Dorothy asked.

"Did," Cecil said pointedly. "No more. The Askwiths don't need a caretaker. They need a general contractor. Good heavens—what they're planning to do with that place!"

"Oh dear."

"Oh dear is right. No, I want no part of it. I retired two years ago from my job with the state in Camden. Got my time filled with the houses I got already. Between caretaking those and my work for the Order of the Eastern Star I'm set. We raised over four hundred thousand dollars last year for the children's hospital. No, I don't need to drive myself crazy supervising construction for the Askwiths."

"What are they building?"

"What aren't they building?—new driveway, summer house or gazebo, whatever you call it, a sauna down by their shore, new roof on the boathouse, whole new dock and swimming float, new downstairs bathroom, updating two old bathrooms."

"Oh my."

"I know. Wears you out just hearing about it. But I guess they're anticipating lots of their children with their grandchildren and guests. You know what Dickie Askwith told me he really wanted? This'll kill you."

"What's that?"

"A lap pool."

"Lap pool?" Dorothy asked.

"Yeah, I wasn't sure what he meant myself." Cecil took a deep breath as if he were about to ponder something totally inscrutable. "Apparently, a lap pool is a long, skinny kind of pool, rectangular in shape, and they actually build a current into it so you can swim against it for exercise."

"Well, I think that's ridiculous," Dorothy said.

" 'Course it is. I told him so. I said, hell Dickie you can go right off Prebble Point over there and swim between that and Speck Island. Current goes through there at two knots."

Midway through the fog Dorothy visited Rosie Daniels Kimball who was "creating her own weather." She showed Dorothy numerous sketches of something called "Convection Winds" that was to be made from eighty-foot-long swathes of white parachute material blown by industrial fans. It was for an exhibit in Akron, Ohio, in the Firestone Civic Center. "They wanted me to do something with rubber tires, but I said, 'you folks do that all the time,' and besides I'd already done this," Rosie said, gesturing at her bubble-shaped window.

"What?" Dorothy asked.

"The fog. Here." She got out some large sketches that were quite beautiful of gray and white billowy shapes. "It's called "Fog Bank." I did it in Tucson. They loved it. They don't have any fog in Tucson. I like to try and bring in foreign weather to a place. I've always wanted to do a desert, actually. Ever since I saw the movie *Lawrence of Arabia*—sand is so sculptural. So. . . , Rosie said settling back in a glider swing that was suspended from a beam, her feet barely touching the floor, "What do you do, Dorothy?"

The question caught Dorothy completely unaware. A multitude of half-formed answers flashed through her head. They all sounded defensive or plain silly. So very slowly she began to answer. "I do nothing that is ascertainable. In the morning I watch the sun come up. Then I garden, then I swim. I read and I write letters." And finally, without a trace of defensiveness, she said, "It's a very contemplative life."

"You create your own weather!" Rosie said gleefully, and reached down with a pointed toe and kicked herself into a swing on the glider.

"I guess so," said Dorothy, rather startled by the analogy.

"I'm so sick of 'committed women,' those charity ball types and even the volunteers who do it without the ballgowns."

"No, I disagree—not about the charity balls. That is ridiculous. But I think the in-the-trenches volunteer is wonderful. I have friends who work for planned parenthood, help run clinics and work at shelters for battered women. But I can't do that. I don't have the knack for making those kinds of relationships. I don't have the personality. I send money instead."

"I love it!" Rosie said fiercely. Her little face split into a wide grin and looked so chimplike that Dorothy thought she would swing right from the glider up to the rafters.

On her way home from Rosie's she stopped at the post office. There was a letter from Peter saying that he and Ella were supposed to have met in Nairobi but Ella could not get away.

A bad sign, Dorothy felt. She decided that she would write to Peter and share her concern over Ella. Although she prided herself on never prying, she had determined to ask Peter a few questions about Ella's family.

There was also a brief note from Lacey Concannon telling her she was so glad Dorothy had not invested in Yonder, the orbital burial company. It was now in trouble. It seemed that a cease-and-desist order had been issued by the state charging that Yonder was operating as an unlicensed cemetery, and according to state law they were required to have forty-five acres of land and an access road that led to a highway. Yonder was contesting, arguing that it was not a cemetery but a transportation system. The upshot, of course, was that no money was being made or would be, if ever, for a long time.

By that evening the wind had started to back somewhat fitfully into the north. By morning it was northwest and when Dorothy walked down to the point the fog had cleared. The day was limpid with dry air and pale morning light. Sitting on the mooring just off the Starbucks' was a boat that at first glance seemed directly out of Dorothy's Michigan sailing days. It was not a dory but a Herreschoff 12. It had a stalwart charm, still elegant but not too refined. Dorothy stood on a ledge overlooking the water and imagined herself at its helm. There could certainly not be that much sail area. Indeed it must be the perfect boat for these waters. She had never thought of owning a boat just for herself. But this one did not look like too much boat. It had been a long time since she had sailed a boat herself, not since Michigan. Ira had always sailed *Ventricle*. Perhaps she could look into owning a boat like this one. She would ask Andy.

She was not required to look any farther than that mooring. The boat was for sale. Andy himself had planned to sail it over to a yard in Camden. "I can't believe it," Dorothy said as she wrote out the check. "I'm actually a boat owner."

Andy sailed with her on her maiden cruise. It was ten times

simpler than the *Ventricle,* and within twenty minutes she was entirely comfortable at the helm. The biggest challenge would be sailing with tiller in one hand and chart in another. Andy also provided her with some extra charts, and Cecil picked up a few other items for her in Rockland. She began to devote her evening to studying charts and mapping out courses with her parallel rules. Using the compass roses she plotted out various courses in fictitious winds from East Point on Shag to other islands with names like Cat and Hard Head and Eagle.

At first she kept her voyaging within the immediate vicinity of East Point, exploring the coves on the far side of Back Island which was no more than a mile away. Within a week, though, she was prepared for a more adventurous journey and sailed in tandem with the Starbucks who went in their small cruising boat to Loon Island where Chowdie collected her favorite paving stones.

The next day Dorothy sailed there again, this time by herself. The breeze was stiffer but she did fine. She had become so caught up in sailing that she had nearly forgotten her concerns about Ella when a letter arrived from her. She opened it with dread. But this time there was absolutely no news about Ginger or Willy. There was quite a bit about Honest Abe, whose arthritis had become more crippling and who also had a parasitic infection. There was a very long, involved discussion of Murphy who was in the midst of an "alpha-type" struggle with his brother Nutkin. This Ella said was "showcasing" nicely some concepts she wanted her graduate students to focus on. For Dorothy, however, it was a very unsatisfactory letter. It seemed as if Ella had dropped a curtain between them. Could she simply have stopped observing Ginger, Fred and Willy? She couldn't stand it and wrote Ella an immediate reply asking for news.

She received a letter in direct response. It was terse and to the point.

Dear Dorothy,
We feel that Willy will not last the month. He is
increasingly nervous around all large males except for
Fred, who seems more and more distracted himself and less
able to cope. Ginger totally ignores Willy. Harriet, on
occasion, has tried to do a little aunting. However, Mar-
cus has threatened her repeatedly and in one instance last
week attacked and opened a large wound on her left flank.
Sorry that I have no better news than this. Hope you're
enjoying your new sailboat. Too bad about the old lady
being turned out of her own house. There is actually some
very interesting literature on aging and social interaction
within nonhuman primate groups. See Knoedler, 1971
and Atwell, 1978.

Yrs.,
Ella

Dorothy felt alarm and panic. If there had been any way of telephoning Ella she would have done so that minute. In the meantime a letter had arrived from Peter which was equally unsatisfactory in terms of the answers it gave to Dorothy's questions about Ella's family.

Dear Mom,
It sounds like you're having a wonderful time in Maine.
I think it's great that Monica's coming. Work is going very
well here, although for the last three weeks it's been hard
to get anything done because of all the press coming here
to look at the new skull.
About your questions concerning Ella's family. I know
this sounds weird but I really know very little. I know that
her father died years ago, way before Ella was even in high
school, and I know that her mother is some sort of
invalid. Ella said it's an Alzheimer's type thing. She's in a

nursing home. Ella has no brothers or sisters. There was some cousin who lived with them for a while but Ella detested him and he moved away. I think her father might have been an alcoholic. It was not a great life. They lived on a farm and it went bust over the years. I really can't tell you any more. Ella is one of those people whose life seems to have started in college. She is decidedly closed about anything before. She did so extraordinarily well in college and her work in primatology was so distinguished early on that it overshadows anything that went on previously. She seems to like it this way, and as you know the Ella that I know and love is the only one I need to know and love. We'll both see you at Xmas.

Love,
Peter

In her next letter to Ella, Dorothy did her best not to betray her alarm over Ella's tone or the bad news of Willy's apparently impending death. Instead she faced things head-on. She took Ella's suggestion for reading about aging in nonhuman primates as an opportunity to return to her own field observations on Shag Island.

Dear Ella,
I'm really sorry about Willy. Is it as hopeless as it now seems? Could there be any radical changes of course or, I guess, miracles? I can imagine how disturbing this must be for you.
Thank you for your reading suggestions on old age in nonhuman primates. I shall have to wait until I get back in range of the MCZ library to follow up on them. In the meantime I do have a happy old-age story of one who was not turned out, but quite the reverse. Cecil Weed, the island man who takes care of this house and several others, he and his wife Agnes live with Agnes's mother—or

perhaps it is the reverse, she with them. In any case I
stopped in the other day to return something I had bor-
rowed and Agnes was washing Patty's hair. Patty is ninety-
four. It was a lovely day and Agnes had her on the porch.
She was towel-drying the old woman's hair and Agnes's
granddaughter Murlie came out with two combs. Murlie
and Agnes then each stood on either side of Patty gently
combing out her hair in the sunlight. Her hair is terribly
long. There's at least a yard of it and most people would
have cut it off and kept it short. But Agnes and Murlie
combed and combed, rubbing a sweet-smelling lotion into
it, all while telling Patty what beautiful hair she had.

Then Susie, Murlie's little girl, brought out Patty's
afternoon snack, a glass of ginger ale and cookies. Susie
plopped down by her great-grandmother's knees and took
off the old lady's shoes and stockings and began massaging
her feet. They do this to help her circulation problems.
The entire scene was inexpressibly beautiful. This old lady
being combed, lotioned and massaged by three genera-
tions. A nice story, isn't it? And it's true. I only wish Mrs.
Bancroft could look forward to such care and love. She is
being installed this week at the Norumbega Inn with a
"nurse-companion" who is "skilled with hip replacements"
according to the daughter . . ."

The rest of the letter was devoted to her boat and her mini-
voyages and trials with rudimentary navigation. She sealed
the letter and went out to rock on her sunset porch.

It perplexed Dorothy that she had been thinking about Ella
so much. She couldn't imagine what had transpired between
the lines of all those letters that had in some way taken hold
of some part of her. Perhaps she had grossly misread all the
letters. Perhaps there were no real signs of warning or changes.
Maybe she had imagined it all, like the fictitious winds she
plotted on her navigational charts. Perhaps it was just a case

of a meddling fifty-two-year-old woman in need of a project. She, after all, knew women who divided their lives into projects—planning weddings, redecorating houses, buying third homes. For thirty years marriage had been her project, then moving to the condo, then death, now widowhood. But she had been a widow for over a year. Was time lying heavy on her hands? Was this why she had become so focused on Ella? Each letter seemed part of a large rescue effort and she felt an undeniable sense of mission in regard to Ella. But what was she rescuing her from? What was the danger? What was the mission?

26

"**I** can't believe it! You made it!" Dorothy cried as Monica stepped off the *Sea Queen*. They embraced and then held each other at arms' length to savor the moment and each other. Monica's face was wet with tears. "Are you all right, dear? Are you all right?" she kept asking.

"Of course I'm all right. I'm fine."

It had been almost five years since they had seen each other. "You look just the same," Monica said.

"More gray hair."

"No, it's silver, just like your name."

"And you're the same."

"Go on." Monica laughed. "I've gained ten pounds."

"But you look just the same. Not one gray hair."

"Redheads don't grow gray. We fade and get dull."

Dorothy gazed at her friend's full, smooth face with its hectic flush. Monica would always look like a camp counselor or the most ferocious center player on a girl's hockey team She was the essence of the girl's school jock. She had thickened but not aged. One would have never guessed that she had just come from the New York Academy of Science where she had delivered a lecture on the Dark Halo syndrome and galactic stability. "But are you all right, Dorothy?" Monica asked again.

"You expected me in widow's weeds, and not with a tan and in deck shoes. Would you believe that it's the first time I've not had sun poisoning? Tell me, is it possible that the ozone layer is thicker here? Oh Monica, this is Cecil. He'll drive us up with your bags. I don't have a car here. Hardly anyone does."

"I was going to call it *Memory*," Dorothy said. They were close-hauled on a course for Flint Island. "Because of all the good memories of our times in the various *Dory Dears* and *Dory Deluxes*. Then I thought, well, Monica's physicists are coming up with all these new exotic words every day of the week. Maybe she'll have an inspiration. Not Dark Halo, that's rather ominous, but I'm not so keen on *Memory* now as a name. You see when I first saw her moored out front she appeared, well . . . really like a ghost ship from my past. She's of course not similar at all to the sailing dories, but she is about the same size. *Ventricle* was much bigger."

"The *Ventricle?*" Monica asked.

"The boat we had. I sold it after Ira died. It was a big chunky thing. Nice for cruising but I could never handle it by myself."

"So why don't you like *Memory?* It's a lovely name."

"Oh, I don't know. It sounds so, you know . . . well, like in the past I suppose." She laughed.

"Yes, I suppose so. I mean, that is what memory suggests— the past."

"And frankly, Monica, I'm much less romantic about the past. I'm just plain not romantic anymore. As a matter of fact, I think I never really was. It's something I have learned about myself in the last year or so."

"Oh, aren't you? What about your proposal and your prop-osition?"

"Hardly romantic, either one, believe me."

"Do you think you'll ever remarry?"

"Why should I?"

"Dorothy, you shock me. You and Ira had such a good mar-riage. I would think that—"

"I'd want to duplicate it."

"Not duplicate it. That's impossible."

"You are thinking in corollaries, Monica," Dorothy said, steering a bit closer to the wind.

"What are you talking about?"

"This might really shock you but I have come to realize that my whole life has proceeded as if it were a geometric corol-lary."

"And what the hell is that supposed to mean?"

"It has been with me a matter of consequence based on a proposition with little or no proof," Dorothy said succinctly, as a young student might respond to a teacher's question.

"So what's wrong with that? How do you think we get from here to there in theoretical physics? Hunches, guesswork, proposition."

"But there's no proof. It just happened. I took it all as a given."

"You took what as a given?"

"My marriage."

"But it was a good marriage," Monica replied.

"Of course it was, and I have two great kids."

"So what's the problem?"

"The problem is that—oh God, this is so hard to explain and I can only talk about it with you! Look, whatever I say in the next few minutes I don't want you to think that I am one of those tiresome women who believe that they could have made more of their lives if they had stayed single—that I would have become a great scientist, artist or whatever. I'm not that much of a fool," Dorothy said slowly, keeping her eyes straight ahead as she pointed the boat as high as possible into the wind while keeping her moving smartly. "I think I went into marrige without a real reason, which was quite typical of me. I am, I now realize, a person who accepts easily the kind of general narrative forms and fits my life into them and so it never really becomes my story but just a kind of stock scenario. You see, I think that I am the most conventional person in the world—that I don't mind. But what I do mind is the lack of passion. That's the fee you pay for living your life not by rules but by corollaries."

"You mean you didn't ever love Ira?"

"Monica," Dorothy whispered, "I'm not sure." She turned her head and muttered into the wind. "But I'm very ashamed."

"Ashamed? Why?"

"I don't know. Possibly I've lived a lie." She brought the boat into the wind and came about.

Monica sheeted in the sail, then turned and looked straight at her friend. "You're no liar. But you're more of a romantic than you'll admit."

"I am, am I?" Dorothy sighed. "What about you?"

"Oh, I'm hopelessly so," Monica replied.

"Yes, that's what Peter's girlfriend says—scientists are the most passionate of all."

"But being romantic isn't the same thing as being passionate. There are some very dispassionate romantics."

"But you consider yourself a romantic."

"Yes."

"And Rupert too?"

"Yes, I have my physics and he has his flings, but we're still very romantic."

"Flings? You mean other women?"

"Yes."

"I can't believe it. He seems so devoted."

"He is. It's only occasionally that he does chase off."

"But Monica, why do you tolerate it? That's not romantic at all."

"Simply this: we think, I don't know for a fact, but we think we are in love and we think we've been that way for thirty years which is good enough for me. Rupert is the only person who has ever understood me for who I am, an entity, a being apart from that loony family of mine with all those airy aesthetic types that have wound up suicidal, alcoholic or both."

Dorothy knew that this was true about Monica and her family. There was a dark side to the family's creativity and iconoclasm. Whereas Monica was a robustly normal sort. She remembered how Monica's mother referred to her as a "disgustingly cheerful child." Despite her brains, Monica was regarded as somewhat suspect within her own family for her levity and common sense.

"And I," Monica continued, "am the only one who really understands Rupert as a discrete individual apart from that absurd eight-hundred-year-old baronetcy of his family that has absolutely crippled every other male member. You can't imagine what a handicap it can be—being a peer of the realm. I mean, they either take it very seriously or try to reject it in a way that has a kind of tabloid banality to it. I told you about our nephew Lonnie, who is a legal heroin addict. You know they do that in England. You can become registered as one and the state helps support your habit. Anyhow it takes a profound kind of valor for a normal individual to come out of that kind of heritage."

"And is that why you love him—his normalcy in spite of all, his valor?"

"Partly. But I think, I suppose you'll call this a corollary, but love for me comes with a kind of exclusive understanding of someone. I am the only one, at least so far, who understands Rupert, and he is the only one who understands me. If the universe is an accident, if intelligent life is an accident, then Rupert and I are following in that venerable tradition. Together we are like accidental riches in a random world. Apart, Rupert and I just don't make all that much sense."

Dorothy could not help but wonder if she and Ira together added up to such riches.

They sailed every day, packing their lunches of crabmeat or tuna sandwiches in a brown paper bag. They laughed that in their middle years their bladders seemed to have increased their capacities: they could now each handle an entire beer. Once more they switched off taking the helm and Dorothy now steered them down the Fox Island Thoroughfare in a very light wind. Looking at Monica she could not help but wonder if, by some quirk in time they could have gone back to being teenagers and been given a preview of themselves at fifty-two years of age, they would have been recognizable to each other and to themselves. Monica was a thickened, slightly blurred version of what she had been. But she was essentially the same. Dorothy, however, felt herself to be quite different. She certainly was physically. Her dark brown hair was entirely gray. As a young woman she had never been plump but just right. Now she had to fight to keep weight on. It was as if her whole body had been drawn out along the line of time into a thinner, more sinewy form. She could see the cords of muscles in her neck. Her knees were knobby in her shorts.

In the evening they sat out on the sunset porch until late. Monica pointed out the constellations within the shoals of stars. But the visible was lackluster next to the invisible that Monica described—that world of dark halos, icy nuclei, galaxies cannibalizing one another, voracious black holes, collapsing stars. When Monica spoke of the edge of the universe, Dorothy felt herself teeter in the night.

One morning Dorothy had just finished putting a load of laundry in the dryer when Monica ran breathless into the house.

"There is a rather impressive vessel off your dock and a small woman with a bullhorn calling for you and asking about the depth of the water."

"Good Lord, who could it be?" Dorothy said, dropping the lid on the dryer, and ran out the door. She could see the spars over the treetops. As she came around to the front of the house she whispered, "For heaven's sake!"

"Who is it?" Monica asked.

"Halsey Winthrop's mother, Betsy, on *Djinn.*"

The eighty-foot-long jet-black Hinckley yawl had its sails aback as it held thirty feet off Dorothy's pier.

"That you, Dorothy? I got the right place?"

"Yes, Betsy, it's me."

"Well, I've come to hijack you, dear."

By this time Chowdie and Andy were down on their shore. Andy had brought his camera.

"I'm sending in my crew to pick you up," Betsy called through the bullhorn. "Pack a bag. It's my annual croquet tournament. Bring any guests you want. Plenty of room."

"If you say no," Monica whispered, "I'll kill you."

"All right. Is Halsey up?"

"No. He's fishing in Norway."

Betsy Winthrop was a squat woman in her mid-eighties. She wore a white culotte, polo shirt and, Dorothy was pleased to note, Reeboks. On her head she wore a khaki hat with a narrow brim. There was absolutely nothing superfluous about Betsy Winthrop in dress, word or physique. In the tradition of many upper-class women of her era, she had not been to college. Widowed relatively young, she had taken over the administration of her family's vast wealth and managed the estate better than the family-owned banks could.

She came from an uncommonly handsome and rich family. The one thing that began to appall her early on and that grew into a profound disgust was what she called "the lack of usefulness"—in the most practical sense, if not moral sense—of many of her relatives. She saw their own fortunes shrink through inept management by trust officers. She saw many of her relatives satisfied to live in houses they could not properly maintain, supported by staffs of decrepit servants and family retainers because they could do nothing for themselves.

Although Betsy's own family had not allowed her to attend college, she made a point of piecing together almost surreptitiously a practical education of sorts. She had lived in Boston in the time when high-born women sent their cooks to the Fanny Farmer School of Cookery and on occasion attended a lecture designed for the lady of the house. She convinced her mother to let her go to one of these and came away disgusted after a session on color-coordinated meals, a phenomenon then in its heyday. It had been a Valentine's Day menu; beet juice had been used promiscuously in the preparation of decorative glazes and tints for everything from cottage cheese to cakes. There had been a demonstration on how to carve a radish into a tulip form. One session was enough. Betsy decided that if what constituted a higher education for women in college was anything like her two hours at the Fanny Farmer school, it was a blessing that her parents had refused to let her go.

From that point on, she began her impromptu curriculum which resulted in an interesting patchwork of the liberal and practical arts. She learned how to cook by horning in on fishing trips with her older brothers and cousins in Canada and cooking what they caught. She badgered the captain of the family schooner to teach her celestial navigation. When he finally confessed that he only knew how to navigate coastally, she talked him into teaching her that, and then got herself copies of the navigational classics Bowditch and Blewitt and some star charts and taught herself the rest.

Betsy still did all the navigating on *Djinn* and, as the young college boy cleared up lunch, she took the helm and managed to make the mooring in front up Wind's Way with precise steering while calling out orders concerning running backstays and backed jibs.

Three hours after Dorothy and Monica had left Shag Island they were slamming wooden balls around on the Winthrop lawn. Betsy was Dorothy's partner. Monica had been paired with a very elderly man who played in a golf cart with a canister of oxygen on the seat.

"You see, Charlie," Betsy said, "aren't you glad you aren't up at Northeast at the cousins'? Binny would never let you on their court with that thing. My cousin Binny Althorpe has this half-million-dollar croquet court. It was written up in the *Times*. But it's ridiculous. He practically makes you play in bedroom slippers. It's too perfect. There's no challenge to it. Whereas here we let the moles tunnel about . . . just like over there"—she pointed to where the lawn swelled into a ridge. "You're going to have to really whack it to get over that."

"Poison!" Charlie called out.

"Oh no!" Betsy moaned. "I think we should handicap him!"

"Handicap him!" Monica exclaimed and rolled her eyes. "What does she want to do? Cut off his oxygen?"

Charlie had just taken a whiff from his tank and started up the golf cart. "Watch out for me now, Betsy!" he cried as he rolled the cart up to where Monica was standing. "We're a team, kiddo!" he said, punching her in the arm.

There were four teams, Monica and Charlie eventually lost out to two college-age youngsters. Dorothy and Betsy were left to play off against an eight- and ten-year-old brother-sister team.

"I know you expect me to be nice," Betsy was saying as she lined up her next shot, "just because I'm your great aunt, but I'm not nice." And she then proceeded to whack the little eight-year-old girl's ball into the oblivion of the tall grass at the edge of the lawn. "There's another thing I'm not nice about either." She looked directly at Dorothy and Dorothy felt something clutch within her as she saw the anger in the old woman's eyes.

"What's that?" Dorothy asked.

"Cocktails are at five-thirty. Meet me at five o'clock on the south porch."

Dorothy could not imagine what could have been the object of Betsy Winthrop's anger. It was unbelievable to Dorothy that Halsey could have said anything to his mother about his proposal to Dorothy and, even if he had, she knew that Betsy was not the kind to hold it against her.

Dorothy arrived promptly at five on the south porch to find Betsy already there. She was standing with her back to Dorothy, gazing out at the Thoroughfare. She stood looking out for the better part of a minute toward the water. She turned around slowly and Dorothy was shocked. The anger had dissolved in Betsy's eyes and they appeared old, dull and sad. She is going to tell me something about Halsey, Dorothy thought. He has cancer. She is going to tell me that and she will describe our worst fear—outliving one's own child.

But that was not it.

"I have a friend," Betsy began. "An old, dear friend, I believe you know her."

"Who's that?" Dorothy asked.

"Elsie Bancroft."

"Elsie—you know Elsie?"

"Yes. I've known her for eighty-two years. You probably know that she has been put in the Norumbega Inn."

"Yes. Yes. I know the story."

Betsy eyed her carefully. "Yes. It is a story, isn't it? These despicable children of hers!" The fire crept back into her eyes. "He's bad, the son-in-law, but just in a conventional way. All he did was marry up, if one can call that little creep 'up,' and as they say, probably sleeps down. But the creep, little Elsie, is worse than bad. She has always been a malicious little thing. Nobody could ever understand it. Boy! Did she have her sights set on Halsey for the longest time. But he caught on to her number pretty quickly. In any case, and don't ask me how I know this—I'll just say the Penobscot grapevine—there seems to be a movement afoot to reinstall Elsie on Shag Island. I'm all for it, of course. She was doing fine until she found out that she would not be going back to Shag, but to Camden instead. That was a real setback. My spies tell me she is pretty depressed. You can get away with depression under sixty-five, but in our age bracket, upper eighties and nineties, it means death. I've seen it, believe me. It's as fatal as a heart attack or cancer, simply not as efficient."

"Oh God!" Dorothy murmured.

"Wait. It gets worse. I now find out that little Elsie and her husband had managed to get big Elsie to sign something several years ago, a kind of inheritance-tax dodge, so that the Shag house is actually in their name. It then comes down to the fact that we are not dealing with a simple reinstallation of a legal owner."

"She certainly wouldn't evict her own mother."

"She would, and basically she already has. I've got my lawyers checking the legal implications of all this. I've even got an A.C.L.U. fellow on it. I've contributed buckets to that outfit over the years so they owe me one. We're going to get her out of there and back where she belongs, come hell or high water." Betsy jabbed her hands into the pockets of her dress. "But when we do it we're going to do it right. There's a lot of romantic souls over there on Shag who are dreaming up all sorts of escapes. Well, this is not some swashbuckling Errol Flynn adventure. We're dealing with a ninety-two-year-old lady with pots of money but no power at the moment and in ill health. I don't want anyone jumping the gun. Letha? That's her name, isn't it?"

"Yes. Letha Hardy. I know her."

"They're trying to keep her away from Elsie. Would you believe that there's an approved visitor's list and not only is this Letha not on it, but neither am I. In any case Letha has a relative who works at the Norumbega and she's able to get messages through. So I want you to tell Letha what I've told you. She's part of the group working to get Elsie back and she can tell the others. They have to know that legally Elsie no longer owns the house and this could cause problems. So they're going to have to hold it.

"Secondly, tell Letha, and have her tell the rest, that I'm working on this with my lawyers. They're treating it as a civil liberties case. That seems to be our only hope for doing an end run around these despicable youngsters.

"Finally, tell Letha to get word to Elsie that Betsy is going to do something. She should not fear. I'll get her out of there if I have to . . . to"—Betsy shook her fist in the air—"chloroform the goddamn nurse and row her to Shag myself. Letha must tell Elsie to hold tight. She cannot go into this spiraling depression. We'll fight them!"

Dorothy felt something thrill deep within her. She could have been a wartime waif in the streets of London watching Mr. Churchill walk through. And indeed although there was now silence as they stood there on the porch, it was as if a ghost voice had continued to speak. . . . "We shall fight them in the Norumbega, on Shag, on the oceans. We shall fight with growing confidence and growing strength . . . we shall defend our island, whatever the cost may be. We shall fight on beaches. We shall fight on the landing grounds . . . the town piers. We shall fight in the fields, and in the gardens of driftwood. We shall fight in the hills and on the ledges. We shall never surrender. . . ."

Dorothy stood silent, mesmerized by the presence of such moral tenacity. She felt linked with everything that had ever been weak and had grown strong through the example of courage.

She took the message to Letha and, figuring that Chowdie was behind the rescue mission, told the Starbucks directly.

They were most pleased to hear of Betsy Winthrop's involvement but expressed concern about any lengthy delays as it had been reported that Elsie was declining.

Monica had picked up the mail that morning while Dorothy had sought out the Starbucks and talked to Letha. She came into the kitchen. "A letter, my dear, from your favorite primatologist, I believe."

"Oh God!" sighed Dorothy. "I don't think I'm up to it. I just know that Willy's dead. I can't read it."

"I don't believe how intense your life is on this tiny island," Monica said, putting the mail down on the table. "For a widowed lady with two grown children and plenty of money, you are hardly leading a retiring or emotionally complacent existence. You seem, if not stage center, to have more than a walk-on part in a lot of dramas."

Dorothy rested her chin in her hand and shook her head. "Maybe it's just that I have more time now to fill up so I get more intensely involved. Who knows? Dramas might have been swirling around me, around all of us, but there just wasn't time to pick up on them before." She was not really sure exactly what she had been doing before this anyway. Her kids, after all, had been on their own for years. And Ira had still worked twelve-hour days. She felt it was more a question of insulation. In some strange way, within the thirty years of her marriage she had so expertly played her role of homemaker that she had amputated herself from larger experience.

It was paradoxical: a worldly family like theirs, the husband a cardiac surgeon of international repute, whiz-kid daughter on Wall Street, son distinguished in one of the most competitive corners of academic research. By all rights the home should have been a microcosm of that macroworld of medicine, high finance, and academia. Yet it had not. She had insulated it too well for that. She had never thought about it until now. She did not resent it now. But she felt that for all people there must be a time when the nesting act, the homemaking, ends.

She had simply not realized it. Only cathedrals had indefinite schedules of construction. There must be a point in reference to homes, however, when the nesting, the basic construction, ends. After that there is only maintenance. But if one continues to construct the nest, it does not get qualitatively better, just thicker. It is all insulation from that point on.

Dorothy picked up the letter from Ella and opened it. She read the first few lines. "Oh!" she cried.

"Willy died?" Monica asked.

"No! It's wonderful. To the contrary. Listen to this. 'Dear Dorothy, I know you will be pleased and relieved to know that there has been a fortuitous turn of events. Ginger has resumed her cycles. Whatever baboon god you prayed to, it listened. This seems to have done the trick. Marcus is consorting with her in normal fashion and no longer keeps the vigils. Willy is making a comeback as Ginger is growing more attentive every day. We are most pleased. Will write more later on. Yours, Ella.' Oh this is stupid!" Dorothy put down the letter. "But I think I'm going to cry. I feel so relieved." Dorothy flopped back in her chair. "I just had the most dreadful feelings about the whole business. It wasn't just Willy. It was Ella. I felt so sorry for her through this whole thing. You know, if you'd see her you would think she was indestructible. She probably is. I mean, my God, she goes off to these godforsaken places. I told you about her milling grain with a trailer hitch. She has to 'hyena-proof' her camp and drive one hundred miles for drinking water. She once wrote me about watching out for 'crocs' while she bathed in a river. Of course, Peter has written me about crocodiles for years. Oh dear, I hate to think about it! What if my children get eaten by crocodiles!"

"Sophie won't."

"Oh boy, Sophie! Never! Did I tell you?"—Dorothy began to laugh—"Ira got such a kick out of this."

"What?"

"Sophie was interviewed a couple of years ago as one of the

top young women on Wall Street for an article in Ms. magazine and the quote they highlighted, the one they put under
her picture, was 'I never really go out of my way to screw
anybody.' "

"That's priceless!" Monica said "When are they coming?"

"The day after you leave. I'm terribly excited about meeting
this Rob. I guess mainly because I feel that she's . . . Well,
for Sophie this seems serious. It's been going on almost a year
now, and for her to bring him all the way here . . ."

"One that she's gone out of her way to . . . in the best
sense, of course."

"Of course." Dorothy laughed.

Two days later Dorothy stood on the town dock waving
good-bye to Monica who was aboard the Sea Queen bound for
Rockland.

27

Rob seemed just a tad embarrassed that first morning when he came out of the bedroom that he and Sophie shared. Dorothy liked that about him. It suggested a kind of vestigial courtliness which Dorothy interpreted as an assumption that certain people were special, namely, herself and Sophie; that making love to a woman under her mother's roof was a special situation.

Rob Fitzsimmons was in fact even better than Dorothy had anticipated. He had a rugged elegance and wonderful blue eyes which were a little tired-looking under heavy lids. His dark, reddish-blond hair was flecked with gray, and she guessed that he must be a good ten years older than Sophie. His nose was slightly beaked which was a blessing because, with the heavy-lidded eyes, it saved him from being a pretty boy. And finally there was the wonderfully angular jaw. Dorothy was strongly attracted to men with chiseled jaws. She had a theory about that which she once used in an examination in logic class as an example of a nontautology in which the first sentence does not imply the second: All men who are honest have strong jaws, but not all men who have strong jaws are honest. Rob Fitzsimmons had a strong jaw. He also loved Jane Austen. He recently had reread *Pride and Prejudice*. He was wonderfully helpful in the kitchen. Unlike most people who try to help, he never seemed to have to ask what to do or where things went. He simply went ahead and did things and found things without asking. And something had changed within Sophie because of this man. Dorothy could not quite put her finger on it. Sophie was still just as tough as ever, but something inside her had opened up.

Dorothy had just sliced a potato in half and had begun rubbing the grate on the grill.

"What are you doing, Mom?"

"Cleaning the grill before we put the steaks on."

Sophie's eyes widened and she looked at Dorothy as if she were some sort of alchemist. She then turned to Rob. "She knows all these secrets for stuff like this. She does this thing with baking soda and vinegar and it takes out any kind of stain."

"Take notes, Sophie," Rob answered.

"I don't want her tips on that stuff as much as on the market. Tell Rob about the Reebok thing and Expeditions Unlimited."

Dorothy told Rob a bit about her successes and out of the corner of her eye she caught Sophie looking at her with a kind of wonder. It was not the first time she had seen such a look in her children's eyes. Certainly she had seen it in Peter's and much more rarely in Sophie's. It was the way, as newborn babies just able to focus, they had studied her face while they nursed, or when later on in their childhood she would make something right for them that had seemed irreparable, solved the unsolvable. Dorothy believed that for most children, mothers were a mixture of the knowable and the slightly mysterious. On the conscious level a certain part of the child was attuned to the knowable; another part, on a subconscious level, was in a thrall to the mysterious. It was not a frightening kind of mystery of all, as Dorothy saw it. Therefore it cast a happy kind of spell rather than a grim bondage. The knowable and the mysterious were not polar opposites. That the knowable was predictable did not mean that the mysterious was unpredictable. It was simply more unfathomable, more convoluted. In fact, Dorothy saw the knowable and the mysterious as akin to the unequal scaling between surface and volume. The mysterious, the hidden dimension, was the volume, which increased much more rapidly than the surface, the knowable dimension. It was this hidden dimension that added weight to the knowable. Sophie, however, had never really succumbed to this dimension of her mother, this mystery, until now. Perhaps she had never needed to. Dorothy credited Rob with the change.

Rob and Sophie were to stay for a week. On the sixth day of their visit they went for a late afternoon sail. It promised to be a beautiful sunset as a northwest wind was blowing, bringing in with it crisp, limpid air that gave the end of the day an autumnal brilliance.

Dorothy had decided not to go with them, claiming she had some chores to do. In truth she felt that they should have the sunset for themselves. She did not like to think of herself as one of those omnipresent mothers who saturated the very air with her being so that the young lovers could not maintain some of the their own style of intimacy when on a visit.

She watched the little boat sail out of the channel, close-hauled, pointing for Cat Island with Rob at the helm. He was a captain for poets. It seemed to Dorothy that a complete navigational system was built into his mind and soul. He could sense the wind by its angle on his neck. He could smell a danger through the loom of the fog. He had no need in Dorothy's mind for the standard equipment. He had compass roses in his brain and retinal star charts. She could not help indulging in a magnificent proposal scene worthy of Jane Austen, slightly updated, and occurring on Cat Island. She could see them both emerging naked from swimming in the secluded cove, briny and glistening. They had taken a bottle of wine and two cups with them. She knew that the nude swimming and Chardonnay were the staples more of Danielle Steele than of Jane Austen, but the conversation would elevate the proposal to Austen's level. The tone would not be one of simpering acquiescence but sparkling negotiation. Dorothy felt that Sophie had at last truly met her match. She tried not to let herself be carried away by her fantasies, but she felt that this was not idle dreaming. It seemed more than merely possible.

She had just finished switching a load of laundry to the dryer and was wiping her hand around the inside of the drum of the washing machine to see if there were any stray socks when she felt a plastic card. She took it out and saw that it was a driver's license—Rob's. She looked at it quickly and then uttered a small shriek. In the photograph he wore a clerical collar. The license gave his full name and then the initials O.S.B. The address was in New York, far uptown.

Dorothy walked straight to the bedroom where Rob and Sophie slept. His wallet was on the dresser, a credit card holder beside it. She opened the holder. A long plastic strip with cards unfolded. She studied them. There was a MasterCard, a gold American Express card and Diner's Club, and a myriad of personal identification items, the latter giving the final irrefutable truth about Robert Hugh Fitzsimmons, O.S.B., Catholic priest, Order of Saint Benedict.

Father Fitzsimmons had three addresses—two Benedictine abbeys, one in New York and one in Washington, D.C., and a third address in Rome. There were two sets of business cards. One set had his name with his three initials and gave the organization name in Italian—*Istituto Per Le Opere Di Religione*. There was a Vatican address on this card. The other card had the name in English, *Institute of Religious Works*, and gave both the Vatican address and one on Wall Street.

268 / THE WIDOW OF OZ

Dorothy sat down on the bed stunned. The cards lay in her
lap. Waves of incredulity swept over her, and each wave brought
a more fantastic image—papal robes, monks kneeling in prayer,
crucifixes, Sophie in bed, a mitred head on the pillow beside
her. Good Lord! What would they do to Sophie if they found
out! Dorothy stood up trembling. She caught sight of a very
elegant black leather case with Rob's initials. Just R.H.F., no
O.S.B. She flipped the clasps. A long white raw silk band lay
neatly folded. Dorothy picked it up. "This ain't no tallis!" she
muttered. In it were two small bottles of clear fluid. Holy water
and oils, she assumed. And then there was the book with the
word *breviary* embossed in gold on the outside. She opened it
up. There was a bookplate inscribed, "To Father Rob, from
his friends at Precious Blood."

"Precious Blood!" Dorothy whispered. This was too much.
A queasiness welled up in the back of her throat.

Dorothy looked around the room. She did not know what
she was searching for—a crucifix? A cassock? She hardly needed
more proof. All she saw was the lovely cashmere sweater he
had worn the previous night for dinner, a pair of topsiders
and—God!—a jockstrap! It was hanging on the doorknob of
the closet. She felt a rising tide of panic. What in the hell was
Sophie doing screwing a priest? What might they do to her?
This was no small-potatoes parish priest by any means. This
fellow had a Vatican address—and her Sophie! "Oh God, I
wish Ira were here!" Dorothy blurted out. And Rob was so
charming. She felt like such a fool. Why couldn't he be Jewish! Jewish, what was she talking about? Presbyterian would
do. Lutheran, anything but a Roman Catholic priest. She had
to collect herself. They would be back soon. How could she
face them? She mustn't let on that she knew. She had to
think clearly. If she showed up with his driver's license he
would know that she knew. Better it stay lost or, better yet,
slip it into the pants pocket of his slacks as if it had stayed
there through both cycles of washing and drying—a small mir-

acle, but after all that shouldn't strain a priest's credulity.

She had just poured herself a very stiff drink when she spotted the sail coming into the channel. At the same moment the telephone rang.

"Mrs. Silver?"

"Yes."

"Mrs. Silver, I hate to disturb you but my name is Julian Raymond and I'm an associate of Ella's at the Berkeley Primate Center."

"Yes. Yes, is something wrong?"

"Well, yes. We've just had word that Ella's mother has died."

"Oh dear, no."

"Yes, I'm afraid so, and as you know she's at her field site in Kenya. We've tried to get a message through. But it's very hard. We were wondering perhaps if we could reach her through your son Peter in Olduvai."

"Yes. Yes." She was watching Rob and Sophie make the mooring.

The rest of the evening was a blur. Rob took over the helm of the communications operations. He had a contact in the Bank of Nairobi, in the embassy, and the bishop just happened to be a close friend. This last piece of information was given with astute casualness. "I just happen, through some friends, to know the bishop of the diocese down there." Dorothy let it go. She could not even follow the labyrinthine channels of telecommunications through which Rob seemed to be threading this message. She merely watched with amazement as he worked calmly. She imagined that this equanimity was all part of the priestly package. It came along with the breviary, the stole and the holy oils. By midnight, when it had been confirmed that a message was definitely on its way to Peter, they all turned in for the night.

At three in the morning, unable to sleep, Dorothy got up,

put on a heavy sweater and went out to the sunset porch. Unhappily, she could not concentrate on Ella's loss, even after being so curious about her family. Too much had happened in the last twelve hours. Her children led complicated lives and there was nothing much she could do about it—Peter involved with a girl who devoted her life to shaking down the secrets of evolution by staking out baboons; Sophie sleeping with a Benedictine priest. She heard footsteps behind her.

"Mom!"

"Sophie!"

"Couldn't sleep?"

"No, I couldn't."

"I know you and Ella are so close," Sophie said, sitting down in the rocker next to Dorothy.

"Sophie!" the name rang out like a clarion. Sophie's eyes widened.

"What is it?"

"Sophie," Dorothy said. "I know." Her voice trembled.

"You know what?"

"I know that Rob is Father Rob of the Order of Saint Benedict."

"Oh, Mom." Sophie's voice was a whisper.

"I don't understand, Sophie."

"Mom, I don't know what to say. It just happened."

"Do you love him?" Sophie bit her lip and nodded slowly. "Well, what can be done about it? I mean, he's broken his vows. Where do you go from here? Does he get defrocked or what? How in the hell did you two get together anyway?"

"It was easy."

"Easy? Have you become a nun?"

"No. It was a deal."

"A deal!"

"It was the Serona Pharmaceutical deal."

"But he's a Benedictine," Dorothy said.

"Yeah, but Mom, do you realize that the Vatican is the

largest stockholder in the world? It's got eleven billion dollars invested in the market. Rob does the same thing I do. I mean, you know, they aren't all tucked away in monasteries illuminating manuscripts."

"Or making Benedictine. No, apparently not. I have some, by the way, in the liquor cabinet."

If it had to be religion she might have known that Sophie would not nickel-and-dime around with any of those born-again TV ministry types. No, she'd go for the Fortune 500 of the lot—Catholic Church, a Benedictine with Vatican connections, first-class all the way.

"You upset, Mom?"

"Well, not upset exactly. I imagine that His Holiness would be more upset than I am. I mean you're sleeping with a prince of the Church. I'm confused, though."

"He's not a prince. You have to be a cardinal for that."

She had forgotten what a quick study Sophie was. She would already be well versed in the political structure and administration of the Vatican, not to mention its portfolio. "Is that more of a sin . . . uh, sleeping with a cardinal? I mean what can they do to you—burn you at the stake?"

"Mom! They can't do anything to me."

"I don't understand any of this. The celibacy thing is only part of it. I don't understand his cashmere sweater, and the Ralph Lauren shirts and how you two manage dinners at—where was it you told me you went the other evening?"

"Texarkana."

"Yeah, Texarkana."

She would have to revise the nontautology:
Some men are priests.
Some priests screw around.
Rob Fitzsimmons is a priest . . .
Indeed, that was a truth table tautology.

28

❧

The next few days for Dorothy were a blur of bad news and stories poorly finished. The order of the events did not seem to matter. She had waited all day for a call from Ella until finally she gave up and went out alone for a late afternoon sail. When she returned the phone was ringing. It was an associate of Ella's. Ella had tried to call herself but there was no answer and she had had to drive back to camp. The message was that Ella would not be returning for her mother's funeral. She "did not see the need." Dorothy had simply replied, "Oh."

It seemed as if she had just hung up from that call when the news of Elsie Bancroft came. She could not remember whether it was Betsy Winthrop's phone call or Chowdie running breathlessly down the path that informed her first that Elsie had died. Dorothy had images of the old lady's heart breaking and her sleeping away into death during the night in her strange bed at the Inn. But that was not the case at all. She had wandered out of her room at the Norumbega and with her walker had managed to get down to the shore. Her body was found washed up the next morning. "They're not calling it suicide," Betsy Winthrop had barked. "They're saying she was just demented, confused." But Dorothy could tell that Betsy did not believe that her old friend had become so deranged. It had been so foggy that night, as Dorothy recalled, that Elsie could have just gone for a walk, lost her way and fallen in. Dorothy tried to imagine the fragile lady walking on her new hips over the fog-shrouded bank. In her imagination Elsie seemed to float rather than walk.

And then sometime after this, whether it was one day or three or four Dorothy was uncertain, Cecil Weed came huffing down the path. "Dorothy, special delivery, air express letter from Africa."

"Oh, good God!" She supposed if it were really bad news they would have telegrammed her.

"You want me to stay a minute, Dorothy?" Cecil offered.

"Oh, no! Don't worry. It's just from my son's girlfriend. Her mother has just died so I'm sure it's about that."

Although the letter had been sent air special, it had been four days coming. Before even reading the letter Dorothy counted back in an attempt to set her mental calendar straight. It had been written before Ella knew about her mother. Rob and Sophie had left only three days before. She could not imagine what would have prompted a special delivery letter from Kenya. She opened the letter and began to read.

Dear Dorothy,
I lied. Four weeks ago Willy died. Marcus attacked in broad daylight. There was nothing anybody could do. It was so fast. He just swept down on him and bit him twice in the skull. There were four deep puncture wounds. Ginger screamed and ran off. Fred just sat there on his haunches stunned. It was immediately apparent that Willy was dead but Marcus picked up the little body one more

time and slammed it down as hard as he could and then
casually walked away. I tried to approach, but Fred would
not let me. He not only flashed the white skin above his
eyes in the conventional gesture of threat but he actually
chest beat in the style of gorillas and then, like a chimp,
began "drumming" (pounding the ground). I've never seen
this done before. It was as if he were borrowing every
alpha male threat signal in the primate repertoire regard-
less of species. I quickly retreated. After a few minutes he
went over to Willy's lifeless body and picked it up. Hug-
ging it to his chest, he set off. I followed him for twelve
hours. Somewhere near midnight, Fred must have dropped
the body because he began making tighter and tighter circles. By the first light of dawn I could see that he was
empty-handed and in spite of his exhaustion was still
hunting for Willy in a desultory manner.

He never did find him and he eventually rejoined the
troop. Several days later, when the troop was traveling
near the spot where Fred had dropped the body, he again
seemed to grow agitated. He rushed about, showing more
energy than he had for days and making wahoo barks
which is a signal of alarm. Ginger became very alarmed.
She seemed to sense that this had something to do with
Willy. She had by this time resumed cycling as is often the
case after a mother's infant has died or been killed. The
troop moved on but Fred stayed behind. Oddly enough
Harriet circled back and stayed with Fred that first day,
but then she moved on. Fred stopped eating and grew
quite listless. Several days later a graduate student found
his body in the brush near the last place we had seen him.

Now I suppose you're wondering why I never wrote you
all this in the first place, or perhaps you already know.
This little piece of history happening out here on the
savannah with these nonhuman primates has echoes
within my own life. Mine was a different kind of infanti-

cide. *The child was not "killed" in the conventional way.
(I only use the quotes grudgingly.) Out of the scraps that
were left, an adult was pieced together. Of course, the
story is not a one-on-one literal translation. But there was
a glazed mother. She is now in a home for alcoholic and
demented old folks. Her brain is totally gone. There was a
Marcus in the form of a slightly retarded grown cousin
who came to help out on the farm, and there would have
been a Fred. But Fred drank too, and after he found out
what Marcus had done to his daughter he got drunk one
night and set off on his tractor and turned it over in the
Niobrara.*

*Like almost anyone engaged in research that looks at
ancient beginnings, I suppose we all come with our own
personal baggage and set up ad hoc all sorts of comparisons. I didn't actually intend ever to become a primatologist and certainly did not think I was trying to unravel my
own history through it. Remember I went to aggie school
to begin with—cattle, soil programs, etc. Somehow I got
to Berkeley and monkeys. I know that a lot of people go
into primatology to grind an ax. It's a very easy field for ax
grinders of all varieties. But I didn't go into it for this reason. I had no illusions or agendas at hand when I started
out. I never even dreamed of trying to figure out anything
about my fucked-up family. I have been terribly drawn to
all the primates I have observed over the last ten years,
drawn to them not simply because of what they tell us
about understanding ourselves but because in their own
right they are so wonderful, so complex, so vividly individual. If there are any parallels to be drawn here between
species it is only the basic one that underlies everything—
life on Earth is a crapshoot and so is your family and
whoever you get as your parents. But I would be lying
again if I did not tell you that I have been caught off guard
out here, and what I have seen has shaken me. I try to*

read nothing into it, or at least not more than I should. But I feel it all—this terrible, inexorable pressure of the crapshoot and the victims.

I have enjoyed writing to you over the months. I am sorry that I have recently misused the exchange.

With love,
Ella

"Ella, Ella, Ella . . . ," Dorothy whispered. She went and got a piece of paper. It was odd. She seemed to know exactly what to say. It was as if through all these months of correspondence, there had indeed been an agenda and that she had been tutored on some subliminal level for this moment.

Dear Ella,
First of all, don't worry about lying. You did not misuse anything. I think the closer we get to people the more we might lie. We often lie for the best of reasons. So, although you lied I do not feel deceived. I am of course shocked by what you have told me. And I am profoundly angered. I am angered as a mother—a crapshoot mother, but still I am angered by the abuse you endured. It makes little difference to me that your family was shot through with alcoholism. Where were the loving, responsible adults? Were there no grandparents? No aunts, no uncles? Neighbors? Teachers? I know that I am naive. I don't care. For every weak mother I imagine posses of gallant ones, riding in to save babies.
It is not so. I am left with only one thought. Motherhood might be a crapshoot (from a child's point of view) but friendship is not. What you have been writing me all these months, a central theme of the Savannah Soaps, is friendship. It is friendship pretty much relieved of the Darwinian burden or at least the visible part of that burden which has to do with reproductive effort and sexual com-

petition. Did you not say yourself in one letter that it was
not so much a chicken-and-egg question, as some might
think? Nor is it a clear-cut case of a close bond of friendship arising out of economic need, i.e., food sharing.

Didn't you suggest that there was a kind of inherent
capacity for close bonds, for friendships that allowed for
reciprocities to follow? Isn't this exactly the case of the
spandrels of San Marco that Gould writes about?—current
utility cannot explain original functions, i.e., friendship
did not necessarily evolve from needs to share food. We
look at the "spandrels" of these friendships, these bonds,
and assume their purpose, the end product, the current
utility, is an economic or sexual one. You have said that
perhaps the whole bond comes rather from a purely social-
emotional need that cannot be assessed strictly in terms of
economic benefits. We catch our breath then not over the
usefulness of friendship and the accrued benefits—these
are the side consequences, like the paintings in the spandrels—but the fact that the friendships as you have
described them seem to evolve for such unaccountable reasons, out of unexplainable feelings of mutuality and sensations of comfort. Friendship therefore can have none of
the randomness, the crapshoot aspects of blood relations.
There is choice and intention for reasons that go beyond
the obvious benefits to be derived.

Ella, dear, I cannot replace your mother, the one who
never seemed able to mother, but I can be a friend in the
noble tradition of Honest Abe, Harriet and Fred.

> With deepest affection,
> Dorothy

She had no sooner sealed the letter than Sophie tele-
phoned.

"Mother, I know you're really upset about me."

Dorothy had to pause. She honestly for several seconds could not remember why she was supposed to be upset about Sophie. "Mom?"

"Oh, you mean about Rob and you and the Catholic thing."

"The Catholic thing?" Sophie repeated.

"Well, rather, his being a priest."

"Mom, are you all right? You sound kind of weird."

"No. I'm fine and I'm not very upset."

"You aren't?"

"No. I mean, it seems rather simple to me. If you two are really in love and want to pursue this, well, he just resigns, turns in his cards or whatever they do. I guess you've already defrocked him." She laughed.

"Mom!"

"Well, why are you so surprised? I do worry about you having to keep all this so hidden. Although I guess you don't hide it all that much if you go to all those fancy restaurants."

"No. We are kind of careful when we go out."

"Well, that's what I mean. If I had a gorgeous hunk like that on the line I'd want to show him off."

"Oh, Mom!" Sophie paused. "Did you ever reach Ella?"

"Not exactly."

"What do you mean, not exactly?"

"It's a long story—believe me, next to hers your problems pale. Want me to call up the Pope for you?"

"Mother! Are you drunk? What in the hell are you talking about?"

"It's too long to go into now, but Ella is not coming back for her mother's funeral and I don't blame her. She had the grimmest of childhoods."

"Really?"

Sophie sounded so naive, so vulnerable. "Yes, sweetie. It's very sad." She suddenly wanted to hug Sophie, to mother her, to tell her bedtime stories, to protect her, to lie to her. "Listen, tell Rob that I know about him and still think he's great and that you never have to hide anything from me. He can come in all his paraphernalia for all I care—crucifixes, hats, the whole bit."

"Oh, Mom." Sophie laughed. "You really are too much. Okay. I'll tell him. Talk to you soon, then."

Dorothy hung up. It seemed as if a whole day had passed but actually it was just past noon. A light breeze had come up. She decided to go for a sail. She packed up a lunch for herself and grabbed her sweatshirt and charts.

The wind was out of the southeast. There was a wetness in the air that the sun, weak that afternoon, could not dry out. She had no real course in mind. She was in the habit of sailing out close-hauled and saving the easy run, the downwind part, for coming home. When she had come abeam of Thatcher's Island, which was beyond where she usually sailed for a short afternoon run, the boat clung to the wind at a slant that felt good and made it hum a bit so she decided to keep on for a piece.

She had, she felt, dealt handily with both Ella's and Sophie's problems. She was, after all, she thought ruefully, a good advice giver, a good mother, a good wife, too, once upon a time. It had not been that long ago.

She shuddered. She had vaguely been aware of a loom off Bent Island, beyond Bent really. But now she realized that the southeast point that curved out like a claw had been swallowed in fog. Indeed the fog seemed to be rolling in rapidly and scrawling a script of mist around the boat.

She came about, and almost as she had tacked, the wind died. The sails suddenly hung slack and the boat went dead in the water. She now realized with a sudden horror that the fog had stalked her all the way out. The way home, the islands, every rock, ledge and buoy had dissolved into the milky whiteness. Like a fool she had not even noticed her compass course sailing out. If she had, it would have been easy to follow the reciprocal course home. But the breath of the fog was on her face now and perimeters had vanished. The world had become rimless, without reference points.

The vapor grew thicker and more impenetrable. What wind there was had shifted. The boat moved slowly now, but toward what she did not know. She felt only that she was being drawn deeper into the throat of the fog. She looked at her compass but the needle mocked her as it swung without heading in the lassitude of the calm.

She felt the panic welling inside her. Her sails slatted noisily. She lowered the main. Now only the jib was up. Still there was no direction and no speed. The wind had vanished. Dorothy felt lost, totally and completely lost, without any physical sensations of movement, without reference, without framework. Steeped in the thick billows of the fog, she could have been in the sky or in space. For all intents and purposes she had slipped her gravitational orbit. Perhaps, she thought, she had spun off into one of the multiple universes that Monica had spoken of.

Now she was alone, out of human reach or, for that matter, the reach of the Pleiadian sisters—Maia and Electra and Acyone and the rest. Her panic increased. She tried to calm herself by thinking of Sophie, of Peter, of Ella, but they dissolved like the islands into the thickness of the fog.

She had never felt so isolated. A chill began to creep over her body as she realized that this indeed was the isolation of death. There was a starkness. It came with no comparison, without metaphor, because, a voice whispered in the back of her brain, there is no "like" with death. She had fought that hard. She had fought it on the short drive to the hospital that day as she had locked herself into the icy trance. And even when they had told her the worst, she had in her discrete, inimitable way, so neat, so fastidious, tucked away the actual images, the signals, not the symbols, of finality—the dark, ragged hole that was a mouth in the ashen face now sunken in death. "That image will fade," the nurse had said. But these were not just images, not representations. The darkness of that hole was palpable. This was not just life stopped. This was life no more, or never had been. For there was suddenly that awful question. Had life ever happened here? Been contained within that dark, stiffening vessel?

She had stood there, her arms hanging loose at her sides, in the curtained section of the emergency ward and wondered what had happened to the notion of a last breath passing out of the body and drawing with it the spirit. She had felt cheated, not by death but by God, who had slurred that spectral passage of spirit, of crossing over, and had left only the crumpled dark cold thing that was rumored to have once held life. She had lost the chance to watch its essence dissolve. So alone that passage had been for Ira.

Dorothy bit her lip. She had not been there for him then, or since then, in all of her doubts. A serenity stole over her. She sensed it for what it was. The tranquility that comes to those who have lost everything. The calm thickened like the fog and beckoned. She would not be leaving. She would be joining. It would be so easy. The fog seemed layered now like strata. She could imagine a frozen canal and Elsie Bancroft skating down it. Like a child for whom the clouds seem so tangible in their volume as to be cushions for sitting on, Dorothy imagined the fog enveloping her. She would just slip quickly over the transom. She stood up unsteadily and began to unzip her life jacket. The cold wet air hit her chest. She sat down hard on the seat. She wiped her cheek with her hand. It slid across her face. She looked down at her hand. It appeared wet. Then it blurred. The jib wavered in its whiteness. Her whole face felt raw in the mist.

There was water everywhere. The spars dripped with beads of water. The air rolled with vapor. Tears and condensation mingled in varying degrees of saltiness eventually to join the water of the bay. There was no dividing, no separate rivers. There was only the wet shimmer of grief and the knowledge that she had been loved. Suddenly she was aware of a tidal odor. It was an exposed ledge, she was sure, off to port, and the scent came on the edge of a new wind. She hauled in on the jib sheet to sail as close as she could to the ledge without fetching up on it. The smell came up sharp now. She was skimming under the lee of the ledge. She knew it was there even though she could not see it through the blur of her own streaming eyes. *Faith*—that is what she would call the boat, not *Memory*. A door in the wind opened, and Dorothy tacked and sailed through it smartly for home.